The Prince
of
Mirrors

ALAN ROBERT CLARK

Leabharlanna Poiblí Chathair Baile Átha Cliath
Dublin City Public Libraries

FAIRLIGHT BOOKS

This paperback edition was published in 2019

Fairlight Books
Summertown Pavilion,
18–24 Middle Way,
Oxford, OX2 7LG

A CIP catalogue record for this book is available from
the British Library

1 2 3 4 5 6 7 8 9 10

ISBN   978-1-912054-12-1

www.fairlightbooks.com

Printed and bound in Great Britain by Clays Ltd

Cover design by Sarah Brody

In memory of Sue Townsend and Rebecca Swift.

Also, as always, to Robert Palmer.

PROLOGUE

December 1891.

A man, young, nudging his prime, sits on a train as it hurtles across the bleak, black landscape of a late afternoon just before Christmas.

He is tall, slim and very neat, polished and sharp as the pin that holds his ruby-red cravat. He has countless cravats, but chose this one because it is cheerful, festive even. He thought it might be an antidote to the misery of the mission from which he now returns, but the stratagem did not work.

The young man's suit is a poem to tailoring; his proud valet can recite every pocket, pleat and tuck of it. From its sleeves, his shirt cuffs poke out to precisely the fashionable length above his long, flimsy fingers; an extravagantly high wing collar cradles the neck of a swan. His moustache waxes upwards at its ends into a perpetual smile. His hair, which to his distress is thinning a little, is parted, neatly, in the middle. The features, too, are symmetrical, angular, pinched almost, except for the lips which seem to have strayed from another face entirely. They are the lips of a voluptuary. It is the lips which give him away.

Everything shakes and shudders with the rushing of the train. The gaslight wobbles inside its smoked-glass shades. The gold tassels that fringe the window blinds dance like a chorus of girls in a music hall. An evening paper, folded and unread, quivers on the cushions beside him. But the young man, his spider legs elegantly crossed, sits very upright, very still. He is holding himself together for fear he may break apart.

It seems to him that he has just committed a crime, an inexcusable crime which flies in the face of everything he strives to be. All of his short life he has tried to please people, especially God, and surely God will not be pleased by this. He has abandoned a friend, a friend like no other. He has abandoned him out there in the bleak, black landscape, like some old working dog which has outlived its usefulness. Almost kinder to have shot him through the heart, but the young man's courage went no further than a pat on the head, a hurried, furtive farewell.

'Don't leave me in this place, Eddy,' the friend begs. 'Take me away. Somewhere close to you. I'll get well faster then.'

'But Jem, you must stay here. Only until you're tip-top again.'

To make them both feel better, Eddy, the neat young man, tells kindly lies. He holds out the prospect of happier times.

'You shall be at my wedding,' he says, 'an honoured guest. You shall help me with the impossible burden I must carry one day. We shall go on travelling through this life side by side, companions forever.'

The lies leave his mouth messily, in fits and starts, like teeth reluctant to be pulled. He wishes they were not lies, but the door to the room in which they sit is locked; the windows are barred. Those who command the young man have allowed this one visit; it is not certain they will permit another.

The train, the great, belching, steaming thing, becomes an accomplice to the abandonment. Faster and faster it flees over fallow fields, as desperate as him to get away, to shroud the memory in palls of smoke and disperse it to the four winds.

The half-hearted day gives way to dusk. Eddy catches his reflection in the hazy mirror of the window. He has been fascinated by his reflection for as long as he can remember. In childhood, at least, it was not vanity but curiosity. He studied himself like a detective from Scotland Yard, searching for clues, though they came but rarely. After a time, he abandoned the looking glass and peered instead into the eyes of those round him. In retrospect, this was not a wise move. When he grew into a handsome man, he could at last see what he longed for in those eyes, though his delight would lead him to seek it in places he should never have gone. Oh dear no, not at all. Yet he always knew that this delight was a shallow thing, that there had to be something more. And, to his amazement, it had come to him. It came, like a miracle, from a friend. The friend he had just deserted like the old working dog.

Eddy stares into the fathomless window. He knows this darkness will soon pass. Soon the lights of the city will appear; a pretty sprinkle at first, then dense and dazzling as a sackful of diamonds. He is heading towards the light, towards a future. A future he never thought possible just a few weeks ago. That he now has the courage to grasp it is due to the man locked away back in the darkness.

Tonight there will be yet another ball, another celebration;

Eddy will dance with the girl he is to marry. He will take her by her cool hand and lead her into the waltz, though it will really be she who leads him. They all think him stupid, but he is clever enough to know *that*. He has always been drawn to people stronger than him. His Grandmama, his father, his brother and now this girl. But nobody ever seemed stronger than Jem. Once upon a time, Jem was a god.

When this awful winter is over, just before spring comes, Eddy and the girl will be joined together. And then, oh Lord, what may happen? The possibilities are endless; frightening, too, but at least they are possibilities. There will be no more pointlessness, no more travelling along dangerous roads in search of the way ahead, *any* way ahead. At last, he feels certain that someone is taking shape in all those mirrors. Against the odds. When he had almost lost hope of it. Someone more substantial than the smiling moustache, the collar and cuffs, the ruby-red cravat.

'Happy Christmas when it comes,' his friend says, when Eddy picks up his greatcoat and his bowler. The voice is weak, fractured, as if it has been broken on a wheel. 'Wrap up well against this infernal cold.'

Out in the corridor, he hears the lock turn behind him. How he wishes he had not heard that. A little cry darts out from him. The kindly doctor pats the arm of the perfect suit. And then Eddy walks away. How can he do such a thing? he asks himself. Everything he is, might still become, is owed to Jem. To his care, his dedication, his love. Dare that last word be used? Surely no other will do.

As the train spirits him back to the light, the young

man stops being neat. His body sags against the wall of the compartment. He uncrosses his spider legs, draws them up towards his chest, encircles them with his arm. Though it is warm in here, stuffy even, he turns up his jacket collar against some unknown chill. He buries his cheek in the fat, velvet cushions. The symmetry of the handsome face dissolves. Like the train, he shakes and shudders.

CHAPTER I

December 1872. Windsor.

It is the day of the year when the Earth is required to cease turning round the sun. It must come creaking to a halt and hang suspended in the universe with head bowed and gaze cast down.

Yesterday, from the railway station, a necklace of closed carriages, laden with heavy hearts, curved up the hill. The people on the pavements, half-hidden in the fog of their own frosty breath, did not press forward in the usual hope of a gracious wave from a gloved hand. They had drained themselves of the faintest hint of colour. Bright blue eyes, golden hair, even a florid complexion would be a mark of disrespect. Yet though their mourning was expected, indeed demanded, they were shown no thanks for it. The great gates were soon slammed on their rigid faces, shutting them out and shutting the carriages in.

If the common people felt this exclusion, they might have been comforted to know how eagerly those trapped in the carriages would have swapped places. How gladly the prisoners would have torn off their veils and raven-black weeds, run pell-mell back down the hill and across the frozen meadows towards the far horizon. Locked inside the walls and towers, they were required to embrace death, even to wallow in its clasp. It was like being bricked up alive.

'Dear God, deliver us,' sighed the fat man as he heaved himself down to the ground.

'You're looking rudely well, Bertie,' said his mother, her lips pursed tight as a reticule. It seemed more of a rebuke than a welcome.

At his house in the city, the fat man had hardly left his study for days, hardly spoken except to snap out some cross command. In the stables, his coachmen wandered like lost souls; his horses pawed the ground, eager for the proud, showy spaces of Piccadilly or Rotten Row. Once again, the anniversary of the sudden, shocking departure of his father was rolling in from the west; a thundercloud that would not dissolve until eleven days later when everyone, even his Mama, would be obliged to celebrate the birth of baby Jesus, an imposition she distinctly resented. Inside her battlements, the Messiah outranked her lamented consort, but only just.

Now at breakfast, the fat man mutters to one of his sisters.

'Well, here we go again. The Dreadful Fourteenth.'

'Hush, Bertie, or she will hear.'

The sister glances towards the little woman at the far end of the table, nibbling at a thin biscuit as if it might have been poisoned by an anarchist.

'The execution of Charles I, the loss of the Americas, the

Charge of the Light Brigade,' replies Bertie. 'What were these disasters compared with the passing of our sainted Papa?'

He whacks his egg so hard with his spoon that yellow yoke splatters the tablecloth. His younger son laughs out loud. The little woman's gaze sweeps along the table and leeches onto the child. Then suddenly, the granite face dissolves and she flees the room. Another of the sisters flutters in her wake.

'Naughty Georgie,' murmurs Georgie's mother.

'Yes, bad boy,' says Bertie and slaps his hand so lightly that the child laughs all over again. Georgie can do little wrong in his father's eyes and he knows it.

Bertie is eating a breakfast fit for a shoot rather than a requiem: porridge, bacon, chicken with mushrooms, rump steak, boiled eggs stuffed with truffles.

'Why do you eat so much food, Papa?' asks Georgie.

There is silence at the table. The fat man looks at him as if this is the most difficult question he has ever been asked, the answer unreachable as a star.

'It's something to do,' he says at last.

Georgie's mother, a young woman, lovely as lark song, slender as a reed, crumples into giggles.

'Alix!' says another of her husband's sisters. 'Not today.'

The young woman blushes and bites her lower lip. Beside her, another boy, taller than the first, the very image of her, rubs her arm to smooth away the chastisement.

This boy has not said a word at breakfast. He has scarcely eaten either. A truffle, extracted from his boiled egg, sits like a gallstone on the edge of his plate. He is nervous. He longs to be in Norfolk, riding his pony.

'Are you quite prepared, Eddy?' asks his father. 'It's a great honour that Grandmama does you today, inviting you to the special place.'

'Yes, Papa,' says the boy. 'Thank you, Papa.'

But Eddy dissembles. He is not prepared. He has no idea what preparations he is supposed to have made. Nobody has told him. How is he supposed to know? He is still only eight. Grown-up people are so unfair. They expect things of you but do not bother to tell you what they are.

Eddy has never been to the special place before, but his Grandmama has declared it is now fitting for the child she calls Albert Victor to join the pilgrimage. Whenever he visits Grandmama, he has to remember that he is a boy with two names – well, three to be precise. Grandmama had decreed these names at birth. His parents were outraged, but she would not be gainsaid. In all things, the little woman is as immoveable as the great circular keep of her fortress. 'It is my right to interfere,' she had said. 'We are not like other people.'

'She can call him what the hell she likes,' Bertie had growled to his wife. 'Oliver Twist. Wee Willie Winkie. I don't give a tinker's cuss. To us, he will be Eddy.'

After breakfast, Eddy is dressed in his kilt and sporran, his *skean dhu* strapped against his long woolly socks. His little brother watches, arms tight across his chest. Georgie is not yet allowed to go to the special place. He is the younger by a year and a half and begrudges every day of it. Georgie keeps clouting him until their mother pushes herself between them and clouts them both.

'I forgive you, Georgie,' says Eddy. 'That is what the Bible teaches, so I forgive you.'

Georgie, freshly enraged, spits in his eye, so they are both clouted again. Eddy does not mind. If this is the price he must pay for having a brother, then so be it. He cannot imagine a world without Georgie. He loves him more than life.

In the special place, Eddy's knees are cold. He has never known anywhere as cold as this. He wonders if a boy in a kilt might be at particular risk of death by freezing. Perhaps if he dies here, they would simply leave him where he falls and go back for luncheon. It is a church, after all, so it would be quite appropriate and save everybody trouble. He does not like to cause anyone trouble.

In his cosy little church in Norfolk, they sit on pews of warm, dark wood and kneel on the pretty prayer cushions his Mama has embroidered. There, everyone is so tightly squashed you can smell the rain steaming off the greatcoats. But this place, the special place, is like the pictures of Roman temples he has been shown in the schoolroom. There is no steeple, no tower, just a funny roof shaped like a lantern, as if some giant had dumped it there in passing. There are no pews either, only a big, empty chamber. All round the walls are paintings on the stone, the colours bright and blazing; reds and pinks, yellows and greens. The roof is dotted with golden stars against dark blue, like the sky at night. Usually, he likes bright colours, but the richness here does not convey joy. His church at home is filled with hopeful hearts, full of joy in the love of God. He does not feel that here.

Eddy holds tightly to his mother's hand. There are so many people and he is the only child. All the uncles, aunts, cousins, battalions of them, and, as usual, a lot of faces he does not recognise, though they seem to recognise him. It is very odd, this not knowing people who know you. He wonders if he will ever get used to it. But the crowd is easily swallowed up inside the echoing space. Even clearing your throat sends a rumble round the walls. He is glad Georgie is not here in case he might do one of his farts; Georgie's farts are quite spectacularly awful. A choir begins singing from a hidden corner; their music heavy as the air. There are several vicars too, far more grand and grim than their jolly old chap at home who has hairs growing out of his nostrils.

It is only now that he reaches the centre of the chamber and sees the squat lump of grey stone. It is a glum thing and no mistake. What could it be? Angels kneel at each corner, their wings spread wide, their faces tired as if they had just flown across the sky with it and only put it down a moment ago. Now he notices something on top of the grey lump. Made of stone too, but pure white and flawless as fresh snow, carved into the shape of a man asleep.

One of the grand vicars starts to speak. His voice is light and squeaky; it trills round the painted walls and up into the roof like some trapped sparrow. A soft sigh escapes the lips of Eddy's mother. Perhaps she longs to sit, maybe her bad knee is hurting her today, so he squeezes her hand as hard as he can. On his other side, his father stands as tall as he is able to, his expression as cold as the stone at which he stares.

Now Grandmama appears. Behind her trail two thin, beaky-nosed women, their eyes lowered, prayer books in their hands. Grandmama is wrapped in clouds of black bombazine, a long veil curtaining her face. She walks alone up to the great, grey stone. There is silence in the chamber. Eddy wonders if she has turned to stone too, like everything else in here. He worries in case it is infectious and that he might be next. Turned to stone! Frozen to death! He wants to be back in the warm with Georgie, eating crumpets and farting.

A finger of pale winter sun pokes through a window and points straight at the sleeping man carved in white. For a moment, the shape glows with light, the rays flicker across it, stirring it from its sleep. From behind Grandmama's veil comes a short, sharp cry, like the yelp of a puppy when you tread on its paw. And suddenly, the sun illuminates the boy's foggy, unformed mind. Suddenly he knows what the big grey stone is, and that there is something inside it. And when he sees the trembling of his Grandmama's shoulders, he knows that he is right. In an instant, he is filled with horror and pity. This cannot be allowed, he thinks. Someone must go to him.

He is a slim, slight boy, but he climbs trees even better than his brother. Pulling free of his mother, he runs past his Grandmama, clambers up on an angel's wings then onto the dazzling white figure. At last he can see the marble face, strong and beautiful, dreaming its dreams. But now he has grasped the reality. For the first time it comes to him, as it must to us all, what death means, and he aches at the cruelty and the waste of it.

'You told me he'd gone to Paradise,' he calls down to his grandmother. 'But he's really here, isn't he? Inside this stone. We can't leave him in this awful place; it's so cold. We must take him home where it's warm. Please, Grandmama.'

The little woman has thrown back the dark veil, her eyes as wide as if the earth had just tilted beneath her feet. Behind her, Alix and everyone else has indeed turned to stone. All except Bertie. For once, the fat man runs. He stretches up his arm to the boy, tells him to come down, but the boy is not listening.

Again, Eddy begs his Grandmama; again, Bertie reaches out. When Eddy finally takes his father's hand, he calms a little. But before he comes down, he leans forward and kisses the cold white lips.

Bertie pulls him away and passes him to one of Alix's women. As she steers him towards the great high door, Eddy sees every face turn away as if they no longer know him. The woman holds his elbow as they go down the steps, past the regiment of waiting carriages, to a little bridge that crosses a stream. They stand by the parapet and look into the water. The woman points out the fish darting beneath the lily pads and the squirrels racing through the tall, damp grass. It is pretty in the gardens, even in the wastes of winter. He feels a bit better now. He tries to free himself from her but she will not let him go.

At last, they all come out of the special place. It is drizzling now. Umbrellas sprout like a forest of toadstools. Horses stamp their feet in the cold, breath puffing from their muzzles. Alix reclaims him from the woman, kisses his forehead but does not speak. Now Bertie is here. He looks at his son as if he is seeing something that is beyond his understanding. He talks so quietly in his deep voice, it seems that the words surface from some dark well inside him.

'This will never be forgotten, Eddy. Never. Are you going to be up to it, eh? Are you going to be up to the mark?'

Bertie takes his hand and leads him back towards the carriages where Grandmama stands waiting. Eddy feels his father's palm sweat into his own, slippery as the slugs he and Georgie dig up in the garden. But Grandmama's eyes are kind and the plump hand reaches out and cradles his chin.

'Your son has a good heart, Bertie,' she says. 'That is a gift from God.'

'I am sorry for the disrespect he has shown today, Mama,'

he says. 'To you, to me, but above all, to my dear father.'

In an instant, the eyes freeze over.

'Disrespect? I saw no disrespect,' she says. 'All I saw was love, which is more than *you* ever showed your father.'

The little woman almost spits the words at him. Bertie seems to wither into the hard ground. She seizes Eddy's other hand. He will ride back with her, she says. When Alix goes to climb in with them, she is dismissed. Inside the carriage, Grandmama is still agitated. She twists and turns on the dark green leather, then pushes her head back out of the door.

'Disrespect?' she says again, almost shouting now. 'That's a fine choice of word coming from a man who killed his father and left his mother only half-alive.'

Round them, people quickly contemplate the laces of their boots, hide underneath their umbrellas. Nobody can look at Bertie.

It had been a dull little scandal, really. The heir to the throne losing his virginity to an actress. Such a cliché. But its impact had been catastrophic. Bertie's father, distraught, robbed of all perspective by the fetid memory of his own licentious parent, had dragged himself across the worst of winter to the university city. A long walk was taken across the fields in the rain. You must not be lost, his father had begged. Everything your mother and I have worked for. The good of the country. The peace of Europe. Not to mention the judgment of God. Though indestructible within his own rectitude, the body of Bertie's father was already worn down by too much work, driven by his devotion to a demanding wife and to a land which had never much cared for him. The chill caught in the Fens finished him off in weeks. In the heart of Bertie's mother, it was not so much a death as a murder. And though the murderer must be permitted to live, he would be condemned forever.

As yet, of course, Bertie's own two boys know nothing of all this. It is something never spoken of, certainly not before children. Let them go on playing in the bower of childhood for as long as possible, before they must face the wickedness of the world. But today, in one angry moment, it has poured out and people are sheltering under their umbrellas, aghast at the force of it.

As the carriage, its blinds pulled down, trots back towards the grey and ochre battlements, Eddy begins to gulp and sniffle.

'But why did Papa kill Grandpapa? Why? Was it in a battle?

'Indeed it was,' she says. 'Your grandfather was battling to save your father's soul and he lost. Then he died of a broken heart.'

'So Papa has no soul now?'

He is not exactly sure what a soul is, but is somehow certain it is much worse than being without an arm or a leg. He sniffles even more.

'Hush,' says Grandmama, scooping him into her arms. 'God forgive me. I should not have spoken of such things before an innocent boy. Hush now, hush.'

Eddy surrenders to the folds of black bombazine. As his eyes slowly dry, her own flow forth. Holding his head against her breast, she weeps and weeps until he thinks he might drown in her hopelessness.

'For a moment,' she says, 'for just a moment, you made me feel he was alive again. Thank you, dear child.'

*

1875. Sandringham, Norfolk.

If he waits long enough, his Papa will come home again. He knows that now. They all know it now, like they know their ten-times table, the Latin names of the plants in the garden and that God sees everything.

Eddy, Georgie and the three little sisters have come to understand that their Papa is not like the fathers in the story-books who go to work on the morning train and return again at six-thirty. Their Papa goes away for days, weeks even, but he will always return, bringing them little presents, hugging them as if he has found the separation unbearable. He is Santa Claus in Norfolk tweed.

'Gosh, Eddy! How tall you're getting,' he laughs one day. 'We'll soon have to put you in a circus with the Bearded Lady and the Dancing Bear. Eddy, the Human Pipe-Cleaner!'

Eddy laughs back. He has learnt to do that by now, to live with these little chaffs like a dog lives with its ticks.

Often their Papa would bring visitors from his other life. His children would prefer to have him to themselves, but they have learned not to be greedy and expect more than their due. Bertie's new house of buttery stone and cocky red brick wakes and stretches itself, puts on its best clothes.

'Come along, my darlings,' says Alix, clapping her hands. 'Let's show these grand people that we're not country cousins. We must dazzle.'

And so she does. She lights every room she enters with the glow of a thousand candles. She reminds the world what it misses by the exile she has imposed on herself, charming them all over again as she did before the terrible fever that brought in its wake the deafness and the limp. They may become weary of having to shout, but they yearn to take her back with them, back to where they want her to belong. Yet the intruders will bore quickly, they will tire of visiting her stables and her dairy and her pretty gardens. And soon they will pull her Bertie away again. It will not be difficult. There will be no heel marks in the gravel.

'So sad,' Eddy hears one man murmur to another. 'She is much more beautiful than all his other women put together.'

Eddy knows their type; he recognises it now from the way they dress, how they carry themselves, even how they smoke their cigarettes. Papa calls them his 'wicked boys'. Eddy hates them all. They are taking his Papa away. How he wishes he understood why his father always has to go. He wonders what he has done wrong this time, why he is still not up to the mark.

At breakfast, on the day Bertie leaves for the city, he announces that they will play theirf favourite game. Eddy's heart beats faster. It is an opportunity. He must seize it.

A man stands beside Bertie's chair, holding the silver tray. Criss-crossed piles of new-made toast, sliced thin as fingers, dripping with butter. The yellow-golden goo glints in the morning sun, the smell beyond heaven.

'Now then,' says Bertie, 'choose your runners. Look for endurance, flexibility and just the right degree of sogginess.'

The man with the tray bends towards five small faces. Dutifully, they inspect the candidates.

'Come on, come on. Conditions are perfect for the off. The course has been pressed this morning, hasn't it Palmer?'

'Yes indeed, sir,' says the man with the tray, as if he finds it a ridiculous question.

'So the going will be exceptionally smooth,' says Bertie.

Georgie and the girls make their selections. Eddy chooses his last, staring at it, trying to make some judgement but not knowing how. His Papa's fingers are drumming on the arm of the chair and he knows he must be quick. These moments are so rare and precious, they must never be spoiled.

'Oh, hurry up, Eddy,' says Georgie.

'Place your runners at the starting gate,' says Bertie.

Each finger of toast is placed onto Bertie's knees, buttered side down. At once it begins to seep into the grey-black stripes of his trousers. His gaze moves across the five of them. His face is never graver than now; the heavy lids half-closed, the eyes no more than tiny rents in the fleshy fabric. Apart from the crackle of the logs in the fire, there is silence in the room.

'They're off!' cries Bertie.

He throws his legs forward, turning his calves into gentle slopes. The fingers of toast start to slither down the trouser legs towards the winning post of distant shoelaces.

'Is Louise edging in front?' he shouts. 'Or is it Toria? No, Georgie is overtaking them both.'

Eddy's spirits are already sinking. His own piece of toast has hardly shifted from Papa's kneecap. He has picked a poor runner. He should have understood what flexibility and endurance meant and been able to spot them. He should have been cleverer, but of course he is not clever at all.

Georgie's face is pressed right up against Papa's leg, watching his runner ooze down the course. His bottom lip juts out above his hard little chin.

'Move, move damn your eyes!' he hisses at his toast.

'Georgie!' says Bertie. 'Where do you get that language?' He speaks sharply, though the bud of a smile forms inside his black, bushy beard.

Eddy knows exactly where Georgie gets his language. It comes from the stables, from his friends, the grooms. Like trophies, his brother carries back new rude words he has heard in the tack room. The latest one is 'cunt'. Neither of them knows what it means, but they are pretty certain it is incredibly rude. Eddy would like to be friends with the grooms too, but he never knows what to say. Anyway, it is Georgie they like.

Now the melting butter is dripping off Bertie's legs onto the piece of matting which has been placed there by the man with the tray. Georgie, Louise, Toria and little Maudie are whooping and shrieking now, but Eddy stands frozen, waiting for the sentence which is sure to come.

'Eddy, your runner is not running. It has scarcely shifted at all.'

'Yes, Papa. Sorry, Papa.'

His throat tightens and tears jab inside his eyes, but he must not let them fall. It really would not do. He is not certain why, only that such is the case.

Georgie and Toria are neck and neck, but his brother's toast just slides ahead and hits the shoe first. Georgie's eyes are ablaze; he pummels his knees with his little fists.

'Yes... yes!'

'Well done, Georgie,' says Bertie. 'I think you've been studying form.'

The man with the tray dabs the sopping trousers with a napkin. As Bertie rises to go up and change, Eddy is desolate.

Papa will be gone soon. Who can guess when he will have time to play with them again? He really wanted to do well in the race today, so that Papa might have a special word for him, a word all to himself, unshared with the others. Instead, like his finger of toast, he is stuck where he was before.

'Poor old Eddy,' says Bertie as he turns away. 'Not even as good as the girls.'

'Useless cunt,' whispers Georgie.

CHAPTER II

1876. Sandringham, Norfolk.

'Wake up, Eddy!'

The piece of chalk bounces off the schoolroom wall three inches above his head. It hits a signed photograph of the late Emperor of the French and cracks the glass. The Emperor has only been dead a few years, so it seems most disrespectful.

'What's so interesting about the pattern of the carpet?'

'Sorry?'

'You've been staring at it open-mouthed for the last half-minute.'

'Have I?'

'Don't you remember?'

'Sorry.'

No, Eddy does not remember staring at the carpet. The Reverend Dalton looks at him for a moment; a strange look. The same look he gave him yesterday when Eddy suddenly stopped eating, his fork frozen in mid-air, the bacon fat dripping onto the tablecloth. Eddy does not recall that either.

Dalton booms at him from behind the big, square table, piled high with the books he uses to teach them. Sometimes Eddy hears Dalton's boom in his dreams, like the thump of the waves from the German Ocean breaking on the beach. Grandmama believes he models himself on Mr Irving, the actor. Nobody, she says, could ever doze through one of the Reverend Dalton's sermons. Eddy appears to be living proof that this is not the case.

Eddy and Georgie have come to believe that they are sentenced to Dalton's sermons through all eternity. And not just on the joys of the good Christian life, but also on English, history, geography, algebra, Euclid and so on. They are incarcerated with him from seven in the morning until eight in the evening. Apart from the people of the house, Dalton's is the first face they see in the morning, the last they see at night. He seems to be everywhere. There is no escape.

'Maybe he'd like to watch us have a shit too,' says Georgie.

Sometimes, as he gazes through the schoolroom window at their Papa's carriage rolling off again towards the station, Eddy thinks it is Dalton who is really their father. It is booming, boring Dalton who is here with them, who is bringing them up. Why can't their Papa do that? Why has he paid Dalton to do the job, just as he pays those who look after his horses and his hounds? Do Eddy, Georgie and the girls have no more value for him? For a moment, Eddy hates Papa, hates Dalton, hates the world.

Yet, with the insight of children, he and Georgie know that Dalton is not a bad man. They know that he cares for them and this makes them care for him too. He is doing his best. And so they strive to please, but the yoke of him is heavy as they pull themselves uphill into being educated men, men worthy of their place at the summit.

Sometimes Eddy struggles to see the purpose of it all. In their spanking new house where the books were bought by the yard, the shelves feel no other touch than that of feather dusters.

'*East Lynne*,' says Bertie to any guest unwise enough to raise the subject of literature. 'Now *there's* a novel. I knew nothing could ever top it, so I've never tried another.'

Alix reads only the scriptures and the tales of Hans Christian Andersen, her beloved countryman. The world of Eddy's parents is a place where book-learning hardly matters. A world of passing the time between the snipping of ribbons and the planting of saplings. So Eddy cannot understand why it is supposed to matter to *him*.

What's the point of learning the thoughts of Cicero, he shouts at Dalton in his head. How the devil can Cicero ever help *me*?

How can anyone ever help him? When he is staring at the pattern of the carpet, when the fork freezes on its way to his mouth, this is usually the thought he is thinking. He is seeing that long, narrow chamber in Grandmama's vast house. The great chair of blazing ivory, carved and patterned with such delicacy that it looks like lace; on its arms the heads of mythical beasts standing guard, a gilded canopy of scarlet and gold soaring above it.

'Is that not the loveliest chair you've ever seen?' said Grandmama that day to him and Georgie. 'It was given by my peoples in India.'

They were allowed to walk round the chair, even to run their fingers over the fretwork of the ivory, on the strict understanding that their fingers had not been engaged in anything unpleasant. But then Georgie plumped himself down on the green velvet cushions, kicking his legs in the air.

'King of the castle,' he chanted. 'King of the castle.'

'Remove yourself at once!' shouted Grandmama. 'That chair is not to be sat upon by just anyone and certainly not by *you*!'

Georgie stuck out his tongue and was cuffed for it. Then she held out her hand to Eddy.

'Albert Victor, *you* may sit.'

Oh dear, Eddy did not want to do that at all. He tends to be a little clumsy. He breaks things easily. He had an awful vision of the ancient ivory crumbling beneath him, the heads of the mythical beasts rolling across the floor. But Grandmama required him to sit and so he must. She came close to him, took both his hands in hers, stared into his eyes. It was most uncomfortable. He wanted to look away but she did not break her gaze. And then she made a long, slow bow of her head.

And so the penny dropped. The realisation of what his future held. The thing he was required to become one day. Dear God. A terrible fear lanced into him. A new fear, freshly minted, one more to add to those already seeding inside him. In the years to come, as he grows to be a man, there will be times when he is able to pretend it is not there, times when he can chloroform it away with many distractions, even times when he can persuade himself that he has learned to live with it. But, from that moment, as he wriggled on the great ivory chair, it would never ever leave him.

'Wake up, Eddy!' the Reverend Dalton says again.

This morning he is expounding on the status and achievements of their great nation. He returns to the subject often, as if scratching an itch. The facts crack out from him like the cannon in the park on Grandmama's birthday. The British Empire covers nearly ten million square miles of the earth's surface. Boom. Britain produces two-thirds of the planet's coal, half its iron, steel and cotton. Boom. Our people earn the highest wages and eat the cheapest food. Our navy is the most powerful in history. Boom. We are the land of freedom, opportunity, an exemplar of civilisation to the primitive. We are the greatest power since the Romans. Britain sits on top of the world and on top of that sits this family, the most venerated since the Caesars. Boom. Boom. Boom.

The facts are blasted towards Eddy's brain, where they are supposed to lodge for all time. But they are too big, so he pretends he has not heard them. He shields his memory against them and thrusts them back out into the wide blue yonder, where they may circle aimlessly, forever unknown.

I am just a slow boy in Norfolk, he thinks. Nobody else. Truly, I assure you. A slow boy, not up to the mark. He feels sleepy. His head droops to contemplate the carpet.

'Wake up, Eddy!'

The chalk takes flight once more.

That night Eddy dreams. He is on his favourite pony, riding out through the gates of Grandmama's castle. The soldiers salute as usual. Before them is the broad, endless avenue that ribbons out towards the southern horizon. It is a lovely warm day; the trees are blowsy with leaves, the grass speckled with wild flowers. Eddy and his pony trot gently at first, then break into a canter. He can hear voices behind him, familiar voices, loved voices, calling his name, telling him to stop, to come back. But he does not. The canter erupts into a gallop; the wind streams through the pony's golden mane until it is almost horizontal.

'So where are we going?' shouts the pony.

'Anywhere, anywhere. Just away!' he shouts back.

'If that's what you want,' says the pony.

It gallops faster and faster until they are nearly at the southern horizon where the avenue runs out, where the land itself runs out. What will happen then? It will be any moment now.

'Stop! What are you doing?' Eddy asks.

'You said you wanted to get away,' says the pony.

'I do, I do... but we can't...'

'Nonsense! Of course we can,' says the pony. 'We can do whatever we want, go wherever we want, be whoever we want. Are you game?'

'Oh, yes!' Eddy shouts into the wind. 'Yes!'

'Hang on, then.'

As they reach the hazy line of the horizon, Eddy's heart pounds in his head. He clings on for dear life, but for once he is not afraid. He can feel the pony's every muscle tensing under him. It gives a wild, wonderful whinny. He wraps his arms tighter round its neck as it takes off into the clear, welcoming air. Still Eddy is not afraid, not at all. As they climb higher and higher into the sky, he even dares look down. The avenue disappears, the towers and battlements are veiled beneath the wisps of cloud in a forgotten life. He wonders where they are going, but he does not really care. All he knows is that he is free of every thought and feeling that has ever troubled him. He will never go back; he cannot go back.

*

1876. Eton College.

A flock of happy crows in their black tailcoats, they perch along the length of the high, red wall. A hundred or more, he reckons. As he walks out onto the pitch, they begin the usual chant:

'Big Jem. Big Jem. Big Jem.'

Smiling down on him, it is as if they are bowing their heads. The champion of the Wall Game has taken the field. All hail.

He certainly looks like a champion. God, in whom he has decided not to believe, has blessed him with the height, weight and strength of a warrior. That massive head alone is enough to scare his opponents. The rest of him is as unyielding as bricks and mortar.

'A veritable Hector,' sighed his tutor, Oscar Browning, on the day they crowned Jem Stephen as Keeper of The Wall. 'The son of Priam has risen from legend and is amongst us again. The college has never known such a player.'

'Stuff and nonsense, O.B.,' he had replied, blushing.

In time, he will learn not to blush, to coolly accept the bouquets scattered at his feet. But for now, the reddened cheeks and the shy grins only make them adore him more. Besides, he knows that a gentleman must at least pretend to modesty. Yet inside the huge head, he is certain that it is true, that his prowess will be remembered down the ages. He pictures the young crows on top of the wall shrivelled into old men, nesting in the leathery warmth of the House of Lords or a club in Pall Mall.

'Did you ever see Big Jem Stephen play?' they will wheeze.

'There was nobody like him, before or since. He was kissed with magic, that boy.'

It is as well his shoulders are broad; they are so laden with the expectations of others that a lesser man would crumple. If he follows his estimable father into the law, they say, it will be Lord Chancellor at least. Prime Minister even. Indeed, if the House of Saxe-Coburg-Gotha were removed by revolution and a republic declared, why not Big Jem for President? They laugh of course, but they are not entirely joking.

Sometimes, on his pinnacle, he feels a little lonely. But he is accustomed to that from an early age, when the estimable father, in pursuit of his own apotheosis, goes to ply his trade in the governance of India and takes his wife along with him. It is ambitious blood that flows in the veins of the Stephens. In three generations, they have come from nothing to prominence, wealth and respect. So the furniture is put into storage, the children into schools. Whatever pain his father may feel at parting, ambition is his opiate.

'One day, it will be your turn to run with the baton,' his father writes from Delhi, 'and carry our name to even greater renown. You must begin to prepare at once. Make yourself fit in mind and body. Gain wisdom from your studies and humility from the love of God. Waste no time. Failure is not to be contemplated.'

So they abandon him to this ancient jumble of brick and stone beside the snaking river. In revenge, he finds here the home he has never known. Somehow, the soul and spirit of the place comforts, nurtures and raises him. Its past becomes his past, its beliefs his own, its heart and his beat together.

And there is no shortage of others willing to father him;

those single gentlemen who hide themselves away in the safety of ivy-clad courts. From a sweet, shy boy, Jem Stephen roars into a fine-looking youth. Among the single gentlemen, there is much competition for him, but it is only under the wing of Oscar Browning that he permits himself to take occasional shelter. Only to dear, silly, clever O.B. will he ever show a chink in his burnished armour. Only to O.B. does he show his first faltering verses.

'My dear, the poem is not without flaw, but it has the freshness of dew on a May morning,' says O.B. one night on his usual round of the dormitories. 'In truth, there was a star danced and under that you were born.'

A fat finger reaches out and brushes his cheek. Like the other handsome ones, he is practised now at dealing with these things.

'O.B., you go too far again,' he laughs.

'Then I suppose I must be punished.'

All those in the dormitory know the form. O.B. bends his fat arse over Jem's bed. Jem laughs again and reaches for the slipper.

As the years pass, he heeds his father's instructions. He wastes no time. That head is so large, they joke, because it is stuffed with brains. He wins scholarships, sails through examinations. His intelligence is respected, his opinions valued, even by the most distinguished masters. His company is sought by all. Everyone wants to be his friend, his disciple, his admirer. He has more passionate love letters than he knows what to do with. He reads them in bed at night, under the quilt. They excite him, but they frighten him a little too. He is always quite sure of what he knows, but not of what he feels.

And when his parents finally return and come to inspect him, it is they who are inspected. They find themselves the objects of curiosity, feted even, as the begetters of someone quite remarkable. Jem never forgets the look he catches on his father's face; on the lips a smile, in the eyes a fury.

Now on the pitch, under the high, red wall, the whistle blows. Like a lion, Jem powers through the jungle of arms and legs. He likes the bitter tang of fresh sweat, the pliant warmth of the other bodies. He likes the feel of their arms round him, their hot breath, their damp, flushed faces close to his. He never feels lonely then.

'Big Jem. Big Jem,' they chant again.

The very next morning, a boy is found dead in bed. The doctors come but they cannot isolate a reason. God has called him, they say, shaking their heads to excuse their ignorance. It was his time. Everyone is shocked of course, but Jem Stephen, Keeper of The Wall, is shaken to his core. The boy was strong and vigorous. It was only yesterday that they had grappled together on the pitch. For days he worries, in case he himself has been somehow touched by death.

In the churchyard, O.B. and the younger boys weep like women. The chaplain trumpets the appropriate lines over the open grave.

'Fear no more the heat of the sun...'

What bloody nonsense, Jem thinks. He loves the heat of the sun. It is his natural place, his birthright even. He will fly as close to it as he can. His wings will be invulnerable. He tells himself that he fears nothing. If golden lads must come to dust, then so be it. But he, Jem Stephen, will not go before his time. He simply has too much to do. Lord Chancellor, Prime Minister, whatever. He will outshine them all.

But whichever path he takes, he will always be Keeper of The Wall.

CHAPTER III

1882. HMS Bacchante. The Mediterranean.

He knew the moment would come, but when it does, it is no less of a shock. He and Georgie are to be parted at last. It is like a chasm opening at his feet.

A letter is waiting at Malta. When they reach home after this long voyage, Georgie is to be turned round like a freshly victualled ship and sent right back to sea. A career in the navy; the age-old albatross of the second son.

But the letter has not yet done its work. It also decrees that Eddy himself will go to a university. For a moment, he thinks he has misread it. But no, there it is in black and white, in his Papa's hasty, thoughtless hand. A university? Are they serious? Surely not. It is a missive from a madhouse.

'So what do you think?' asks Eddy, as they steam west towards the Pillars of Hercules on a piss-wet morning.

Georgie is staring out of the porthole; the tough midshipman stroking his baby beard. But he has thrust a finger in his left ear and is wiggling it frantically. Eddy knows what that means; Georgie has been doing it since he grazed his first knee. He is nearly seventeen now but, being so small, he seems much younger. Eddy wants to reach out, put a hand on his shoulder, but that would not be welcome any more.

'Well, I'd rather stay at home and shoot, but got to do something, I suppose. Grandmama expects every man to do his duty.'

They avoid each other's gaze. Eddy looks out of the other porthole at the curtains of rain. The only sound is the distant dull heartbeat of the engines.

'Damn and blast!' cries Georgie suddenly.

He rushes to the white porcelain pitcher and vomits. They are both wizened old mariners by now, used to the most merciless of storms. Neither of them comments on the fact that today the sea is flat calm. Georgie throws the sick through the porthole, wipes his mouth, laughs.

'And you to a university. Christ almighty!'

For three years, this tiny cabin, squashed beneath the poop, has been their home. It is their only bulwark against the others. Life is rough for everyone on this ship, but it is rougher for the boys they call 'Sprat' and 'Herring'. Nobody else has their parents' portraits hanging on the gun-room wall. Nobody else must take so many beatings now on the principle that they will be untouchable in years to come. Nobody is treated with less respect when they are initiated into the sailor's life, stripped naked, their buttocks caned and soap shoved up their arses.

It does not take long for Georgie to learn to fight back. The others taunt him with the penny dreadful magazines they hide in their sea chests, the stories of his Papa and Mrs Langtry, his Papa and some other.

'Ignore them,' says Eddy, as he cleans up yet another battered lip, another bloody nose. 'We should be used to it by now.'

'Ignore them?' Georgie shouts. 'Don't you love Mama like I do?'

'Don't be silly.'

'But you won't fight for her? Oh, I forgot. You can't fight, can you?'

Georgie is ashamed that his elder brother cannot fight. Goodness knows, Eddy has tried, but his efforts are ungainly, devoid of nobility. They incite laughter, not fear. Georgie even tries to teach him, but it is a lost cause.

'Oh, Eddy,' he says, after flooring him yet again. Eddy lies on the planks, all arms and legs, like a crumpled marionette.

But Georgie picks him up. Georgie always does. And now they are taking Georgie away from him.

In the night, he cannot sleep, though he is on early watch at five. He looks across at Georgie in the hammock beside him, rocking gently in the swell. He reaches out and almost strokes his brother's cheek, his fingers a hair's breadth above the skin. Georgie half-opens his eyes, smiles, closes them again. Eddy blesses him, thanks God yet again for him. Without Georgie, he will surely crumble like a rotten spar.

When he drags himself up onto the deck, the dawn is breaking. In less than a week, their lives at sea will be over. How odd it will seem not to stand here alone at sunrise any more. He will miss the peace of it, a peace he finds nowhere else in the maelstrom of the ship. In truth, these solitary hours do him no good. Too much time to think and be afraid. Too many big black clouds.

'What a misery you've become lately,' says Georgie one day. 'A real curmudgeon.'

'That's rich coming from you,' Eddy replies. Sometimes now he answers back, but not as often as he should.

As he stands at the prow in the rising light, he thinks how little their lives really changed on this ship. They merely swapped their beloved red-brick house for four thousand tonnes of wood and iron. HMS *Bacchante*, as she hauls them across the oceans, under steam or sail, is just another prison. Still the endless boom of the Reverend Dalton and his dreary catechisms. The moments when Eddy drifts into some other place and does not remember it. The chalk flying through the air.

This great voyage was supposed to turn him into a grown-up, but he knows he isn't really. How absurd that he might achieve such a thing. Nevertheless, he has somehow learnt, with Dalton at his shoulder, to give the appearance of it.

In Australia, Albert Victor opens fetes and hospitals, creaks down a mineshaft to hear a gang of blackened men sing *God Save The Queen* in a fetid tunnel. In South Africa, he meets the King of the Zulus; in Japan, the Mikado. He and Georgie have their arms tattooed with red and blue dragons, just like Papa's, so now they carry at least the markings of a man. With trembling hands, Eddy delivers dull little speeches written by Dalton. But the crowds cheer them as if they were the words of Solomon. As the months pass, he notices that it is to him that the huzzahs are directed, on him that their eyes mostly rest. He thinks Georgie sees it too. Often now, when they are on display, Georgie puts some space between them, ebbing back, stranding him on his own. Each time, Eddy feels a flutter of fear in the pit of his stomach.

'Gibraltar on the horizon, three degrees to starboard.'

A voice shouts down from aloft. Eddy sees it now, rising from the curve of the earth, a limestone lion dozing in the early sun. But its people will long be out of their beds, ready to welcome them. The Governor's Lady will be taking her bath. The ceremonial horses will have been buffed until their coats shine as brightly as the soldiers' boots. Fat men in gold chains will be sweating already, wishing it were all over. The town will be all of a flutter with flags and bunting, like a tart with no taste; its dignity tossed away to welcome two scrawny boys. Eddy's heart sinks.

'We sailors might go round and round the globe,' says the old salt who teaches them their knots, 'but we are never really *in* it.'

He and Georgie had been sent away to see the world, but how can that be possible when the world will never truly show itself? It will always wear its gold chains, its big feathered hat, its vacant smiles. The world will always be nervous in their company and, when they have passed by, it will breathe out and go back to being itself. And Eddy and Georgie will move on to the next place, embalmed in their blissful ignorance of what that really is.

But it is not quite accurate that he has learnt nothing of the world. This is the navy after all. In the depths of the night, it is not only the weevils and spiders that sneak and scurry below decks, seeking out the darkest corners. In his hammock, he thinks of these things, is excited by them. At the same time, he is excited by the postcards of the beauties which his brother hides in his sea chest. He wonders why his body steers such a wild, erratic course, why the violent expulsions that soak his thighs in the night are triggered by such diverse images. He does not understand; just as there has been so much else in his eighteen years he has been unable to understand.

'Will it always be like this?' he asks God, as he watches the bow slice through the waves, a cleaver of proud black iron in the burgeoning morning. 'Am I to reach my grave no wiser than I left my cradle?'

Across the deck comes a scratching sound. Georgie's kangaroo has woken up and frets to be let out of its cage. It is only a baby, no bigger than a small dog. It wants to hop to the galley where its breakfast is being prepared alongside everyone else's. Georgie is fussy about what it eats and is cross if it is not provided. It is his special present for his mother, an exotic addition to her little menagerie at home. It will be feted and fussed over, exhibited to visitors, photographed with Grandmama.

Eddy releases it. Head tilted to one side, it gazes up him with wide curious eyes. In a few days, they will both go down the gangway at Cowes. By then, a blanket of cloud will have pulled itself over the ship. Papa and Mama will be on the jetty with his three sisters. Grandmama, too, black and white as the weather, ready to embrace him back to her bosom. The little kangaroo will find itself in a cold, grey land; the ground under its paws will feel strange to it, the skies oddly dark. When it grows up, it will try to run free, but it will meet fences, walls, barriers it cannot cross. As it stares at him, Eddy wonders what it sees or what it wants.

Something inside him lurches and shifts, strains against its ropes. He has some nuts in his pocket. He stretches out his hand. When it comes close, he thinks how simple it would be to pick it up and go together into the sea. To be spared from the half-lives that await them. They would feel no more than a few seconds of fear then all would be done with. A blessing, really. After all, he himself has lived with fear for years now, the fear of almost everything. A few more seconds would hardly signify. How easy the fall, how swift.

Instead, he strokes its head as it nibbles from his palm then hops off towards the smells from the galley. After breakfast, Georgie will put it back in its cage, then they will don their dress uniforms and go to smile at the Governor's Lady.

It is a few days later, on the very morning when The Lizard pushes itself out of the Cornish mists, that the cry goes round the ship. Georgie's little pet has gone missing. The latch of its cage hangs limp and broken. For hours they search from prow to stern, under every bunk, in every corner of the hold, until they are forced to draw the tragic conclusion.

Georgie's glance moves between the broken latch and the stone-grey sea. He refuses to weep of course, but his voice quivers in his throat.

'Why did it want to escape?' he says. 'What a life it would have had.'

*

1883. Sandringham, Norfolk.

In the bedroom they have shared since childhood, at the little table where they used to wade through Dalton's swamp of homework, Eddy picks up his pen to write to his brother. It is such an odd thing to do. They have never had to write to each other before. Until now, they have scarcely been apart, have breathed the same air. The space that Georgie has left is the emptiest Eddy has ever known.

My dear boy,

I can't tell you how strange it seems to be without you and how much I miss you in everything all day long. I know tough old mariners like Sprat and Herring don't care for soft talk, but I hope you'll forgive me at this turning point for us both.

The single thing I'm most grateful for in my life is that Papa and Mama recognised how much I depend on you and that we should be brought up closely together. This has been a godsend for me, but I'm sure it must have been tedious for you. Sorry for those countless times when I've infuriated or disappointed you. I do so yearn to be more like you, dear old Georgie. How often have I wished that you were the elder, and I'm quite sure Papa wishes that too. You'd certainly make a better fist of things than I ever will.

Dear boy, wherever you wander, Sprat will be thinking of Herring constantly and praying for your safe return. You are so much more than a brother to me; you are my best friend. It seems, however, they've found me some new 'friend' to guide me through my time at the university (Me? Ha!). He's a few years older than me, some brainbox they've hunted down to tutor me and shake me awake (as Papa puts it). He comes here to tomorrow to meet us all. His name is Mr Stephen. I'm dreading it rather, so I hope he'll be a decent chap. But even if he's a saint, he can never replace my beloved brother (who most certainly is not). Anyway, I've vowed that I will do everything I can to please him.

Sorry again for all this soppy stuff.
Yours affectionately,
Old Eddy

When he lays down the pen, he notices it is one that Georgie often used. He decides that he will take it with him to Cambridge, a little piece of Georgie in his pocket.

He looks out of the window at the view he has known all his life. It is a May morning, but a fierce wind is whipping round the red-brick house, decapitating the petals from the regiments of tulips. Eddy gives a little shiver.

He lies down on one of the two beds, stares over at the other. The coverlet is smooth and crisp and clean, the pillows white and puffed as the chest of a cockerel. How he wishes everything were rumpled and smelling of those spectacular farts.

He aches to be asleep again. He has not slept well for nights on end yet, during the day, he can hardly keep his eyes open. Outside the window, the wind is carrying in more clouds off the German Ocean. They are black as storm waves at midnight. He closes his eyes and clings on to Georgie's pen as if, like some piece of infinitesimal flotsam, it might save him from drowning.

CHAPTER IV

1883. Sandringham, Norfolk.

'He's out in the garden talking to Buddha,' she says. 'Shall we go and interrupt them?'

The beautiful face, the face that launched a thousand postcards, smiles up at him. She slips her arm through his and leads him out onto the terrace. Jem Stephen can scarcely believe this is happening. What a stroke of luck. Just when he needed it.

When he ascended from Eton to Cambridge, he cut a swathe through the Fens as easily as he had taken the meadowlands by the Thames. The competition had been fiercer, the challenge greater, but he had conquered again. Everything on which he set his mind fell to him. The cynosure of all eyes. The object of desire. The presidency of the Union. Even, lest he almost forget, the law degree that his father, now the eminent judge, had demanded he take. Now, at twenty-four, fragrant with the scent of all his garlands, he is ready to go to the Bar. But to Jem Stephen, those law books are the tombstones of ambition. He does not want a profession. He wants so much more than that. He *is* so much more than that. He is a poet. He is an orator. He is a great mind. He is not to be labelled, not yet at least.

'Take me. Use me,' he wants to say to the world. 'I am ready for anything.'

And now it has come to him. In a letter from that tedious Reverend Dalton. The old saying is of acorns that grow into mighty oaks. But this is an oak full-grown already. Within its shelter, he may climb higher than he ever imagined.

Dalton has told him the boy is dozy, impossible to rouse. Unteachable almost, retaining next to nothing. The job will not be easy. But Jem Stephen is undaunted. With Alix on his arm, chattering about nothing like some pretty bird, he strides towards his destiny along an avenue of pleached lime trees.

Suddenly, though, he breaks out in a sweat, his head swims, his heart bangs, he feels a little faint. Damn it! Not again, not now. He breathes slowly from his diaphragm, calms himself in the way he has taught himself to do. In a minute or so it passes, as he knows it will. What a fool you can sometimes be, he says to himself, as Alix prattles on. These stupid moments of darkness and terror. Nobody doubts you except you.

The Buddha is a great fat fellow with a big belly and breasts like a woman. The statue came all the way from China, a gift for Bertie, on a specially strengthened boat. Having travelled so far, Buddha seems content to rest here for eternity, smiling benignly at them all. But if the giver of the gift had hoped that such a presence might inspire them all to be more spiritual, he must be sadly disappointed. This is not a house where the opening of the mind is considered of importance.

The three sisters are romping on the lawn, throwing balls

for little dogs. Jem gives them his attention for a moment. The girls are curving into women now, but it is clear that none will ever be beautiful, none will ever threaten their Mama. Looking out at the world with Bertie's bulbous German eyeballs, they must all see that by now, he thinks. At the very moment of their blossoming, they must know that they are already doomed to the shadows. When they see him approach, the girls stop romping and cower into the shadow of the Buddha. Are they nervous of people from beyond the walls of the park? Jem wonders. He absorbs all this in a second, feels sorry for them, dismisses them from his mind.

Now he spots the boy, propped against the base of the statue, cap over face against the glare of the late morning sun. As Dalton predicted, he appears to be asleep.

'Come, everyone, and meet Mr James Stephen,' calls Alix. 'The poor man is going to help us deal with our darling Eddy. Oh Eddy dear, do wake up.'

The boy lifts the cap, stifles a yawn and blinks against the light. Jem is surprised. Dalton had not mentioned his beauty.

As Jem walks towards Alix's children, his head blots out the ball of the sun. A halo of yellow and gold shimmers round him, as in some religious painting. The sisters sigh, almost in unison. Buddha is dethroned at once. This new god, just off the train from King's Lynn, wears a white linen suit and a white hat, its floppy folds only emphasising the geometric perfection of his features. When the hat is respectfully removed, it releases a tousled mop of fine brown hair. He shakes the sisters' hands as if trying to dislodge their teeth. They blush and retreat once more into the shade of the pleached limes. The boy uncoils long legs and stumbles to his feet. He extends his hand, looks uncomfortable when Jem pumps it hard and does not release it, staring into Eddy with sharp blue eyes. The boy mutters some words of welcome.

'I hope, sir, that you'll soon call me Jem, as my friends do.'

He says it firmly; more a command than a suggestion. Jem Stephen is used to being listened to. He sees no reason why anything should be different in this case.

'Do you think, Mr Stephen,' asks Alix, 'that you can coach our silly Eddy so he doesn't disgrace us among the clever people in Cambridge?'

'Everyone has gifts Ma'am,' replies Jem. 'Everyone can make a contribution to the greater good.'

'Well, Eddy's gift is a kind and loving heart,' she says, 'given to him by God. And we rejoice in that. But *do* see if you can find a trace of anything else.'

She breaks into peals of laughter and raises her parasol. He is to be honoured with an inspection of her little dairy and to see the Brahmin cows which Bertie brought back from India. She takes his arm again and leads him back along the avenue of pleached limes.

Jem looks over his shoulder. The girls follow silently, but pregnant with giggles. Eddy trails behind them, fanning his face with his cap. Jem waits until he catches his eye and sends him a smile to outshine the sun.

'*There is a position to be filled*,' said Dalton's dull letter.

But what might that be exactly? Could he become more than a tutor, more than a companion? Could he become a new brother? Is not *that* the real position to be filled? Surely, Jem Stephen is the perfect candidate. Surely, he is entitled to nothing less.

'I am ready for anything,' he repeats to himself.

Bertie is at home today, flown in from his other world. As they pass in front of the house on their jaunt to the dairy, he is standing by the window of the Saloon, belching his cigar into the innocent air. With a fat finger, he reels his son inside.

Despite the heat of the day, the Saloon is chilly. In these months, no spitting fire offers any comfort; the great hearth is dead-eyed and dark. It is a house that seems to carry the cold in its bones. Long before Bertie raised his new mansion of buttery stone and cocky red brick, a far simpler home stood here. A quieter, less obtrusive one, long weathered into the flat fields, accepted by the landscape. Might the spirit of those old walls still haunt the new ones? This is, after all, a spartan place of spartan people, where the sandy earth trudges out bravely, unadorned by many hills or forests, to drown itself in the waters of the German Ocean. It could hardly be claimed that this family is in any way spartan, in any sense unadorned.

'Houses have souls,' Alix had laughed in the winter, drawing her shawl more tightly round her. 'Maybe it disapproves of us, frivolous and spoilt as we are. Maybe it's even trying to freeze us out.'

Today Bertie sits in his favourite armchair, a raddled, chintzy thing, its chubby arms faded to grey with rubbed-in ash. It is a broad chair but, as time has passed, Bertie had expanded to fit it. Now it is hard to tell where Bertie ends and the chair begins. He looks up at the vast portrait above the dead hearth; he and Alix, the two boys. Painted as they need themselves to be seen. Together. Contented. No champing at the bit. Bertie sighs.

Eddy presents himself. They do not simply 'meet'. That is the way these things are done. It is this way between Bertie and his mother and the way it must be between him and his sons.

Eddy is commanded to get down on his knees. He is alarmed. Papa has never struck any of his children. What in God's name might he have done? But Bertie merely places his hands on Eddy's head, as if he is going to bless him. The fingers wander back and forth across his skull.

'What are you doing, Papa?'

'I'm looking for peculiar bumps. Bumps which might tell me what makes you tick. Because I'm damned if I know.'

Bertie searches some more, leans back in the raddled armchair with a sigh.

'It's called phrenology. The analysis of character through the protuberances and indentations of the cranium. Your grandfather ordered it done to me. Several times in fact.'

'And what did they say, Papa?'

Bertie pauses, blows out a long, slow puff of smoke.

'That I was a disaster. A calamity waiting to happen. It looked like I might be given a one-way ticket to Bedlam. Indeed, your Grandmama is still firmly of the opinion that would have been the best course. She tells me so frequently.'

Bertie glares at the ash gathering on the tip of his cigar. A sudden breeze from the window dissolves it onto the arm of the chair. He rubs it into the fabric with his thumb.

'Well, that's just silly, Papa,' says Eddy. 'How could you be a disaster? You are a great man.'

His father rises out of the chair. He goes to the window again, belches his smoke out into the garden. Eddy is left holding the edge of his Mama's piano. *Love's Old Sweet Song* is on the stand. She is driving them mad with it.

'You are a great man, Papa,' he says again. 'I wish I could be just like you.'

Bertie's free hand twists the tasselled border of the heavy velvet curtain.

'No, that would be a terrible mistake. I don't want you to be like me. Oh dear no.'

'Well I think you could do anything Papa. Anything you set your mind to. One day you'll show them all.'

The words tumble out of him on a wave of love.

'And I'll do whatever I can to support you. Georgie too. We will be by your side.'

Bertie stubs out his cigar on the window sill and throws it out onto the gravel, safe in the knowledge that someone will spot and remove it within the hour. He lays his hands on Eddy's shoulders.

'Georgie doesn't matter,' he says. 'It's you who matters. It's who you become that matters.'

Bertie stares hard into him, runs his fingers across the skull again.

'So who *are* you?' he asks. 'Where's the ruddy bump or crater which will tell me that? We sent you round the world for three whole years in the hope that, when you came back, we'd somehow see you more clearly. But when you walked down the gangway at Cowes, I still couldn't. I could see your brother of course. He's a fairly simple soul. Brightly lit, few shadows there. But you?'

Bertie lights up another cigar, throws the match out of the window.

'And you give us no help. Most of the time you're half-asleep and when you're awake you hardly say a word. Dalton has all but written you off. He came to me the other day, confessing that he can hardly get a damn thing into your head. I thought the poor man was going to weep.'

'I'm sorry Papa. I've always done my best.'

'Look, I don't much care about all that. I hated school too. But you're nearly a man now. I need to see where you're heading. For God's sake boy, give me a clue. Show me something of you. Anything will do.'

Eddy does not know how to answer. He is torn between distress at his father's disappointment and elation that he is talking to him about anything of consequence. Bertie is an emotional soul; he cries at the opera or when some old animal must be put down. But he rarely opens the door to himself. Now Eddy wonders if there is a chink of light.

And did he hear rightly? Did his Papa say that Georgie does not matter but that Eddy does? Did he say that? Of course Eddy knows the reason why it is said, the awful, unthinkable reason. But it has never actually been put it into words before. So Eddy matters more to Papa than Georgie? His heart is bursting, but the words will not come. Bertie still stares at him. Then his shoulders are shaken, roughly, violently even. But still the words do not come. Bertie sighs and pats his cheek, smoothes down Eddy's jacket where he has creased it. He cares about such things.

'Alright son,' he says, as if Eddy were a pony frightened by a wasp. 'Alright.'

Bertie goes back to his window. On the lawn, Alix and the girls have stopped on their way to the dairy and are playing catch with one of the little dogs. Jem Stephen stands and watches, a rock of serenity in the whirlpool round him.

'Come here,' says Bertie. 'Look, there's your model. Not me, him. Young Mr Stephen seems to be an excellent fellow. A scholar and a sportsman. Brains and brawn. Sound in mind and body. The perfect young Englishman. Just what we need you to become too. He even writes poetry apparently, though I'm not expecting you to go that far.'

Eddy looks out at Jem Stephen. For a moment, the usual black cloud hovers over him again. How absurd. How could he even begin to compare? But he is aware of a strange excitement too. Perhaps, being a god from Olympus, Jem Stephen can even move clouds.

'I've had a long talk with him about you,' says Bertie. 'Study him in everything. Follow his lead. Let him guide you where he will. Let him make a man of you.'

Out in the garden, little Maudie throws the ball too far, almost up to the window. But the dog flies off after a rabbit so Jem Stephen runs to fetch it, scooping up the ball like an eagle on a lamb, lobbing it back to Maudie in one perfect movement. Jem Stephen is at one with his world, with the earth and the trees and the sky. Eddy tries to imagine what that must feel like.

'Splendid throw,' shouts Bertie.

Jem throws them a cheery grin, as effortlessly as he had thrown the ball.

Eddy wonders if he is found or lost.

*

Jem Stephen squats on the top step of the staircase. Under his arse is a wooden tea tray, but he is so big it is invisible beneath him. At the foot of the stairs, Alix and the girls gurgle with excitement. They have all clattered safely downwards in a tangle of hoots and screams and now Jem must do the same. Eddy stands a little apart, watching him. All day, Jem has noticed how closely he is being studied.

He is certainly having a hectic day. Before luncheon, he is shown the Brahmin cows and how to make a pat of butter in the dairy. He is introduced to each of the horses by name and allowed to feed them sugar lumps. After luncheon, a fat old nag is found for him and they all trot off on a tour of the park, the woods and the coverts. They stop at the cottage of a sick labourer where Alix and the girls fuss over a new-born infant. They make Jem take it in his arms, whereupon it pisses all down his linen suit. The women shriek while the labourer and his wife near die of shame.

Now the man who has passed every test that Eton and Cambridge could pose him, must pass this one if he is to be truly esteemed under this roof. The girls clap and chant, like the crows at the Wall Game. Jem grins and pushes himself downwards. The sheer weight of him propels the tea tray down the stairs faster than they have ever seen it go, but it is also his undoing. Little Maudie had specially selected the tray as appropriate for a god. A gift from the Mayor of Norwich no less, but it cannot bear its responsibility. It splinters under him, its shards shooting out to left and right, abandoning him to tumble down the rest of the staircase in a windmill of arms, legs and flying hair.

Four perfumed handkerchiefs rush to stop the blood oozing from a cut on his forehead; four fans flutter to cool any fever which might have suddenly broken out. He is smothered in concern. For a minute or two, he tolerates the indignity then gets to his feet, rising like a colossus from a sea of silks and satins. He gazes down on them with a hearty smile from which he has not completely succeeded in erasing a twinkle of contempt.

'Really, ladies, please don't fret,' he says.

'Are you really sure you're alright?' asks little Maudie.

A deep voice roars into the hall.

'Of course he's bloody alright,' yells Bertie. 'He's a man, not a silly girl. Now go up and change for dinner and leave the men in peace. Mr Stephen needs a brandy.'

But in the Small Drawing Room, Bertie is as solicitous as his womenfolk. Jem is escorted to Bertie's own chair, given a stonking brandy, has his wound personally dabbed by Bertie's own handkerchief, embroidered with the three feathers. They smoke together, wrapped in a fug of solidarity against the silliness of women. Bertie speaks of his own brief time at Cambridge. The cruelty of being exiled to a villa outside the town, watched every moment by stuffy old men, not able to be a real undergraduate, not able to have fun.

'But Eddy here will be allowed to live in college,' he says. 'These days the young don't know they're born. Everything handed to them on a plate.'

Eddy lurks behind his Turkish cigarette, says nothing. He crosses and uncrosses his legs; the fingers of his other hand drumming on the arm of the sofa. Jem sees a muscle twitching in his jaw.

'On a bloody plate,' says Bertie again.

Jem shifts in his chair and winces. Oh dear, he groans, there must be quite a few bruises coming up.

'It really was incredibly stupid,' Eddy explodes without warning, his voice almost a shout. 'Any fool could have seen that the damn tea tray would never take Mr Stephen's weight. He could have been killed. I cannot think what got into Mama. Perhaps, just once in her life, somebody should say no to her.'

From the park, a peacock shrieks in outrage. In the Small Drawing Room, Bertie looks at his son, the frog eyes never wider. Jem protests that his injuries are nothing compared to those he suffers every Saturday on the football pitch, but Bertie does not hear him.

'You will withdraw those remarks,' he says, in a voice so quiet it can hardly be heard above the peacock. 'I am amazed that you should speak that way of your dear Mama who loves you so much.'

Eddy is still panting with rage. He throws his spent cigarette away and tries to light another. But the match trembles and dies in his hand. Jem Stephen hobbles over and strikes a new one. He leans in close to Eddy, the flame making the scarlet gash even more livid.

'Really, sir, I will be fine,' he says gently. 'But thank you.'

Bertie rises, muttering that it is time for them all to change. Jem Stephen bows, trying not to wince again. Eddy inclines his head in the required way.

'Well well,' says Bertie as he brushes past.

At dinner, the grander neighbours come and a show is put on for them. But Jem is not to be outshone by titles, jewels and decorations. Besides, his show is better. At first he says very little. He is gracious to the women and defers to the men. But he is like one of Bertie's thoroughbreds, trapped in the starting gate, pawing the ground. Then, with some question addressed directly to him, Bertie sets him free. He races away with the topic, blue eyes ablaze, body straining inside his evening clothes as he jumps over every interruption, every contradiction, using each phrase and sentence like muscles to power him forward. The table is riveted.

Though he himself would never claim to be clever, Bertie likes such people round him. Bertie catches Eddy's eye and raises a meaningful brow. Jem sees it, sees the expression on Eddy's face. It is a sad look, a hopeless look. Damn. Has he gone too far with his showing-off? Has he scared the boy? Dazzled everybody except the one person he must impress?

'*He is affectionately regarded by all,*' Dalton had written, '*but perhaps not by himself.*'

I must not forget that, thinks Jem Stephen. If I cannot raise him up to me as yet, I must lower myself a little to him.

With the guests gone, the lamps in the drawing rooms are turned off, the ashtrays emptied, the open windows closed. Bertie has decided that, as an aid to concentrated study, Jem and Eddy will work and sleep in a small villa in the grounds, so now they are shown out of the great front door and expelled into the night. With a rumble and thud, the bolts are thrown behind them. For the first time, they are alone. Perhaps now, Jem wonders, he will begin to talk to me.

With a sweeping gesture, he indicates the pathway through the gardens, inviting the boy to follow him as if he, Jem, were the owner of this little kingdom, not Bertie. From now on, he must make Eddy feel that his old life is shut away behind the bolted door. From now on, Eddy must feel that Jem is in charge, that only Jem can lead him forward.

It is just a few hundred yards to their place of exile. The moon is high and the night beginning to cool as they walk through the corridors of shrubbery. Jem says nothing. He waits. At last something comes.

'I do hope you enjoyed yourself this evening, Jem. You certainly seemed to.'

'Yes, indeed. Very pleasant.'

'I often worry that outsiders may find us a little trying *en masse*. All that shouting so Mama can hear.'

'Everyone was most gracious.'

The shrubbery opens out to display the little villa used to accommodate single gentlemen whenever a large party consumes the big house. Bachelor's Cottage is a plain edifice, suitable for some unimaginative merchant in a city suburb. Eddy's man is cross that they are to be banished to such a common outpost.

'There simply won't be enough room to lay out your clothes properly, sir. They will be permanently crumpled and it won't be my fault,' he says.

But tonight, the place looks almost pretty in the moonlight; its image reflected in the little lake that laps against its sloping lawn, a rowing boat tied to a post.

Jem stops and lights his pipe; Eddy yet another cigarette.

'Will there be another dinner party tomorrow evening?' Jem asks.

'Oh, I imagine so.'

'And the evening after that?'

'I imagine so.'

'And tomorrow you will ride out again with your mother and sisters?'

'Probably.'

'And visit another sick farmer with a revolting child?' Jem laughs.

'Perhaps,' Eddy laughs too.

'And will you make some time for yourself?'

'What for?'

'Nothing special. To sit alone. To be silent. To think.'

'Think about what?'

'Anything. The universe. The meaning of life. Yourself.'

Eddy does not answer, but looks out across the moon-white lake. Jem senses that he flees from such reflection like a fox from a hound.

'So what did you think of the world then?' asks Jem.

'The world?'

'You sailed round it for three years. What did you think of it?'

'Jolly interesting.'

'And what did it teach you?'

As they stroll round the edge of the water, Eddy tells him about learning to tie sailors' knots and climb the rigging, about the mine in Australia where the miners sang *God Save The Queen*, about meeting the King of the Zulus, the Mikado of Japan, the Khedive of Egypt.

'And what did it teach you about yourself?' Jem asks.

Again, Eddy does not answer. There is something like panic in his eyes. He shrugs and turns away towards the little house.

'Well, it must have taught you something,' Jem calls after him. 'And I shall make it my business to find out what it was.'

Inside the villa, Eddy's man waits for him, stifling a yawn. They say a polite goodnight, then, at the door to his room, Jem turns and beckons Eddy inside.

A fat trunk sticks its head out from under the bed. Jem's

clothes bulge from the little wardrobe. His shaving things are laid out by the washbasin. A portmanteau stands in the corner. He dumps it on the bed and pulls it open. It is bursting with books. Books of every size, shape and colour. Books mint-new or in crusty leather bindings that carry the smell of old, damp libraries.

Eddy stands uncertainly on the hearth rug. Jem throws a book at his feet, then another and another. Eddy steps back but Jem keeps on hurling them until his ankles are surrounded.

Ha!' Jem says. 'Like Joan of Arc at the stake. And it's high time we set your imagination ablaze.'

He comes right up to Eddy. Warm, pipe-smoke breath hits Eddy's face.

'There are many worlds, Eddy,' he says. 'Not just the geographical one you've already seen. But worlds we can visit inside ourselves. They are lying at your feet, waiting for us to enter them. Will you come and explore them with me?'

Jem Stephen holds out his big hand. Eddy blushes, the muscle in his jaw twitches again. Jem waits with his hand rock steady.

'Other worlds, Eddy.'

The boy reaches out, clasps it and holds Jem's gaze for the briefest moment. Then he extricates his feet from the pyre and eases himself out of the room.

CHAPTER V

Autumn 1883. Trinity College, Cambridge.

He is sick in the night. Twice. He flings the window wide but the stench still curdles the air. He pulls the covers over his head to escape it, to escape the terror of the day to come: his first day at college. The muscles of his stomach are as tight as the skin on a drum. He rubs them with his fingertips but they will not yield.

He had been dreaming of Papa at the moment he woke and had to sprint for the basin. Papa was holding his skull, searching for the bumps.

'Who are you, boy?' he asked. 'I'm damned if I know.'

Through the window, Eddy hears the sounds of the place waking up. He listens for any clues which might help him understand it. Voices reach him from the quadrangle or clatter up and down the staircase beyond his door. The voices of strangers who he must get to know. He will smile, shake their hands, say a few words in the way he has been taught. Of course they will be curious about him. He is used to that. But he wonders how it will be before he is discovered. In the quads, on the staircases, along the corridors, the judgement will take shape and be quietly spread. Allowances will be made as part of the judgement, but the judgement will stand.

He had watched it forming in Bachelor's Cottage. Jem Stephen asked if he might invite some others to join their summer weeks, to help Eddy get used to an atmosphere of what Jem calls 'lively learning'. Nice chaps, all of them. Harry, Patrick, Montague. And all so like Jem. Satellites round his sun. They meet Eddy with eager, unguarded eyes, excited to be there. But as the days pass, the eyes glaze over; the friendly grins still present but are now fixed and with the tiniest creak of an effort in them which was not there before. Soon he notices how they slow themselves down for the dawdler. Only Jem's expression never changes. Sometimes a flicker of impatience invades it, but he does not try to hide that. He explains the thing to Eddy again, urges him on, keeps faith in him.

But still Eddy struggles to see the point of it all. The world already mocks him not only as a fool but as less than a man. The magazine lies on the floor where he threw it last night, split open at the pages where someone, someone he has never met, let alone harmed, has drawn clever cartoons and penned nasty lines.

'*Oh don't hurt him!*' says one, as Eddy is shown playing hockey with the daintiness of a girl.

'*Isn't he beautiful? Too lovely to look at!*' says another, while Eddy combs his hair at the mirror.

He is sure that everyone here will have seen it. They will be laughing at him now, before they have met him, before he has even left the sanctuary of this bed.

Again, his stomach muscles tighten to imprison his rage. It is absurd that he is expected to do what he cannot do. He cannot learn French and German. He cannot understand Euclid, damn and blast him! He cannot remember the date of Agincourt or the building of Hadrian's Wall. Just as he could hardly master sailors' knots or the correct way to polish with linseed oil. Apart from shooting the birds down from the sky, he does not know what he is good at. He aches to find it, but perhaps there is nothing to find. He rolls over in the bed and punches the pillows until he can punch no longer.

'Rise and shine!' booms the voice. 'Big day. Big day.'

Dalton hammers on his door. The Reverend is here too, in overall charge, while he writes his chronicle of their voyage on the *Bacchante*. Eddy cannot imagine who would ever want to read it. It seems there is to be no escape from the old bore in this life. He pictures Dalton standing at his deathbed; himself ancient and wizened but Dalton unchanged. Still shouting. Still throwing pieces of chalk as Eddy's soul leaves his body.

He buries himself deeper under the covers. The anger ebbs and the fear flows again. But he is oh-so weary of being afraid. It cannot be right. God cannot have put him on this earth to live in fear. His only real peace is with his Mama, the silly sisters, his beloved brother. But where is Georgie? Which sea is he scudding across, tasting the salt in the wind, his mind clear and contented, worrying only about how many miles they will make before sunset. Where is Georgie?

'Rise and shine!' bangs the fist at Eddy's door.

In his bed, he cowers and whispers to the pillows. 'Leave me alone. I mean no harm to any man. Leave me alone.'

'Other worlds, Eddy.'

After the vastness of the oceans, Eddy's world shrinks to two battered leather armchairs in a dusty room. Every morning they sit here for four whole hours. Even when he is not physically there, it is at the centre of his thoughts.

The armchairs are pulled close together, as if proximity might speed up the transfer of knowledge. Books are scattered across the little tables and on the rug round his feet. He is Joan of Arc still. Tobacco smoke is so thick that, even in an icy November, they must open a window. Eddy watches it waft in little wisps across the broad face of the god.

Eddy still does not say much, though he believes he is saying a little more. But there is a problem. The thought which runs crystal clear in his mind trickles from his mouth clogged and muddy. Jem's own reflections gush forth, sparkling and perfectly formed. Eddy thinks how hard it must be for him to have to deal with this dullard. He feels the same guilt at being Jem's pupil that he feels about being Georgie's brother and his Papa's son.

They talk mostly of history and genealogy.

'Your family business,' says Jem, 'so you'd better learn the trade.'

Eddy still does not remember the dates of great battles, but Jem says that does not matter much. Bertie's boy is not required to take examinations anyway, so why don't they just enjoy the fun of learning. The fun of learning? Dear God.

But sure enough, after a while, he realises that he does not ache with boredom. He no longer stares at the pattern on the carpet, open-mouthed. No piece of chalk flies. Jem talks about the people at Agincourt, at Flodden, at Marston Moor and why they did what they did.

'So what do you think?' he asks.

'How do you mean?'

'What do you think about poor old Charles I? Saint or sinner?'

'My Grandmama always calls him the great martyr.'

'No, I want to know what *you* think.'

How odd. Eddy does not recall having been asked that before. Certainly not in Dalton's schoolroom. Never by Papa. Only perhaps by Mama when she has to choose a new bonnet.

But Jem goes further. He wants to know *why* Eddy thinks it. And so they talk about that. And maybe Jem agrees with him or maybe he leads him into some other point of view. Sometimes Eddy feels he is steered in directions which cannot be appropriate. Jem talks about the Earl of Essex and his fateful adventure in Ireland, a dashing chronicle full of blood and thunder. As on that first night at the dining table at home, Jem's telling of it casts a spell. Jem's mind, his body, his whole being are consumed by it and it is impossible not to yearn to follow where he takes you. But then, with the same fervour, he talks about Ireland now, about us still being there against the will of its people. Eddy begins to feel uneasy. He finds a nugget of courage.

'I'm not at all sure it's wise for me to discuss such matters.'

'Unwise? I'd have thought it essential,' Jem replies.

It is the first time Jem has ever acknowledged what awaits the boy. For once, Jem's eyes turn away and look down at the rug.

Then he begins to speak about the Empire, like Dalton used to do. But he does not pulverise his pupil with facts and figures. Instead, he talks about what he calls 'the spirit and soul of the thing'. Despite its imperfections, what a wonderful force for good it is. A beacon in a dark and troubled world. The zenith of our island story. How much he envies Eddy, he says, having the chance to play a vital role in that one day. He thinks he may go into politics himself, though his father, the judge, still pushes him towards the law.

'I want to make a real difference to people's lives,' he says. 'Maybe one day, we might be able to work together towards that goal. Wouldn't that be marvellous?'

Eddy feels a rush of comfort, warm as a bath, at the thought of knowing Jem forever; gratitude, too, that Jem might in some way devote himself to him. Such an absurd notion, he thinks, when it ought to be the other way round. There would never be any question in Eddy's mind which one of them was the god. Then comfort and gratitude are overwhelmed by the spectre of the great ivory chair. But Jem, as Dalton never does, sees the change of expression, the sudden panic in the eyes. He stops talking. He gets up to make a fresh pot of tea. He ruffles Eddy's hair just like his Papa has always done. But the touch of Jem's hand creates quite different sensations.

With his tea and a slice of Madeira cake, Eddy is given a new book to read. They are to discuss it tomorrow. It takes him the whole of a long, grey evening to get through it. Much of it he does not grasp, but those parts he understands are loathsome. It is a horrible book.

'So what do you think of what Mr Machiavelli has to say?'

'I dislike it dreadfully.'

'You could not do bad things, even if they might be for the greater good?'

'I don't understand how hurting people could ever make

life better for the rest of us. We would all be tainted, would we not? In the eyes of God at least.'

'But most of our politicians do it daily,' says Jem, 'with their cunning, their ruthlessness, their self-aggrandisement. They are Machiavelli to a man.'

'Perhaps you are right. I've never thought on these things.'

'A truly good soul, in a position of great influence, might do much to change those attitudes. Such a man might even change the soul of the nation. Don't you think so? What a worthwhile, even miraculous, life that would be.'

'But such a man would have to be strong,' says Eddy. 'Strong as Hercules.'

'Yes. And always true to himself.'

'So he'd have to know himself pretty well, wouldn't he?'

'Yes, indeed he would.'

'Oh well then...' says Eddy, reaching for the Madeira cake, by now a little stale.

Sometimes, when he is set something to read, he glances up at Jem and finds that he is being observed; the busy blue eyes quite still and fixed upon him. At other times, the eyes are closed for a nap and Eddy returns the observation. Though he is nearly as tall, he is a sapling beside Jem's oak. One big hand holds the pipe, the other splays out across a broad thigh. Eddy watches the muscles in the neck as he swallows the tea, the tip of the tongue between slightly parted lips.

From the sanctuary of the battered armchair, he looks straight at the bedroom door. Usually it is closed but from time to time it is half-open. The bed is always unmade, the sheets wrinkled up like old skin, the blankets and quilt half-slithered to the floor. One day, when Jem is called from the room, he goes in. What a mess. Athletics kit is scattered everywhere, shaving things loll about the washbasin, clogged with bristles and dried-up foam. This room, too, is shared with ancient books, forgotten in corners, spines twisted or broken, like a defeated battalion.

But the markings of the body are clear on the bed, the outline of the head on the pillow. When Eddy goes closer, he catches the smell of him; a mixture of cologne, pipe smoke and sweat. There are other odours, too, against which he tries to close his mind. He stretches himself out along the bed, placing his head on the flattened pillow, trying to discern where the arms and legs have been and arranging his own to fit. The scent is stronger now. Perhaps it overwhelms him because he falls asleep, maybe just for a minute or two, but wakes to find Jem standing over him. He mutters about having felt a little dizzy. Jem reaches out and pulls him up, holding onto him for a moment longer than necessary. Since that day, Eddy has never been back in the dishevelled bedroom but, in his thoughts, he rarely leaves it.

Tonight they are dining with some don at Queen's, a friend of Jem's from his time at Eton. Harry, Patrick and Montague will be there; the core of Eddy's new chums. It is silently understood that he is not their equal but they have all embraced him cheerfully. What fools they would be if they did not, but they are far from fools, and anyway the embrace is none the less real for all that.

At dinner, the host is exasperated with a corkscrew. Eddy offers some advice as he is good with corkscrews; a small skill, but his own.

'Go tell your grandmother to suck eggs!' snaps the host.

A gaping silence. The host is horrified, stammers an apology. But Eddy laughs and pats him on the back. His Papa would have been apoplectic, but, of course, Eddy is not his Papa. Jem notices, wonders if, among the quadrangles and the water meadows, the boy is beginning to care a little less about that.

In a moment, the conversation flies off again leaving Eddy behind, but he just leans back with his glass of port wine and his Turkish cigarette. He looks quite happy, Jem thinks. Soon the others will almost forget that he is there, but Jem never does. Jem watches him all the time, sees every little change in him, every chink of half-understood light peeping into his mind.

The conversation is unafraid; it knows no boundaries or inhibitions. It swoops from the glories of ancient Greece to the mess in the Sudan; from the hideous uniform of the Boys Brigade to the disgrace of Eton losing the Cup Final to a team of working-class Northerners.

'The barbarians are not just at the gates,' cries Jem, 'they are now in the changing rooms.'

'Try to think of them as Spartan warriors,' replies Harry. 'I'm quite sure that would help.'

Small smiles are passed along the table with the port, though Eddy is not included in those either. Jem is cross with Harry. The remark is too unguarded. For once, he does not look at Eddy, does not dare. Not yet anyway. The right moment will come.

Harry is a small man, wiry and pugnacious, his mind almost as quick as Jem's but not quite. They joust with sentences but Harry always falls. At once he will jump onto some new topic, but Jem will topple him again. Harry just sighs and refills his glass. He has a good heart and he shares the goodness of it. Jem hopes that Eddy marks these tiny victories, like the pride of the page at the triumphs of his knight.

Somebody's father has just been made a bishop, so a quarter-hour is passed in tearing apart the Church of England. Most of those round the table spend Sunday mornings in a warm, hungover bed rather than the chill of a chapel pew. Nobody here seems much enamoured of God. Perhaps they know that, in this life, the majority of the gods will always be on their side, so the disapproval of the Anglican one is of little consequence. Just as well Dalton is locked away in his rooms, wrestling with his epic chronicle. These garrets are pagan places.

Jem watches Eddy sipping his port, smoking, listening. These dinners, in the warren of rooms at the tops of twisting stairways, are perhaps the most important part of Jem's plan. Things are being said round Eddy, more diverse and alien than he has ever faced before. Jem sees the boy opening up to them, clinging to them like a puppy at a teat.

But then the talk turns to the future, though it is never of the things they will do, merely of what they *might* do. Pure, clear confidence buoys them up like a thermal. They chatter of the different heights to which they might ascend, the panorama of options which will be spread out before them and from which they will take a languid pick. If the first choice is not satisfying, they will simply go on to another. Now Jem sees a sadness pass across Eddy's face, the twitching of the muscle in the jaw. But only for a moment. Eddy pours himself another glass, smiles again in that sweet way of his, the way that melts Jem's heart.

Outside, a blizzard has swept in across the Fens. Snow beats against the leaded window. But here, in the turrets, they are safe and warm, protected from the tempests that batter lesser mortals. For a moment, the candle on the sill flutters in the draught, then burns as strongly as before.

Jem and Eddy totter together back towards Trinity. The blizzard has stopped, the wind has whistled away, the town has swapped its street clothes for a virginal white, as if it were taking the veil. But the journey is treacherous, even in alleyways as familiar as the veins on the backs of their hands. Steps and pavements have vanished entirely and Jem, much drunker than Eddy, soon stumbles and falls face down in Trinity Lane. He lies there, laughing, until he tries to stand up and finds his ankle will no longer support him. A big arm is thrown round Eddy's slim shoulders, half the width of Jem's own. In his old greatcoat, sodden with snow, it is like trying to carry a drunken bear.

'Don't desert me, Eddy. Don't leave me here to die.'

'Of course not, you old lush. What would I do without you?'

'Gosh, do you really mean that?' Jem says, wobbling in his arms, belching tawny fumes.

In the middle of Trinity Lane, he begins to sing *Abide With Me* at the top of his voice. Jem thinks that he has never felt happier. A window above them flies open.

'Abide somewhere else, you drunken bastards.'

As they cross their own quad, Jem nearly topples again. Eddy throws both arms round him to break the fall. They stand there shaking with cold and laughter. But it is very late now; they must try to be quiet. They bury their heads in each other's bodies to stifle the noise. Jem feels Eddy's arms tighten their grip round him. He tightens his own. Then Jem pulls his face away.

'Are we very drunk tonight, Eddy?'

'I rather think we must be.'

The moon has come out from behind the snow clouds and glares down on the naked whiteness of the quad. Maybe, Jem thinks, it wants to make sure that I will always see this moment. He cups his hands to his mouth, throws back his big head and begins howling at the moon. In this, as in all things now, Eddy will follow him. Together they stand and roar up into the stars.

CHAPTER VI

1884. Cambridge.

He is locked in a bathroom with a fat, old man. It is a splendid bathroom, the latest thing, the zenith of Mr Crapper's art. There is much giggling on the other side of the door on which they have banged and pleaded to no avail. They have now been in here for over half an hour. The joke is turning rancid and even though his host rarely pauses for breath, the conversation is beginning to falter.

Finding inspiration in the surroundings, his host falls back on a brief history of sanitation, with particular reference to the privies at Hampton Court in the time of Cardinal Wolsey, a great man with whom he seems to identify to a considerable degree. He has certainly emulated his physical contours. Eddy smiles and murmurs an interest. The host struggles on, describing in detail the death of King George II whilst on the lavatory. A dissected aortic aneurysm.

'A warning to us all,' he says. 'Never push too hard. The arsehole, like the rest of the body, will do everything in its own good time. That has always been my motto.'

Eddy thinks the fat old man is a little tipsy. The host asks permission to sit and plumps his fat buttocks on the new cedar-wood seat, as highly polished as the flanks of a stallion. With his balloon belly, he reminds Eddy of the Buddha in the garden at home. He tells Eddy that his shin is still sore from yesterday's lacrosse when Eddy whacked him on the shins with a stick. Would he like to see? He tries to roll up his trouser leg but his calves are too chubby, so he drops his trousers to display the bruises.

'You don't know your own strength,' he says, wagging a puffy finger. 'What a fool I am, at my age, to play against such a strong, handsome lad.'

Among the spires and in the turreted rooms, the fat old man is indeed a Buddha, worshipped and revered. Mr Oscar Browning, writer, historian, educational reformer, whatever that may mean. There is no greater intellect in Cambridge, says Jem, than dear old O.B. And certainly no kinder heart. Like a father to me almost. But it seems to Eddy that O.B. is also rather a fool, silly in a way which even he himself is not.

When these naughty boys release them, O.B. might be persuaded to sing a few arias at the *pianoforte*. Which one would please Eddy the most? He does not know anything about opera so cannot answer.

'I think for you, sir, there can only be one choice. *Voi Che Sapete*. The song of a young man discovering new emotions which he does not know how to deal with. A heartfelt plea for understanding.'

'That sounds jolly nice. Thanks very much.'

O.B. studies him with rheumy eyes. Eddy is only slightly uncomfortable with this because another change has crept over him since he came to this place. He is beginning to realise that he is not ugly. He had always assumed that he must be. The mirror had only shown him his Papa's bulging eyes, his Mama's fragile neck, elegant on a woman but wrong on a man. But there is no denying it now; he is not hideous at all. His body is tall and lean, taller than most of them, the puppy roundness chiselled away. He may not be a strapping athlete like Jem, but he is well enough made. At last, there is something in which he is effortlessly an equal, perhaps even a superior. This is a revelation. It has filled him with an unfamiliar power.

O.B. is still watching him. Eddy senses that the old man knows what is going on inside his head, that he has seen it happen countless times before. He says that Eddy is welcome to visit his bathroom at any time and use the mirror. He begs leave to say that it will never reflect a more pleasing image. He sees the boy's blushes and reprimands him.

'Enjoy your youth and good looks, my dear. They are a gift from God and you must allow other men to admire you without embarrassment. It is the form of affection most valued by the ancient Greeks.'

He points to a small statue of Plato perched on the window sill, beside a pile of lavatory paper.

'When one's own youth is past, to be able to appreciate it in others, even to share their pleasure in it, is some small compensation. Plato knew that. It is the finest, purest thing, quite untainted by anything untoward.'

Eddy hears a tiny crack in his voice and wonders if it is really possible that he, too, long ago, had been beautiful. O.B. reaches for a piece of lavatory paper, blows his nose into it and gives a little sigh.

'Having said that, we are only flesh and blood,' he says. 'So do not listen to all the rubbish talked nowadays about the perils of spraying the seed.'

Eddy blushes again, which the fat man takes as a confession.

'Enjoy it!' he says. 'It is one of nature's blessings. These killjoys preach that madness lies in doing it to excess, even that empires might fall. Nonsense. Without its blessed release, the British Empire would never have been built.'

Little does he know that Eddy, since his years at sea, is as addicted to the habit as the sad creatures in the dens of Whitechapel are to their opium. With his prick in his hand, he long ago noticed that the real world melted away into some distant galaxy. Yet he is not transported to some heavenly plane. Quite the opposite. In those febrile minutes, he is shatteringly here. Flesh and blood, skin and bone, aware of himself in a way he has never known before. He realises, however, that there is still much more to be discovered and he aches for it. He has no idea when or in what way it is to be achieved, but it must happen. And it cannot be long now. Surely, it cannot be long.

The door flies open and crashes against the newly painted wall. Jem is framed in the doorway, the big hands seeming to push it apart, like Samson in the temple. His eyes are fixed on the fat man with his trousers round his ankles.

'We are undone, sir!' says O.B.

Eddy is expecting to hear Jem's hearty laugh but it does not come. He sees that Jem is angry and trying to hide it but he says nothing, just turns and stomps away into the melee.

They are welcomed back into the party with catcalls and whistles. It is a crowded event tonight. No invitation in this town is more treasured by those to whom it is extended or mocked by those to whom it will never be given. Reverend Dalton is never invited, but lets Jem persuade him it would be an innocent pleasure for Eddy. But Dalton has been duped. O.B.'s Sunday evenings do not really take place on this cool restrained Fenland; those chosen to climb the forty-six steps up from the quad must prepare to enter a much more exotic landscape.

Thick Turkish carpets warm the floor. Any wall not hidden by books is hung with patterns of pink roses bursting through trelliswork. Small tables are crammed with plates of cake, jugs of lemonade, bottles of whisky, syphons of soda. Others carry framed photographs of those lucky enough to be numbered among O.B.'s vast acquaintance; here an emperor may rub up against a sailor in Her Majesty's navy. There is hardly any air to be breathed; it is too thick with conversation. Somebody tinkles badly on the grand piano. Every chair, settee and square inch of Turkish carpet is occupied. The noise is extraordinary. An ancient wizened don, drunk as a skunk, pontificates from an armchair to a circle of spotty acolytes; a beefy soldier in uniform doodles tunes on a clarinet.

Jem sits on a wing chair in a corner, as far as possible from the eye of the storm. A blond boy in spectacles sits at his feet. Jem's hand rests on the boy's shoulder. They talk earnestly together. Eddy catches Jem's eye but he looks away at once. Jem smooths the boy's hair and laughs the laugh that was withheld from Eddy. I am in disgrace, he thinks, and am not sure why. It was not my fault I was locked inside the bathroom. Besides, O.B. is his great friend. Am I not to have any other company unless Jem is there too?

Somebody yells out above the din. The host is going to

perform. Whoops and cheers trickle into respectful silence. Cigarettes are stubbed out. The soldier with the clarinet readies himself. O.B. flops down onto the piano stool like a seal. The firelight flickers on flushed, eager cheeks. Several people shyly offer Eddy their chairs but he chooses to stand against the chimney piece. This is a mistake as it gives him nowhere to hide. O.B. announces that this piece is dedicated to his recent cellmate. More cheers.

He outlines the meaning of the Italian as he knows, he declares, that there are philistines in the room. Somebody makes a noise like a fart. He tells them that first love is a wild, overwhelming emotion, a great wave crashing over us. A wonderful confusion of pleasure and pain, burning us like fire, freezing us like ice.

'But we must banish fear and surrender to it without question,' he says. 'There is no point in struggling; we are lost and stand no chance at all.'

'Oh so true,' sighs the ancient don. 'So true.'

Shy couples, nestled in shadowy corners of the room, look away from each other to study the design of the wallpaper.

But out of O.B.'s gross body comes a light and graceful voice. He translates the unknown language with such expression that Eddy is no longer hearing what is sung, he is feeling it. It seeps into him through the smoky air, over the rows of boyish heads. Jem Stephen still sits in his chair, his hand on the shoulder of the blond. Eddy cannot look at him. He sweats in the heat from the fire. He feels a little faint and wonders if he might pass out. How embarrassing that would be.

As the song ends and applause swells, he manages to glance at Jem. The big man sits icy still among the bravos.

He does not applaud, but he has removed his hand from the crouching shoulder.

The clapping melts into chatter. O.B. berates the soldier with the clarinet for playing a false note. The soldier flicks the spittle from the instrument into the podgy face then pulls him across his knee. O.B.'s trousers are round his ankles once again. As the soldier's rough palm slaps his arse, he squeals with delight. The crowd roars. The ancient don chuckles and dribbles a little. And Jem Stephen vanishes away down the forty-six steps, away into the night. For a moment, Eddy believes he will die of grief.

The American sits on a blue deckchair under a pretty blue parasol. Her dress is blue too, so she seems to melt into the summer sky. Eddy wonders if she planned it. It would not surprise him.

She sits very still, watching them play tennis, moving the parasol to match the arc of the sun. She is not like the other girls. They are colourless sparrows beside a bright blue dove. She smiles and nods, but she is not part of them. She does not require their company or their approval. It is impossible to imagine her intimidated by anything, least of all by the likes of him. Unlike the others, who swoon if he bids them good afternoon, she looks right back with alabaster cheeks and cool appraising eyes. She is tall with tumbling brown-gold curls and, though she is not quite beautiful, she enchants him. He has dreamt about her twice, in the way he used to dream about Mrs Langtry and the trollops on Georgie's naughty postcards.

He and Jem win their doubles match. Dalton and O.B. lead the huzzahs from the deckchairs. Eddy bows low to O.B. as he passes, which makes him gurgle like a fat baby tickled with a feather.

'That was much better than your game last week,' says the American. 'I think you're improving.'

'My dear, how impertinent you are!' exclaims her aunt.

The aunt is American too, the wife of a don, a lioness in lilac silk. Invitations to her tennis parties are as much desired as those to O.B.'s Sunday evenings. Eddy, of course, does not need to be invited, merely to come. In her lilac silk, the aunt stalks softly round her garden, nudging young people together or prising them gently apart, in accordance with her well-laid plans.

'Sir, it breaks my heart that you are *hors de combat*. What a frustration you are to me.'

But her impertinent niece is right. Eddy will never be a footballer or a cricketer, but he has discovered that he is passable at lacrosse and now tennis. Before long, he hopes to be welcomed for his skill and not just his presence. How strange and splendid that would be.

'Shall we take a turn?' asks the American, slipping her arm through his and steering him away. The aunt laughs and shakes her head. The sparrow girls watch, aghast at such presumption. But Eddy is quite partial to presumption; it is like a cool fresh breeze.

They circle the tennis court. Jem and the chums are sprawled panting under the trees, as far away as courtesy will allow from their hostess and the sparrow girls. Their heads are thrown back, drinking cordial, chaffing each other on the weaknesses of their game.

'Your friends seem to enjoy each other's company more

than that of the ladies,' she says, 'which is not what my aunt has in mind at all.'

'I suppose we're all rather shy with women. Apart from our sisters, if we have any, we don't get the chance to meet many ladies.'

'And I suppose the damsels of Girton are a little frightening. Or do I mean frightful?'

As they pass, Jem and the others stand up to shake her hand, compliment her on the parasol and the blue dress, praise the beauty of her aunt's garden. How much they all adore her aunt. A second mother no less. But his eyes are glazed over, hazy as the June sky. By now, Eddy has learned to read him like one of his own dusty books. Jem's mind is nowhere near the parasol and the blue dress. The American sees it too.

'It is so strange in this country,' she says. 'So little is quite what it seems to be.'

She spies a pony in the paddock, claps her hands and breaks away. She moves towards the fence slowly, as gracefully as his Mama. He watches her body move under the fabric. Her hips are wide and generous. She will bear her children easily, with no fear in her mind.

'Are you what you seem to be?' he asks.

'And that is?'

The pony has fallen in love with her at once and is nuzzling the alabaster cheek.

'I don't know,' he blushes. 'Different to most of us here. Sort of free.'

'Oh dear, we're none of us that. I've been sent here to find a husband and mustn't go home without one.'

'Well, I'd marry you, given half a chance.'

'Ha!' she laughs. 'I'd be welcomed back to Philadelphia with rose petals in my path, but your Grandmama would drop dead at the very thought.'

Nobody ever refers to his Grandmama in that context. Her mortality is the great unmentionable, even though it hangs over all of them. The American sees the shock in his face. She asks forgiveness for her rough, colonial ways.

'But you...' she says, 'I suspect you are exactly what you seem to be.'

'I hardly dare ask.'

She abandons the pony's muzzle and runs a finger down his cheek.

'Sweet. And not very sure.'

'Of what?'

'Of anything.'

The aunt is waving at them. Tea is about to be served. They turn back towards the house.

'We can all be free, you know,' she says. 'In our minds.'

'That's what Jem always says.'

'Then Jem, odd man that he is, is right.'

Eddy is shocked again. It is the first time anyone has criticised Jem in Eddy's hearing. It is as if she has blasphemed. He asks her reason, perhaps a little sharply, so she answers with a gravity that only makes it worse.

'He is too good to be true. So he must, in some way, be a lie. Be wary.'

They walk back past the tennis players under the tree. Jem lies stretched out on the grass; the usual floppy hat covering his eyes, Harry's wiry curls dozing on his big thigh. The American studies them again for a moment; an alien species.

'I wonder if Englishmen ever really fall in love. They marry of course, but generally from a prudent motive.'

Eddy searches the pale, open face for a veiled meaning but finds none there. Perhaps she refers to the need for a well-run establishment.

'As I must do one day.'

'Yes, indeed,' she says, 'and I'm sorry for it. But I hope that, within those confines, you will be as imprudent as you possibly can. Remember, I'll be watching you and cheering you on.'

'I meant what I said. I'd love to marry a girl like you.'

In his mind he sees her, kind and generous, as she climbs into his tight little bed and shows him the way. He sees her, stately and graceful, standing by his side as he sits on Grandmama's ivory chair.

The aunt bustles up in her lilac silk. Did we have a lovely walk?

'We are engaged to be married, Aunt,' says the American girl. 'You are the first to know.'

The colour drains from the plump, rouged cheeks. The mouth falls open, displaying the crumbs of cake on her teeth. The niece throws back her head and laughs so loudly that every head turns.

'Oh, you are a wicked young woman,' cries her aunt. She has to sit down in a deckchair and be given a glass of cordial. The sparrow girls look on in disgust.

'What a little Don Juan you are becoming Eddy,' says Jem later. He grins and fans himself with his tennis racket but his eyes are bleak as winter.

O.B.'s angel voice sings out through the open windows of the drawing room. That same damn song again. The wonderful confusion of the new emotions. Pleasure and pain. Eddy finds he is quite reconciled to both; after all, there is something noble in them, the very stuff of fairy tales. It is the confusion which troubles his nights in the tight little bed above the quad.

The other world, the world outside, does not leave him entirely alone. A telegram comes from London. There is a duty to perform. He must leave on the morning train. He goes to warn Jem that the battered leather armchair must sit empty for the next few days.

There is no answer when he knocks on the door, but he hears the weak murmur of voices on the other side. Perhaps Harry or Patrick is with him. They will be deep in the wisdom of Plato or the foolishness of Mr Parnell. He knocks again and opens the door. There are teacups on the little tables and a film of smoke hazing the air. Both armchairs carry the markings of a body and he is suddenly resentful. He had imagined the chairs being pushed apart when he was absent, but they are placed as closely together as always. He calls out Jem's name but gets no reply.

The bedroom door is slightly ajar. He creeps towards it like a mouse, though why he creeps he does not know. Jem is spreadeagled on the bed, eyes closed but still puffing on his pipe. Between his thighs, a blonde head is bobbing up and down. Eddy forgets that the bedroom door has a mind of its own, creaking wide open at the slightest touch. An unkind door, to give him such a view. The blond head, its spectacles still in place, turns round. Eddy can see the wetness framing his lips. The blond grins and goes back to his task. But Jem stares at Eddy, his pipe frozen in mid-air, just like his prick. Nothing about him moves at all, except the tear that begins to trickle down his cheek.

CHAPTER VII

1884.

The train crawls through the countryside between the seaport and the city. It is a glorious spring day, a day to be gazing from the window and rejoicing; the rebirth of the land, the soaring of the spirit. The train should be steaming ahead, blowing cheery whistles, but instead it crawls over the burgeoning greens, a black slug through a lettuce, defiling the landscape. Only ignorant children wave at it from the meadows; on the platforms of the towns and villages, they stand with bowed heads. It is a funeral train.

Albert Victor is escorting his uncle home from abroad. In the compartment next to this one, he lies in a box of darkest mahogany. He was just thirty, poor Uncle Leo. Only ten years older than Eddy. He liked his Uncle Leo. More like a chum than an uncle; not stiff and stuffy like so many of the others. And he had everything to live for. A young wife, one child and another on the way. But he carried his destruction within him; when he bled, it would not stop. Year after year, his chance of a future trickled away. In the end, it was a slippery step which killed him. On his way to take tea in Cannes. He banged his knee and his head and was gone within a day. Eddy feels glad his last glimpse was of a world filled with warmth and light before the darkness closed in forever. At least God was kind to him there.

Eddy pictures Jem, Harry and the others raising their unbelievers' eyebrows. The chap fell and banged his head. *C'est tout*. Let's enjoy life while we can. Get the corkscrew. Open another bottle. He wonders where Jem is at this moment and what he might be doing. He closes his eyes against the possible images. He wonders, too, what his next words to Jem will be. After Eddy had stood at the bedroom door, there were no further words between them. In the morning, after a night without rest, a breakfast he could not eat, he climbed into his carriage and fled from the spires and the turreted rooms.

He looks round at the others in the train. Best uniforms, buttons polished, swords rattling against spurs. Backs are ramrod straight against the seats, faces stiff as his poor uncle's through the wall. Most of them are ancient, their lives near lived through. Why does God let them trundle on yet robs Uncle Leo of the joy of holding his newborn child? He hears Jem and Harry laugh again. He had better ask his Mama. She is sure to have a simple answer which will bring him comfort.

No doubt, one day, he will become as old as the living dead round him. But what if he does not? What if he dies young like Uncle Leo? Supposing all the battles within himself are a complete waste of time because there will not be time to resolve them? Would it not be so much wiser to accept things as they are? To stroll in the sun like Uncle Leo, feel the warmth of it on his skin and never worry about tomorrow? To embrace whatever kind of joy might shine down upon him?

At Eddy's age, his Papa had already fallen into the arms of the actress, yet everyone still treats Eddy as a child. My darling little boy, says Mama. Poor sweet Eddy, coo the sisters. His mind churns so much, but he has done so little. He has sailed round the globe but expressed nothing of himself in the ways that matter. When does that begin?

When the train ends its journey, there are processions and crowds, then the gates of Windsor slam shut in the usual way. Inside them, Grandmama waits to receive her youngest child. They take him to the small chapel that sits behind the greater one; a vaulted chamber of coloured glass and gold mosaics soaring to the ceiling. But even these cannot lighten the gloom of its purpose. It is no place for a young man to rest. There is no spring in here, only an eternal winter.

The black-clothed men stand round the dark mahogany box; the women weep elsewhere. Bertie does not raise his glance from the tiles on the floor. Eddy is not sure what his Papa is feeling. The youngest brother had been a usurper, won the prize denied to the eldest all his life; the ear and respect of their mother. Perhaps Bertie wonders how many tears she would have shed if it were him in the box. Then suddenly Eddy sees that his father is in pain after all, and he is glad of it. The pain lances into him too, and they weep softly together. As the priest frees them to hurry back out into the blessed air, Bertie slides an arm round his son. Eddy is pleased, but damn him. Why can his Papa not be as simple as he needs him to be?

In the early evening the sun still shines, brazen in its new-found strength. He sheds the skin of the navy and puts on a jacket, breeches and a floppy hat just like Jem's. He wanders round the terraces and the courtyards. He tries not to think of the body in the chapel, abandoned to the gloom while he strolls in the sunlight. Then, in the coach yard, he sees it propped against a wall: one of these new bicycles, the pride and joy of some gentleman of the household. It is an odd-looking machine, ungainly, ugly even. But Eddy had watched him from a window, flying off along the path. It did not seem ugly then. He wonders if he could ride it. No, surely not. Surely he would topple, bloody his shins as he always does whenever he tries to be brave.

Nevertheless, he takes it, wheels it towards the gates that lead out to the park. He passes beneath Grandmama's windows. She is looking out across the lawns, a white handkerchief in her hand and she has seen him. Blast. He whips off his hat and bows to the window. But there is a faint smile on the old round face. She clenches her fat little fists, mimics the furious pedalling of the bicycle and shoos him away.

Eddy jumps on the machine and begins to pedal. At first, he swerves and veers and wobbles, but soon he is out of the gates and into the park. The faster he pedals, the more sure of himself he becomes. He does not know where he is going, only that he has to hurry. I must waste no more time, he thinks. If I fall, I fall. If I slip on my way to take tea. If somebody breaks my heart.

'May I offer my condolences on your sorrow?'

As he walks across the quads, along the lanes and through the spring meadows, respectful people pop up in his path like daffodils, bow their heads, mutter gracious words. But in the dusty room with the battered leather armchairs, no condolences are spoken. Instead, the big hand slaps him manfully on the back before it goes to make the tea. There is a new book lying on Eddy's chair.

'We need some fun,' Jem says. 'A bit of a holiday. We are going into Barsetshire.'

'Where's that? I've not heard of it.'

'Barsetshire is paradise. I shall introduce you to Mrs Proudie, Obadiah Slope, Mr Harding and many other delightful people. A week or so there will do us both the power of good.'

But when Jem returns with the tea, there is a change in the room. Eddy's armchair has been moved. Now it sits a clear yard from its twin, and is set at a different angle. When Jem sits down, Eddy's eyes are no longer compelled to meet his own. When Jem begins his lecture of the genius of Mr Trollope, the boy can now look at his right ear or just over his shoulder. Then suddenly, Eddy's eyes begin to fill. He covers them with his hand.

Jem, for all his cleverness, presumes the obvious reason for the distress. He begins to talk of how even the shortest life can be filled to the brim with achievement and lasting legacy. He talks of the other great men who have gone before their time; of Alexander, of Marlowe, of Keats and how the same can be as true for us all.

'Take this sad opportunity to think on these things,' he says. 'Make every day richer than the last. Embrace everything that comes your way. That's the most valuable lesson I can teach you.'

At last Eddy looks him in the eye.

'Thank you, but I've already learnt that lesson from this

tragic loss. You do not need to teach it to me. Anyway, you've already taught it by your own example.'

Again Eddy's eyes fill, but now Jem does not mistake him. He hears the bitterness in the words. Along with Mr Harding and Mrs Proudie, there is another new character in the room. Jem wonders if the blond head will always sit between them now, in the fresh void between the armchairs. It had just been a moment of weakness. An impulsive distraction to take his mind off those feelings which had seeded in him since the morning he had walked along an avenue of pleached limes and a hat had been pushed back off a sleepy face. Feelings which he knew must be squashed or else his great opportunity would end in disaster, the mighty oak tree toppled and splintered on the ground. And yet the bitterness he hears makes his heart leap too. It is the first sign, the sign he has yearned for in the pit of the night.

As it always has, the room smells of ancient books, pipe smoke and the brewing of tea. The sun still shines through the leaded windows and, at eleven-thirty sharp, illuminates the row of Jem's sporting trophies that parade on the mantel. But with the moving of the chair, the room is no longer the same. More than anything in the world, Jem longs for it to be back to where it was.

Oh this will not do, not at all. They must both retreat into Barsetshire at once. He lights his pipe, picks up the book. On they go.

'My condolences on your sorrow,' he says at last.

'She has great buck teeth in a mouth that gapes like the jaws of hell,' the boy says. 'She makes Queen Charlotte look like Lillie Langtry.'

A pause.

'Oh my God. Sorry.'

Another pause. Longer this time. He is a student of history.

'On both counts.'

Once more Eddy is sitting in one chair that faces another. But these chairs are very different. Slim, elegant, Regency perhaps. He is not sure of such things. He is wearing his companion's Chinese dressing gown. Dragons slither all over him joining the one on his arm. The other boy sprawls opposite, naked except for a towel, his long legs spindly as the chair, his feet resting between Eddy's thighs.

'I pray the gorgon may only give me sons,' the other sighs. 'If we have daughters, I will never be able to marry them off. Unless they get their looks from *moi*.'

He does not laugh; he is perfectly serious. And there is no denying he is a pretty thing. Curly hair, red as October leaves, skin like ivory, those long legs with their wicked ways. Eddy has been three times now to these rooms in a quiet corner of King's, on the next staircase to O.B.'s. If he is wise, and he reminds himself that he should be, there will not be a fourth.

'Must you marry her?' he asks.

'She is an only child. Her father's estate is substantial and adjoins our own. My own Papa will set his hounds on me if I don't. Besides, I might as well. I don't really care.'

The red-headed boy leans over to fill Eddy's glass, kissing him briefly on the lips. He smells of wine, an expensive cologne and of the pleasure they have just had together.

'I expect you'll be doing the same sometime soon,' he smiles. 'Though on a rather more spectacular scale.'

He is pushing his foot between Eddy's thighs again, trying

to find the gap in the folds of the dressing gown.

'And this... sort of thing?' Eddy asks. 'Will you abandon it?'

The ivory skin crinkles, frowns, is mystified.

'Lord, no. Whatever for? I shall do my duty, then I will take my amusements as I see fit. Papa has promised us a small house near Hyde Park. Naturally, he is unaware that its facilities extend beyond horse riding and the sailing of little wooden boats.'

His toes are playing with Eddy's balls.

'No doubt, as I wander through the bosky glades by the light of the silvery moon, I shall fall over almost everyone from O.B.'s Sunday evenings. Perhaps even your illustrious self.'

'Have you ever fucked a woman?' Eddy asks casually, trying to baste the question with the implication that he already has.

'Not yet, but I'd imagine all holes are the same in the dark, wouldn't you? It can't be that difficult. In the *Grand Siècle*, the Duc d'Orleans, a notorious bugger, managed it by hanging holy medals round his member. Perhaps I'll try that if I have any problems.'

The red-headed boy stands up and pulls off his towel. His cock bounces up.

'Oh do let's stop talking. I've got an essay to finish for O.B. by the morning. What might have happened if Louis and Marie Antoinette had escaped in 1791. So I don't have much time. Not even for *toi*.'

He drags Eddy by the arm towards the tangled bed. He throws himself down on his back, flings the long legs in the air and grabs hold of his ankles. The hairs round his arse are as red as those on his head. Eddy enters him. The boy's eyes roll upwards. The legs are locked round Eddy's back. He is imprisoned.

How odd, Eddy thinks again. Through the arid years of his fantasies, he always imagined he would be the one on his back, or bent across the table but, from the very first time, he knew that would never be the case. He does not want to lie there and selfishly take. His need is the reverse. In this, as in everything, he wants to give of himself to please others, just as he has always done.

Naturally, that first time had been a little comedy of errors, of nerves and fumbling. But he soon took to it like a foal finding its feet. At once he noticed how the other boy lost himself in the act but that he did not and never does. Instead he becomes ever more present, ever more defined. Any feelings of shame or fear of discovery blow away like dandelions on the wind. There is a power in it. He is alive as never before.

Since then, he has not held himself back. As Jem decreed, he embraces what comes his way and a lot does. These things are arranged for him. His new chums take care of it.

'You must meet so and so. He will be at O.B.'s next Sunday. Reading Greats at Clare. Comes from your part of Norfolk. Terribly nice chap.'

It is all done with the greatest discretion. Each new encounter is like a Christmas parcel wrapped up in many layers. Perhaps a shared liking for hockey, whist or the history of the Holy Roman Empire. Or simply coming from the same part of Norfolk. The layers are carefully maintained to protect both the giver and the recipient. It is not expected that the layers will always be ripped away to reveal the ultimate gift. One can stop at any point, decide not to go further, even replace one or more layers one has already removed. That is done graciously, of course. No feelings need be hurt. But Eddy never replaces the layers. He has wasted too much time. In the vault, Uncle Leo will be rotting already.

There are dangers in this of course, and not just the obvious ones. A boy hanged himself last year in another college. But Eddy believes he is safe from that now, vaccinated forever. What a daft notion it was, that he was in love, that his heart was lost. Silly old Eddy, as Mama would say. Thank heavens things turned out as they did, puncturing these absurd, romantic notions that kept him awake in his tight little bed. How he tortured himself over the impossibility of ever having him, the impossibility of ever being without him. All the soppy Greek nonsense that O.B. and the others talk. Forget the kissing. What it boils down to is a cock in an arse, he tells himself. They should all stick to reading Sir Walter Scott, where men are men and there's none of that gush. You know where you are with *Rob Roy*.

So Eddy vows to unwrap as many parcels as arrive on his doorstep and, in doing so, he will prove to himself that he is just like the rest of them. This is just a bit of fun. He can stop at any time. He will be just like the red-headed whore now beneath him. Like the whore, Eddy will soon marry and do his duty. Unlike him, he will never find himself in the moonlit park, his bowler down over his eyes and his pants round his ankles. All of this will be forgotten, shed like the puppy fat and the pimples which still occasionally mar his beautiful face.

He cleans himself at the basin. Wrapped again in the white towel, the boy is already at his desk, pen in hand, halfway along the road to Varennes. Eddy will be casual in his farewells, let him believe he will come again. Then the boy glances up.

'A friend from town is coming this weekend. Staying here with *moi*. Just a clerk in some shipping office, but he looks like a Botticelli. Might you care to stroll over for a drink?'

Well now, Eddy thinks. Two parcels instead of one. An experience he has not unwrapped before. It is irresistible.

CHAPTER VIII

1885. Trinity College, Cambridge.

'The Cruise of the Bacchante,' booms Reverend Dalton, 'is a humble clergyman's riposte to *The Voyage of the Beagle*. Everything described therein will be irrefutable evidence of the glory of God.'

Dalton ploughs ever onwards through the forest of his notes on their epic voyage. His rooms are crammed with the artefacts and mementoes of their travels. A lump of coal from the mine in Australia, fragments of dazzling coral, the amber ring of the King of the Zulus. Interested parties are invited for tea, biscuits and a tour of these exotic objects. It is fast becoming one of the institutions of the college. He has even produced a short guide.

It is an odd existence for a man of his age, thinks Jem. It is fourteen years now since Dalton first went to Eddy and Georgie. Though still in formal charge, it is clear he has sub-contracted Eddy to Jem and the other tutors. Is it a kindness on Dalton's part, a silent acknowledgement that others must try where he has failed? Jem knows he writes to the pretty sister of one of the midshipmen from the *Bacchante*. Does he long for sons of his own so that he can try again with better material? But would she have him? Would anyone? He is no vision of beauty; but maybe he thinks that being the author of a notable book might give him some allure. Perhaps he has heard the gossip about Mr Dickens and his little actress.

Jem smiles as he climbs the staircase in answer to Dalton's urgent summons, expecting to find him covered in cobwebs, pen flying across the virgin paper. But the room is crammed with people, like a carriage on the underground railway. They squat on window ledges, sit on the carpet, shoehorn themselves in among the pieces of coral and the jewels of the King of the Zulus. Every face is a face he knows. Harry, Patrick, Montague. Even the Master is present. And good heavens, O.B. has been imported from King's.

Dalton calls for hush. He announces that Eddy's father is to visit the college to assess the progress of his son. It is vital, he declares, that a highly positive impression is given. A careful approach must be taken, careful words must be chosen. He has already drafted a programme for the day but would welcome comments and suggestions.

The discussion has hardly started when the door swings open. Eddy stands on the threshold. These days, a whole week can go by without him seeing Dalton. He has been feeling guilty. At the sight of him, the conversation stops. Various people stand but at first nobody speaks, not even the Master. They are naughty boys caught out in mischief.

'My dear!' cries O.B. at last.

'Ah, Eddy,' says Dalton, his voice strangely quiet.

Eddy's gaze trawls over the crowded room. Every eye he catches swivels away from him.

'Excuse me,' says Eddy. 'I will come back later.'

He leaves without closing the door behind him. Everyone can hear the running on the stairs.

'Most unfortunate,' mutters Dalton.

'Indeed,' says O.B. He touches Jem's knee. '*You* must go after him, my dear.'

Jem goes up to Eddy's room, scours the quads, even the Chapel. He walks quickly but not so fast as to cause comment. He acknowledges each jolly greeting and raised hat. It is only when he is out by the river that he breaks into a gentle run. It is half an hour before he finds him, in the meadow near Silver Street Bridge. Eddy leans on the parapet, watching the water crash into the weir, its drowsy progress along the Backs exploding into a million angry jets. Jem's hair is all over the place, his flannels muddied, sweat puddling the armpits of his shirt.

'You'd best not appear before my father like that,' says Eddy, spewing the words out. 'He's extremely fussy about appearance. You really should have asked me to your meeting, you know. I could have given you all some tips. No doubt everyone wants to get the most from the visit.'

'That's unfair,' replies Jem. 'Your friends just want to do their best for you on the day. That's why we gathered together. To discuss how to make sure your father appreciates how well you're doing here.'

'And how well you've all played your parts? Then to sit up on your hind legs like his little dog and receive whatever reward each of you is hoping for?'

Eddy is shouting at him now, with the strange anger that

sometimes erupts so suddenly. Jem sighs and does not answer.

'Besides, I don't have any friends, only employees of my father,' says Eddy. 'I discovered that long ago. Friendliness without friendship. That's the rule Dalton taught me and my brother. And I stuck to it until I came here. Oh well, as everybody thinks, Eddy's a fool.'

'You're very far from a fool.'

'Would Harry and the rest bother with me unless they thought the association might benefit them? Would you, if you weren't being paid for it? Mr clever-dick Jem Stephen. Brilliant at everything. Academia. Sport. Fucking boys.'

Jem takes out his pipe and lights up. They stand together awkwardly by the weir, watching the water tumble and foam.

'You don't know me at all, do you?' says Jem.

'I don't really know anyone at all. They never allow me to. Do you remember that American girl at the tennis parties? She said you weren't what you seemed to be and that I must be wary.'

Jem knows he must gamble now. He takes a deep breath.

'She was quite right. I'm not at all what I may seem to be.'

'So what are you then?'

'I don't really know. Probably nobody very much.'

'Jem Stephen? Keeper of The Wall? Brave as a lion?'

'Oh but I'm not brave at all, you see. I'm quite scared most of the time. And the most frightening thing is that I don't know why. At least you have reason to be apprehensive of the future, the great responsibility that will come to you. But me, well I'm just scared for no reason. I've spent years searching for that reason and sometimes I think I may go crazy trying to find it.'

'The great Jem Stephen is frightened? And of *nothing*?'

'Yes.'

'And you have no clue at all?'

'Some virus in the blood, maybe. Some defective gene. Or maybe just some worm that has wriggled into me on a long distant afternoon when I scarcely noticed it or was too young to have the strength to brush it away. A thoughtless remark. A harsh expression. I don't know.'

Eddy turns away from the tumult of the weir. He strides off along the banks. It is calmer there. Jem follows at a distance. Some swans converge on them, hoping for a titbit. Eddy sits down on the grass, does not move when Jem plumps down beside him.

'And how do you cope,' Eddy asks at last, his gaze fixed on the swans, 'with the fear?'

'I do what I've seen you do. On the bad days, I take to my bed. On the less bad days, I just make a lot of noise. I smash balls against walls, I roar out silly songs. I drink. I smoke. And I take my pleasures.'

'So you're not a god after all, then?'

Jem gives a laugh, cold and hard as hoar frost. The swans hiss and scatter.

'But Papa told me I must model myself on you,' he says.

'Did he really say that?'

'Yes.'

'Gosh.' Jem runs the big hand through his hair.

'Papa says he doesn't want me to take after *him*, so if you're no use either, who the hell must I follow?'

Jem slides an arm round Eddy's shoulder and coaxes him back towards Trinity. But he does not provide an answer. In the cloister, they are to go their separate ways.

'How long have you had it?' Eddy asks now. 'The fear?'

'I can't remember when it wasn't there.'

Eddy turns towards the staircase to his rooms.

'Eddy, what I've told you, I've never told another person. Not even O.B., though I suspect he knows it anyway. Whatever you think of me now, there is no greater compliment I can pay you.'

Eddy nods his head, trudges away. When he vanishes from view, Jem feels it like an ache in his belly.

Jem lies down on his bed. He feels so very tired. He thinks he will doze for a while, but he does not. He lies there thinking about those worms from long distant afternoons. All his life he has fought a battle against them, with his intelligence, his beauty, his craving for life. He has fought heroically, all flags flying. But he wonders how long it will be before they eat him away. Because eat him they will.

CHAPTER IX

1885. Trinity College, Cambridge.

Bertie's little dog is to be honoured by the college. It is given special dispensation to enter hallowed walls and cock its leg on forbidden lawns. It struts in with a suitably arrogant manner, oblivious to the fuss its visit has caused. It is Bertie's dog to the life.

The truth is that he would have been allowed to bring in an ostrich, a duck-billed platypus or his whole damn herd of Brahmin cows. The place is in a fever of excitement, concealed beneath its well-polished detachment from the trivialities of the outside world. With the rest of the jittery welcome party, Eddy greets Papa inside the Great Gate. The cheers from the street press in; a vulgarity swiftly shut out.

'What memories,' Bertie coos, gazing round the Great Court. 'What memories.'

'We are honoured to welcome you back, sir,' says the Master.

'Really?' replies Bertie. 'But surely you never had a stupider undergraduate than me?'

The Master, though venerated as a brilliant man, is quite unable to work out the correct answer. His eyeballs roll round his head until he settles for a sort of giggle. Bertie explodes with laughter and slaps him on the back. As he gets ever fatter, somehow the charm expands to fill the extra space. In a minute, they are eating out of his hand like the damn dog.

'But I come today as an examiner,' he says, adopting a sterner expression. 'To examine the progress of my beloved son and to pass judgement thereon. Lucky for him I can't stay long, so at least the drop will be quick and clean.'

He chuckles again, but nobody else does. He sets up court in Dalton's rooms and they come to pay homage one by one. The Master first of course, then the other tutors, then Dalton himself. As if he is a footman, Eddy is given charge of the dog and shooed away. He drags it across to Jem's rooms, where Jem sits in his usual chair, all tidied up. Bertie has decreed that he will speak to Jem last. It is really only Jem he wants to see; the others are just for form's sake, the observance of which is as natural to Bertie as the breath he takes.

Perhaps because he must talk about him shortly, Jem does not wish to talk to Eddy now. He is nervous. His father, the great judge, the head of the clan of Stephen, has written at length, advising him how to shape and mould the case that must be put before Bertie. The case for the ongoing transformation of Albert Victor into a paragon and for the genius of Jem Stephen in achieving it.

They smoke in silence, watched by the dog. Jem ignores it completely. Unused to such disdain for its status, it sits on the rug and growls at him. Jem growls back. The dog turns the growls into barks and Jem does too. The noise gets louder and louder; the cacophony is awful. Eddy sticks his fingers in his ears. Soon Jem is down on the rug on his hands and knees.

'Good grief, what madhouse is this?' Bertie stands in the doorway, Dalton at his shoulder.

The dog flees to Bertie, whimpering for sanctuary. He picks it up and lets it wash his beard with its tiny rose-pink tongue, then drops it on the floor again when its moment has passed. Jem is on his feet, back in himself. He bows, he grins, he makes a clever joke about dogs, he asks after Alix and the sisters. He sees the admiration ooze from Bertie's eyes. Jem's confidence returns. He will carry it off.

At luncheon, for form's sake, Bertie has the Master on his right and Reverend Dalton on his left. Otherwise, he has expressed the wish to be surrounded by those of his son's close acquaintance. Distinguished noses are out of joint, but Eddy's new chums are unabashed and uninhibited. Harry and the others chatter about him, as if he were not there. He is gently mocked for his uselessness first thing in the morning and at all times in a punt, his ever-increasing passion for clothes, his high collars and long cuffs. Laughter rattles the cutlery and the glasses. Eddy flinches a little, hides it behind the usual gentle smile.

Bertie, as is his way, sits back and listens, his head turning from one to another as if he were at a tennis match. But then he joins in. He tells the tale of the teatrays, of Jem crashing down the stairs, of Eddy losing his temper. The first time poor old Eddy had ever been heard to shout. Bertie tells the table he was quaking in his boots. There is more laughter; only Jem does not smile. Jem is angry too. He throws away the case he has prepared and takes another tack entirely. What the hell.

'I don't think it kind of us all to tease Eddy so,' he says, just a little too loudly.

Silence spills onto the table. Eyes are lowered into wine glasses. The Master twists his signet ring deep into the flesh of his finger. Eddy's heart pounds in his head. Nobody speaks to Papa like that. But Jem has not finished.

'Eddy's anger, even if excessive, came from anxiety about my injury. It was kindly meant and typical of his sweet and caring nature. We all have little failings and vanities which can so easily be derided. It's far more helpful that we should celebrate the best in people.'

Bertie blows a smoke ring into the silence. But Jem is still not finished.

'There are many things at which Eddy is not yet accomplished. He's decidedly shaky on the causes of The Hundred Years' War, for instance. But what he has also not yet grasped is how much his simple goodness has enriched the lives of everyone here and how much we value him for it. I am proud to call Eddy my friend. Not because of who he is, but because of what he is.'

'Well said, Mr Stephen,' Bertie mutters at last. 'Well said.'

The table breathes again. The Master stops twiddling his signet ring. Dalton's jaw returns to the horizontal position.

Harry begins to sing *For He's A Jolly Good Fellow*. Eddy stammers a protest, but everyone takes it up. Jem gets to his feet and leads the singing, his voice blasting out above all the others, unabashed that singing is not among his gifts. Only Bertie does not sing. He contemplates his son across the decanters. At the end of the song, Jem raises a toast to Eddy. As Jem's smile blazes down on him, they both know a moment of pure, unclouded joy.

'Nellie was her name,' he says out of the blue. 'Such a pretty name, don't you think? Not a name to cause any trouble, certainly not to shake the foundations of an empire. But, in her own sweet way, that's what Nellie nearly did.'

Bertie is on his second walk of the day. God knows how he will manage it, Eddy wonders, after a ten-course lunch. Sure enough, he is soon a little breathless and they must find a bench. The dog stations itself between his legs, on guard. Bertie leans his chin on his cane and looks across the river to the rash of towers and pinnacles.

'I lied when I arrived this morning. I had to steel myself to come here. Such a lovely place, but it still makes me shudder, even after quarter of a century. This is where the sky fell in on me. No doubt you've heard something of the matter.'

'Hardly anything, Papa,' Eddy lies also. He is amazed. In their family, it is never to be spoken of.

'They smuggled her in, you see. My friends here. No doubt your chums today are just as naughty.'

Bertie smiles and slaps him heartily on the knee; men of the world together. Then the smile fades.

'Just a rite of passage, dear Nellie. No more. Nothing worse than half the young men of our tribe were up to. But it changed everything. And forever, it would seem.'

A breeze whips up and scuds across the water. Bertie pulls his coat tighter round him.

'Your Grandpapa came here to berate me. He wasn't well; overworked, overtired, old before his time. He believed I'd ruined everything they'd both worked for. The great enterprise of restoring the image desecrated by your Grandmama's wicked uncles. We were to be the perfect example, the stainless family for all to look up to. In such families, fucking a prostitute really isn't done.'

The shock of the word hits Eddy's face harder than the wind. He has waited so long for this sort of intimacy, the intimacy so easily given to Georgie, and now, when it comes, he flinches from it.

'We went for a walk together, just as you and I are doing now. Not far from here. On that walk, he tore me apart. Mind you, he'd been doing that for most of my life. They both had. Tearing me apart, as if to reassemble me the way they'd decided I must be.'

Bertie leans down and strokes the dog. It rolls onto its back, ecstatic at his touch.

'If I were lost, your Grandpapa decreed, the whole bloody Empire would collapse. Can you believe it? It was only a fuck. Then the rain poured down and he got drenched and went home and died. And she blamed me. She still does. The child who killed his own father.'

'Oh, that is so untrue, Papa, but I'm glad that you're talking of it to me.'

The breeze is stronger and there is drizzle in it now. They turn round and retrace their steps.

'I talk of it for a reason. Your grandfather was a good man but he was not always a kind one. Perhaps that is how you regard me, too.'

'Goodness no, Papa.' Eddy lies again.

'It seems to be Mr Stephen's opinion that I chaff and tease you too much.'

'It only distresses me because I so want to please you, Papa. To measure up to you.'

Bertie stops abruptly and laughs the thick German laugh.

'But that's the whole bloody point! You *do* measure up to me. You measure up exactly. You're just as I was. Sleepy, poor at your lessons, can't concentrate, too fond of pleasure. The faults I see in you are the same faults I had myself. And there's nothing more irritating than seeing your own deficiencies reappear in your children. I want you to do better than me, to *be* better than me.'

'How in God's name can I do that, Papa?'

'Eddy, I didn't come here today to rip you apart as my father did me. And you are much the better for being here. Through the things the others say of you, the respect and affection they have for you, you finally begin to take shape in my sight. And I like what I see.'

The drizzle has blown over and a shard of creamy sun thrusts through the splintering grey. Bertie stops and watches it sparkle on the finials of the great chapel.

'I am glad that I came,' he says. 'It is good to be here with my own son and to feel easy in his company. Perhaps the damn ghost might now be laid.'

They pass a young mother with a child in a perambulator. She emerges from the shelter of a weeping willow, shaking her umbrella. Bertie raises his hat. She sinks into a deep curtsey, drooping down like the branches of the tree.

'What a pretty sight,' he says. 'I hope she will always be kind to her child.'

As they cross Trinity Bridge, he looks back at her.

'Parents and children. What chances are lost.'

They walk through the quads towards the Great Gate. It is

almost the appointed time of departure and Bertie is always precise to the minute. He has to get back to town for the opera.

'Enjoy your music, Papa. What is it tonight?'

'I can't remember. It hardly matters. It will fill the hours.'

The party is assembled to say farewell; the Master and the dons, Dalton and Jem, the gaggle of chums. The Great Gate is flung open and the cheering floods in again. At the steps of the carriage, Bertie embraces his son. Eddy's heart is full. He is even beginning to look benignly on the dog. But then, in a moment, it is spoiled.

'Make the most of your remaining time here,' his father murmurs into his ear. 'You know that it cannot be long before we must reclaim you.'

He has saved him up until last. The blond boy with the spectacles. It has not been easy. The boy is always at O.B.'s soirees; he flirts, but Eddy keeps his distance. Eddy has a plan for him. As a rule, he is not a person who has need of plans, but in this it is necessary.

It is a summer evening, the windows open to a muggy blue-white sky. Down below, people clatter through the cloisters taking hampers and rugs towards the river. It is a wrong thing he is doing but he is desperate now. It was a stratagem only to be used as a last resort, but time is running out. This life is almost gone. He has to make something happen.

The note he sends tells Jem that a friend is coming up for a sherry and asks if he would care to join them. There is no reply, but that is not unusual. Jem's mind rarely roosts on such courtesies; it is always busy elsewhere. It does not mean he will not come.

Eddy invites the blond boy half an hour before the time he has given Jem. The blond arrives on the dot, nervous and already excited. This is good, no moment is wasted. Within ten minutes, Eddy is lying back against the pillows, one arm behind his head, the other pushing the blond curls down onto his prick. By now, he has learnt how to hold back, to make these things last. He takes a pride in it. It is one more weapon in his new arsenal of minor achievements.

'Why don't you fuck me?' coos the blond.

'Not yet. You must work much harder to earn such a privilege.'

He can hardly believe he is now capable of speaking such sentences. As the gossamer curls dance a jig against his stomach, he watches the clock on the mantel. It is quarter of an hour after the time he gave Jem. The blond becomes more and more excited. He even takes off his spectacles.

'Oh come on, sir, do.'

Soon, Jem is half an hour late. Eddy's guest is an expert at his trade; better even than the long-legged redhead over at King's. Eddy will not be able to contain himself much longer. At forty minutes past the hour, he knows his plan has failed.

The scene in his mind will not be played out. Jem will not crash cheerfully through the door then freeze in shock. The broad face will not crumple and blink back tears, the big hands will not seize the gossamer blond and throw him down the stairs, his clothes tumbling after him. Jem will not rush towards the bed and take Eddy in his arms, swear that somehow, however mountainous the obstacles, they will find a way, any way, however imperfect, of walking through this life together.

But now the blond is begging and he acquiesces. Oh, why not.

'I am honoured, sir,' the blond grins afterwards. 'Something to tell my grandchildren about.'

When the blond is gone, Eddy stays stretched out on the bed in the sweaty dusk. Below the window, people are drifting back from the river; noisier, drunk on the drowsy pleasures of a summer evening. But Eddy's body is tense and unsatisfied, as if the release had never happened. It comes to him now that his wider plan has failed too. He will not be like all the others; the blond in the spectacles, the redhead with the long legs, so many of his new-found chums. Like them he will marry, do everything required of him, but he knows he can no longer pretend that this is a mere recreation.

God knows he has tried hard enough to convince himself. He has tried to rip his heart from his body, to let that body coldly use as many others as opportunity will afford him. But his heart has been heavy with the guilt of it; the awful crime of striving to kill intimacy when it is the thing he craves above all else. Killing it by poisoning it with people for whom he does not truly care. And all because, for some reason he does not understand, it is withheld from him by the person to whom he would give everything. The god in the floppy hat, with Alix on his arm, strolling towards them along the avenue of pleached limes.

And then the god is standing in the doorway, just as Eddy had imagined him earlier. He is smiling, a bit tipsy, carrying his racquet. He is sorry but he has only just seen the note. There had been an urgent summons for a fourth at doubles, then he had stayed to dine. Eddy tells him it does not matter.

'I bumped into your guest on the Backs,' he replies. 'He says you had a pleasant evening.'

The room is almost dark now. The gaslight on the landing is behind him so Eddy cannot clearly see Jem's face, but the comment is made without inflection. Without irony. He pulls the sheet up almost to his neck and sits up straight on the pungent bed.

'Well, gosh, not long now then,' says Jem. 'The May Ball, then off you go. Out into the big bad world.'

Eddy is unable to answer. Between the bed and the doorway is fifteen feet of wooden floor, a dark and unbridgeable void. Below the window, somebody vomits.

'Oh dear, the party season is upon us,' Jem says. 'Sleep well and rise early.'

He half-closes the door then sticks his head back into the room.

'Your summer is beginning,' he says. 'You know that, don't you? Your sun will never be higher.'

'I don't want it if you can't share it with me,' says Eddy.

He does not care now. Why should he? He has nothing to lose. It does not feel like summer to him, it feels like the end of everything. The time now gone has been his summer, the time when he was able to breathe and smell the flowers. There will never be another like it, of that he is certain. If only he could see Jem's face in this damned twilight, see even the tiniest glow upon it, hear even the weakest words of hope. He thinks that if the door closes now then he does not want to see the blasted summer. He does not even want to wake up in the morning. But no more words are said. The door closes.

Eddy drifts into sleep, wakes, needs to go and piss. Glancing down into the quad, he sees Jem on the grass, his back against a pillar of the cloister, looking up at the window. And when, exhausted, Eddy does indeed wake up in the morning, a note has been slipped under the door.

'*Wherever our roads may lead us, you have my love until my last breath.*'

CHAPTER X

1885. Dublin Castle.

'It's a filthy business, filthy,' says Bertie. 'You're a grown man now, I can speak to you of such things.'

He has finished his kippers, boiled eggs, sliced ham, bread, butter, jam and God knows how much more, and is lighting his first cigar of the day.

'Aren't you hungry?' he asks, eyeing the half-full plate.

Eddy has not been able to chew since the subject was raised. The great scandal of Dublin Castle.

'Not sick, are you? No time to be sick today.'

'Just indigestion, Papa.'

The breakfast room, where they sit dwarfed in baronial splendour, is also indigestible this early in the morning.

'And in this very house, of all places,' Bertie goes on. 'The symbol of our authority on this godforsaken island. Perverts at every level of the staff. Orgies even. The place was riddled with it. Riddled. From top to bottom.'

Bertie allows himself a quick smile when he discovers he has made a joke. He enjoys the wit of others, though he possesses little of it himself. But the smile is swiftly gone.

'I can't understand men who engage in such acts. Any friend or servant of mine would be banished forever from my sight. I could never be under the same roof as such an animal, nor breathe the same air. Don't you agree?'

'Indeed, Papa.' Eddy raises his coffee cup, aware that his hand is trembling.

'Well, we've come to try and make them forget such iniquities. Not to mention the political shenanigans. Home rule? Bloody nonsense. Iron fist in a velvet glove. That's what's needed.'

'Indeed, Papa.' Eddy puts the cup carefully down. 'I had best go upstairs and put on my velvet gloves.'

'Do get a move on, Eddy. I am most particular about appearance, but the time you take to get ready is absurd. You're getting as bad as your sainted mother. God preserve me from you both.'

In his rooms, Eddy's man is waiting. Everything is laid out ready. Eddy casts an eye over it and requests a cravat of another colour. He sees the droop of hurt on his man's face but it is important that he feels confident today. He checks himself in the long mirror. The high collar and long cuffs, so derided by his Papa and Georgie, suit him perfectly. Of course, they are just jealous that they could never carry them off. He has never mocked them for their lack of height in the way they have mocked him for his possession of it, but oh how he longs to do so.

He meets his Mama on the landing and they go down together. Bertie is standing in the lobby with his people, drumming his fingers on a table.

'Oh, Bertie, are we late?' asks Alix.

Bertie swallows hard. She does not bother to listen for any answer; she would probably not hear it anyway. Besides, she knows that on this occasion he must wait for as long as she pleases. Today he needs her. Today is one of those on which Alix has been compelled to leave her dairy, her stables, the little dogs and the white cockatoo. Today she must show herself to the wider world or else there is no point to her. She understands that and so she will oblige. She will grumble and groan, protesting that some mare is about to foal and she cannot possibly leave Norfolk, but in truth she protests too much. She knows she is more loved than anyone else of their tribe. Like an invalid taking the waters, she will bathe in adoration. Envied by thousands of women. Admired, desired even, by thousands of men. Today she will remind Bertie of how others see her. Today she has power over him. And when, quite happily, she shuts herself in again, he will, even for a while, remember that.

'Our task in Cork is as follows,' Bertie commands. 'I am to charm the politicians, the priests and the other serious men. Alix, you will captivate the common people as you always do. And Eddy, you are here to win the hearts of all the Irish maidens.'

At the steps of the carriage, he touches Eddy's arm.

'Think of this as your first day with the family firm, so acquit yourself well. It will not be onerous.'

But it does not turn out quite like that. They take the railway from Dublin to the south. The gale that buffets the train is as nothing to the turbulence that awaits them. It begins even before they get there. As they pass slowly through the tiny stations, the expected crowds are present. But they do not carry flags and cheer. They stare silently, their arms folded tightly across their chests. Some have turned their backs. One man shows them his fat hairy arse.

'Oh dear,' says Bertie. 'Don't look, Alix. It will put you off luncheon.'

In the city there is worse. Far worse. The carriage is flanked by lines of Hussars and, beyond that, by red-faced, freckled policemen. But shining swords are no match for the cabbages and turnips which thump like drum beats against the side of the carriage. Nor can the clatter of hooves and the jingle of harnesses drown out the noise that seethes from the pavements. At first Eddy thinks the rain has started again, but it is a low, unending hiss. They are in a snake pit and there is no escape. In defence, they wield the usual smiles and waves, but these are powerless to protect them. Alix cannot understand it. This has never happened to her before. Today no Irish poet will be picking up his pen to write a hymnal to her beauty.

Eddy slouches down in his seat.

'Sit up straight,' says Bertie. 'You must show yourself. There is no purpose to this otherwise.'

So Albert Victor looks out and smiles, but none are returned to him, only the flutterings of black handkerchiefs. This is a funeral procession. It is the end of something. Even silly Eddy can see that.

They are to visit the houses where the poorest people live. They are to talk pleasantly to them and enquire after their health; perhaps assure them that everything is being done to improve their lot. Eddy feels passably capable of doing this. He has experience. Since all of them were children, Alix has taken them into the cottages of the workers on the estate and he has learned to say the right things. But compared with the sights that greet him now, those cottages are like the bucolic idylls of Mr Andersen's fairy tales. Row after row of shattered houses line up for their inspection, like half-dead soldiers after a disastrous defeat. The people in the doorways stand as silent as those on the pavements, but at least there is no aggression, no black handkerchiefs. In the carriage, the scent of Alix's perfume is soon poisoned by the stench of the place. She clasps Eddy's hand.

'Dear God!' she sighs.

He straightens his cravat, mauve by the way, and adjusts the angle of his top hat. Just a tiny bit, so his Papa will not notice. And then he makes a terrible mistake. As his parents alight from one door, he decides to get out of the other. He does not see the great heap of rubbish. He stumbles and falls straight into it. Rotting vegetables, potato peelings, the carcasses of chickens, long-dead cats.

He lies there, winded. Nobody in his party sees or hears him fall. Only the slum people see. His topper has flown off; the drizzle spatters his hair; the oil from it streaks onto his forehead. His coat is stained with God knows what; sticky, greasy, foul-smelling stains. His trouser legs and shoes the same. The slum people watch him. Their faces have no expression, none at all. In their eyes there is nothing; not even mockery or contempt. He wonders if they have any idea who he is and if they would care.

Then a hand stretches out towards him. It is a little hand, a dirty hand, but he takes it without thinking. It belongs to a boy of seven or eight, his clothes no more than rags and tatters. They could hardly be given the name of shirt or trousers; merely coverings to protect him from this hellish climate and they must be useless enough at that.

'You'll have fallen in the tip?' the boy says, a grin on his grubby face. 'How daft is that, then?'

'Definitely daft,' says Eddy.

'Well, come on, or will you be sittin' there all day?'

The boy tries to pull him up but the weight is too heavy for his spindly arm, so Eddy has to make most of the effort himself. But the boy does not let go of his hand until he is upright.

'Thank you very much,' says Eddy. 'How are you?'

'Me? Oh, I'm fair great. We're just off to play football. My brother Charlie and me. D'you fancy a game?'

'I'm not very good at football, really.'

'Oh, don't worry about that. We'll just be kickin' round.'

An angry woman, thin and sharp as an icicle, erupts from the crowd and drags him away. He turns and waves, grinning his grin again.

'Thank you,' Eddy calls after him.

Now Bertie appears from round the carriage.

'Good God!' he says and turns on his heel.

Somebody in their party wets a handkerchief and wipes the worst mess from his clothes. Somebody else lends his coat and hat. They fulfil the things arranged for them; the school is opened, the factory toured. Duty is done. That is the way of it.

Now they are to go by steamer to an island in the harbour to inspect its fortifications. The quay is long and curves out into the water. The tide is so high and every inch of it so crammed with people that the stone of the quay can hardly be seen. It is as if the crowd is some Hydra-headed creature, crouching on the surface of the water, waiting for them.

When they leave the carriage to board the boat, it begins. The Hydra tells their English rulers to go home and get out of their country. What's more they can take their perverted English ways with them. They are the corrupters of innocent Irish lads. They are buggers and sodomites. They are the spawn of the devil. Eddy's stomach begins to tighten in the way it always does.

'Albert Victor looks more like Mary-Ann to me,' somebody shouts. It brings the first laughter they have heard all day but Eddy nearly freezes on the spot. His legs feel like two dead weights, but somehow he drags them up the gangway and on to the boat. But his mind is racing. What does the Hydra know of him? What has been whispered to it? He tries to remember if he has met any Irish boys at O.B.'s Sunday nights. Blurred with champagne, had he ever gone to a turreted room with one such? Had the object of his affections then returned to his homeland and talked of it? Perhaps inside the scandalous walls of Dublin Castle even. Walls have ears, of course. But do they also talk? What gossip may have been carried out into the wider world by some handsome young cook or stable lad?

But the laughter from the quay is soon gone. As the band strikes up *God Bless the Prince of Wales*, a spasm of fury is unleashed. The Hydra is not prepared to be drowned out. The screaming begins. Every insult, every obscenity. Thank God, his Mama can hear nothing of it. The black handkerchiefs flap like the wings of ravens. The Hussars fix their bayonets.

Someone asks Bertie if they would all like to go below.

Perhaps a brandy to warm and cheer them.

'We have no need of brandy,' he replies. 'My family and I will remain on deck. We have come to show ourselves to the people of this city and we will do so until we are no more than specks on their horizon.'

They chug slowly out towards the open harbour, their heads held high. With one hand, Bertie goes on waving to the quayside. The other, held behind his back, is shaking like a leaf. Alix stands still, her smile beached on her face, bowing her head to left and right. She may not hear, but she can see. She does not wave; her fingers are laced tightly together as if in prayer.

And Eddy? He has told himself that he is not really here at all. He is playing football on a scrap of scruffy ground with a grinning ragamuffin. He has thrown away the mauve cravat, the collars and the cuffs. After all, they impressed nobody. Now he is dressed in rags and tatters. Caked in mud and dirt, he is invisible. He is nothing and nobody. He is content beyond imagining.

*

1885. Balmoral Castle.

'I suppose I don't really have any friends,' she says.

'Goodness, Grandmama. Half the world loves you.'

'But that is not love. Nor is it friendship either.'

She tracks him down, huddled in the window seat, and wants to know from whom his letter has come. Just a chum from college, he replies. He does not mention that the letter is a whole month old now, that it is creased and crumpled from endless reading, that if Jem does not send another soon he thinks he might go mad.

'You were lucky in your time at Cambridge,' she says. 'When I was a girl, I wasn't allowed friends. Perhaps I've never really learnt the knack of it.'

It is time to go out in the carriage, as they do each afternoon, rain or shine. Grandmama is impervious to bad weather. She simply does not acknowledge it, as if it is beneath her. Open windows are beneficial she decrees; so the Highland wind is welcomed in and allowed to tear round like an irritating child. The household bite their tongues to stop their teeth from chattering. But Grandmama is contented, as in no other place. And that is all that matters.

Today, though, it is what passes for tolerably fine in these parts. They drive out to Loch Muick. The breeze bowls fat balls of cloud across the sky, letting sudden shards of late summer sunlight pierce down, turning the sullen grey-black water a fathomless cobalt blue. Folding chairs are set out under the old beech trees. She sits down and waits until the rug is wrapped round her knees.

'Tell me about your friends,' she says.

So he talks about Jem and Harry and the rest of the chums. He tells her about his studies, the books he tried valiantly to read, the debates in The Union which floated above him. He describes the tennis parties, the punting, even O.B.'s Sunday soirees, though he sketches those somewhat lightly. He mentions that Jem is the son of a judge and Harry the son of a parson.

'A parson?' she repeats. 'Goodness. I envy you those

friendships, Eddy, but we must always be careful of flatterers and self-seekers. Didn't the Reverend Dalton teach you that at least?'

'Yes, Grandmama, but I discovered that I couldn't make any friends until I disobeyed that rule.'

His anger, as it always does, comes out of nowhere.

'Anyway, was your late personal servant not a son of the farmyard?' he says.

'You are impertinent, which is not like you at all,' she says, the little eyes lancing into him.

He says he is sorry and he is. They sit in silence looking out over the water. A table is erected and tea is brought; scones and jam, crumpets, Highland shortbread. The ritual calms them both.

'But of course, you are also right,' she says. 'After your Grandpapa, he was my only true friend. Now I have lost them both and I must travel on alone. And it is hard. Dear God, it is.'

She eats a third scone. The jam smears the corners of her mouth, like a child at a party.

'It's the loneliness of the thing. This task which God has given me. Nobody can understand it until it falls to them. Prepare yourself for that, Eddy.'

He does not reply. He lifts his cup and drinks it to the dregs. But the breeze has cooled the tea and it hits his stomach like a chill.

'But here, more than anywhere else, they are still with me,' she says. 'That's why I love it so. Your Papa thinks I'm going dotty like poor dear Ludwig in Bavaria, shutting myself away in my crazy castle. But it is quite the opposite. Here, in the silence, is the sanity.'

'I can't think of anyone less dotty than you, Grandmama,' he replies. 'Have another scone.'

The face dimples and smiles the shy, nervous smile. He feels a rush of love for her; the old lady with the jam round her mouth.

'It is nice to have you here, Eddy. You are easy on the spirit.'

The chirpy balls of cloud look bad-tempered now. The first raindrops dapple the shortbread. In the carriage going back, she takes his hand in hers.

'Your friends are lucky in your affection.'

'Might you not allow yourself some new friends too, Grandmama?'

'Perhaps. But where am I to find them?'

'There's one sitting beside you now.'

'My dear, good boy,' she says.

He speaks from the heart, but there are friendships and friendships. They both know that. They would hardly fill each other's yearnings.

And so, each morning, he takes himself to the window seat that commands a view of the drive. The carriage will come at precisely ten o'clock. The carriage that brings the red boxes, the urgent correspondence, the private letters. Then, as it turns and rolls away out into the world, he stares after it and prays for the opening of the door, the footfall on the tartan carpet, the clearing of the throat, the silver tray bearing the envelope.

He can picture the envelope precisely. His name, his other name, will stride out across the envelope in flamboyant loops and whirls, the letters leaning forwards, hurrying to their destination. There is no mistaking the hand and the spirit of the sender. Despite the distance they have travelled, the pages inside will still smell faintly of pipe smoke. And whatever is written upon them, long or short, trivial or otherwise, it will fill, even for a while, the void in his being.

'It's the loneliness of the thing,' says Grandmama.

The door crashes open and wakes him from another doze. His father, the judge, stands squat in the doorway, silhouetted against the yellowy light on the landing.

'Mr James Kenneth Stephen, you will get up at once and you will come down and dine.'

Jem is not sure what time it is, but the room is dark now so it must be evening. He has not left his bedroom all day. Earlier, he tried to do some work, to write even just one more stanza of his new poem, but it is like climbing a mountain in the teeth of a gale. He had thrown down the pen in disgust and crawled back under the covers.

'Look at yourself,' his father says now, marching round the room, turning up the lamps. 'You will rise, bathe, shave, dress and present yourself before your mother in precisely half an hour.'

And though it is another mountain, somehow he does. But the point of his presence eludes him. They sit in silence at the long, walnut dining table. The only sounds are the ticking of the French clock, the clink of steel on china, the aching creak of floorboards as the servant comes and goes. He keeps his eyes mostly on his plate, though he eats next to nothing. If he looks up, they are watching him. It seems to him they are always watching him lately. His mother's eyes are dimmed with worry, his father's alight with irritation. Suddenly, the judge throws his spoon into his pudding bowl.

'In the morning, you will go to work,' he barks. 'You are to be a barrister, not a damned poet. Who will give a brief to a man who stays in bed writing silly verses?'

Jem looks up at him, does not answer, rages inside at the insult of the adjective. For all his father's cleverness, he is a boor, a yahoo. He signals to the servant to refill his wine glass.

'In the morning, you will go to chambers,' says the judge. 'Even if I have to drag you there on the end of a dog leash.'

When he kisses his mother goodnight, he can feel the trembling in her bony shoulders. When the judge erupts, the whole house shakes, from cellars to attics, the very joists and timbers, everything that lives and breathes under his roof. It was always thus.

In his room, he sits again at the little *escritoire*. He pushes the useless poem aside, takes out the bundle of letters. All through the summer and into the autumn, they have arrived thick and fast. At first, he replies to them at once. But as the months dawdle by, he waits a little longer before he answers, hoping to slow down their passionate frequency.

When he does reply, he writes with harmless news of Harry and Patrick and jolly dinners in chop houses off The Strand. He writes comical descriptions of his gloomy room in Lincoln's Inn, where a previous occupant, having failed to save a woman from the gallows, hanged himself as well. The mark of the rope is still on the beam. He writes of anything, in fact, anything but what he imagines the recipient is hoping to hear. His letters must not, like bellows, fan hope where there can be none. Christ, he should never have pushed that note under the door.

His father puts him in the witness box about the letters. How often do they come? How many pages? Do they remain warm and friendly? The connection must be maintained, built on, never allowed to cool. His father asks to read the letters; he is a judge after all. But Jem pleads the bonds of the confessional between tutor and pupil. Florid effusiveness is acceptable between young men of privilege but, even by those standards, Eddy's letters are open to misinterpretation.

Jem locks the letters away, slides back into bed, lies awake in the dark. How did it go so wrong? Again, he turns the pages of it over in his mind.

At first, all had proceeded as he had planned. So easily had he won the admiration, the awe even, and then, in time, the dependency. It came to him with no more difficulty than all the examinations passed and the sporting trophies that sparkle on the mantel. But then it had gone further. He had lost the reins of it. He had not calculated for devotion.

For most of his life, for good or ill, Jem Stephen has lived in his head. It is his head which engineers both public triumphs and private terrors. For most of his life, his heart is a passive, sleepy thing. Then it sees a young face peeking out from under a floppy hat in the morning sun. And when his heart awakes, it roars.

He panics. He does not know what to do. Above all, he must not lose control, the thing he fears the most. The romantic view decrees that love makes everything possible. In this case, he is certain, irrevocably certain, that it makes everything impossible. To reach out towards it might bring discovery, scandal, disgrace. Exile from any hope of a respectable future. The name of Stephen marked forever, diseased like a whore.

And so he begins to draw himself in. He tries, gently, to rebuild the wall which should have been there in the first place. He takes refuge behind it, tries to get his breath back. It is a lonely place, but he is steadfast in his conviction.

Only once does he weaken and let the heart win. On that warm, perfect evening, right at the end of their time together. When, a little drunk, he props himself against a pillar in the cloister and keeps watch over him through the night. And then, as the dawn comes, he pushes the damn note under the door.

Now, on this hard October morning, the judge bangs in, shakes his son awake and shouts his commands. Jem knows he must obey. He must leave this room, hail a cab and ride out towards another life. His head tells him that. But oh, why can't he stay where he is, the curtains tightly drawn? Why won't they just leave him to mourn? After all, there is a sort of death in the house.

CHAPTER XI

1886. St John's Wood, London.

The house is small and low, tidily symmetrical, white stuccoed Regency, identical to every other in the street. A green-painted front door matches the leaves of the little laurels planted like sentinels along the garden walls. Perhaps they are to guard the secret it contains.

For a suburban avenue on a sultry afternoon, it is surprisingly busy. Their hansom is only one of several others, disgorging gentlemen into the houses. Gentlemen with their heads tucked into their chests, scurrying like squirrels. Eddy pays the cabbie, dropping some coins into the gutter. He has every right to be nervous after all.

'You've still not done it yet, have you?' Georgie had asked, as they smoked together after dinner in the Marlborough Club. 'By God, I don't believe it.'

'Of course I bloody have.'

'How often?'

'I don't know. A few times maybe.'

'I don't believe you,' says Georgie. 'I've always known when you're fibbing.'

'I'm not fibbing.'

'Then look me in the eye and tell me you've had a woman.'

Eddy looks at the floor.

'What the hell did you and your college friends get up to then?' Georgie asks. 'You can't have spent two whole years in a punt.'

'Such things were impossible to arrange,' says Eddy, risking another fib. 'Dalton was always there as usual.'

'But don't you want to?'

'What a damn fool question.'

Now, in the suburban avenue, instead of ringing the bell, Georgie opens the door with a key. No servant appears, which seems very odd. Eddy has no idea where to lay his hat so he clings to it tightly. A hat can be a comfort sometimes.

Inside it is cool and smells faintly of new paint. Doors open off the long, narrow hallway; if he were to stretch his arms out, he could touch both walls. Georgie instructs him to wait in the back parlour and disappears into the shadows.

Eddy is a giant in a doll's house. An upright piano is squashed against one wall. There is only space for a chaise and two armchairs. A bookcase reaches right up to the low ceiling, peopled with crisp volumes of new novels. Everything in the room looks new; the furniture shines with fresh varnish, the carpet is scarcely trodden on, just off the loom. Velvet-draped tables are crammed with photographs of the same family, strapping boys and girls of different ages, a mother whose eyes avoid the camera, a father in a clergyman's collar. A pad of sketch paper lies on the piano stool; a half-finished portrait of Georgie. Eddy takes out a cigarette then changes his mind.

He goes to the window that looks out to the back. The garden is narrow but long, ablaze with red and yellow roses. A marble bird bath stands at the furthest end beneath a trellised arch of jasmine and honeysuckle. Here Georgie stands with a dark-haired girl. A Labrador puppy dances round them, demanding attention but not getting it. Georgie and the girl talk earnestly together, his hands on her shoulders. The girl pulls away from him and turns her back. He wraps his arms round her waist, talking into her ear. The girl dabs her eyes with a white handkerchief. They turn and come back up the lawn. Eddy hides in the folds of the curtains. The girl stops again; she grasps Georgie's hand and holds it against her breasts, but he takes it away from her and points towards the house. She pats her hair into place and walks slowly up the pathway of grass.

When she enters the parlour, she is quite another person. For a moment, she stands smiling in the doorway, looking him up and down. Then she curtseys, rises and extends a long arm, white as the arm of the Lady of the Lake.

'I am Rose, sir,' she says. 'You are most welcome in my house.'

The voice is soft and lightly Scottish. She invites him to sit on the chaise longue and, to his surprise, joins him upon it. He cannot think of a word to say, but she looks at him as if he is the most interesting person she has ever encountered.

'My maid is not here today. A sick mother. So George is kindly making the tea.'

'Good grief, are you serious?'

'Is he not renowned for the making of tea then?'

'Not since we were humble midshipmen years ago and he always did it with very bad grace.'

'I can't imagine our wee George as a humble anything,' she smiles. 'But there'll be many things about him I don't know. Then again, there are quite a few that I do.'

They laugh together and the flimsiest bond is formed. Our wee George.

She is a pretty girl, almost but not quite beautiful, though perhaps she does not need to be. Her hair is black and shiny as tar, piled high above an oval face that wears no rouge. She is just a little plump; her breasts look large and firm, even behind the loose fabric of her tea gown. In repose, he would find her a bit intimidating, like that American girl, but when she speaks and smiles, that is all gone. And when she laughs, her nose crinkles and she becomes a child. She is graceful, polite, educated. She might be a nice young governess, but he knows she is not. He knows what she is.

'You've got lots of books here.'

'They're my companions when I'm alone. The books and the dear dog. Your brother is a jolly tar after all. Never here. And you, I'm told, are now a soldier?'

'The Hussars. The 10th. Our father's old regiment.'

'I hear it's a right dashing uniform,' she says. 'You'll be making female hearts flutter like washing in a gale.'

He blushes. She asks if he might send her a photograph of him in uniform and he promises that he will. He admires the sketch of Georgie, compliments her talent.

'You have quite caught him.'

'Oh, his is not a face that's difficult to catch. Whereas *you* now...'

'But why is he easy and I am not?'

'Because he is already set and I don't think that you are,' she smiles. 'Just like a big jelly.'

She peers at his face, titling her head from side to side.

'I would like to draw you one day. Might you let me?'

He is aware that nervousness is seeping away and that tremors of excitement are taking its place. The girl wears a light perfume, but on this humid day it cannot quite disguise the scent of her body. On the little chaise, he allows his knee to brush hers. Rose smiles and pats it gently. Would he like to see her lovely garden?

She leads him out onto the lawn. Through a window comes a crash of china and a gale of sailor's profanities.

'Such a clumsy clod,' she says. 'Though, I must admit, not in all things.'

He is given a tour of the flowerbeds and introduced to the red and yellow roses by their Latin names. It is as if she were acquainting him with her friends.

'George had it all done for me. A tribute to my name, he declares. Would you credit it?'

She tells him she has lived here for almost a year. George was so kind in finding her the house and helping her to furnish it. Aren't all the things just perfect? A long way from what she was used to back home, she says, in a dour and chilly manse. But, of course, this is home now; though only really when George is here. Eddy does not ask how they met.

'It's nice to see brothers who are close,' she says. 'Mine were always squabbling like hens in a coop.'

'We've done lots of that too. Ask Mama.'

'Fat chance of that, d'you not think?' she smiles, picking up the puppy and kissing its head. The stumpy tail throbs with pleasure. He notices that its teeny prick is hard. Rose notices too.

'Dearie me, would you look at that. Men!'

'Has Georgie spoken of me then?' he asks

'Oh yes, often. I know how much he cares for you, worries about you. That'll be why he's brought you here today.'

Georgie appears from the house carrying a tray. It is such a bizarre sight that Eddy cannot hide his grin.

'Bugger off!' says Georgie.

The three of them sit at a small, white garden table. Rose pours the tea. Georgie taps his biscuit against the table. Checking for weevils, he says as usual, as we always had to on the ship. Rose laughs, squeezes his forearm and lays her head against his shoulder. He flushes and draws back. For a moment, pain shadows the girl's eyes then is gone again.

She demands that they tell her tales of their perils on the sea. So they talk of the *Bacchante*'s damaged rudder, how they floated helplessly towards Arctic oblivion until the crew climbed up into the masts and forced her about with the sheer weight of their bodies and their prayers. Rose pretends she is about to faint with the terror if it. They tell her of the Mikado of Japan and Eddy shows her the dragon on his arm and she declares it far superior to Georgie's, then colours at the revelation that she is able to make the comparison.

But then Georgie tells another tale. Of his pet kangaroo which vanished from its cage and was never seen again. Rose bites her pretty finger and furrows her brows.

'Well, maybe it was for the best,' she sighs. 'No life for a creature like that. To be shut up in a cold English zoo. Its soul is roaming free across Paradise.'

Eddy is ridiculously pleased by her words. He decides that Rose is a person who might understand him. Like Jem used to. Suddenly he is glad that he came here today to this small street in the unknown wilds of the city.

He throws a ball for the puppy which chases it then simply stands and contemplates its catch. Georgie strides towards the dog, his jaw set firm.

'Right then,' he calls over his shoulder. 'I'm going to teach this useless creature how to fetch. Rose, you must show Eddy the rest of your dear little house.'

But he is not to tour the rest of the house. He is led back along the narrow hallway directly to a boudoir. Rose leads him by the hand, smiling brightly, as if she were coaxing him towards a dance floor. Inside the room, he is offered a glass of lime cordial. He notices it is ready prepared on a silver tray, in a jug beside two tall glasses. The bed is prepared too; the covers pulled neatly back, pillows of silk and satin neatly propped against the brass headboard. Vases are filled with so many red and yellow roses that it feels like they are still in the garden. But this is not a garden. It is the boudoir of a woman and now he must be a man. Who would have imagined such a thing? He drinks the cordial in three gulps but it does not prevent the sweat breaking out all over him.

Will he be able to play the role? He is terrified of failure, expecting it. Even if he were to beg her not to tell Georgie, to pay for her silence perhaps, would she keep her promise? Might she not let it slip out when she next lies with him on this very bed? Might he not ask the question directly and, even if she were honourable and refused to answer, might not the look in her eyes or the faint smile on her lips provide it anyway? Oh dear.

He suddenly thinks of the boy with the long legs and the red hair; his tale of the sodomite duke who managed to pleasure his wife by hanging holy medals round his member. Too late for that. Maybe if he had searched out some potion; but he would not have known where to acquire it. Too late for that too. He sends a small prayer to God, short and curt as a telegram.

The girl is still smiling as she sips her cordial. But when she turns away to lower the blinds against the sun, he catches her reflection in a mirror and the smile is gone, the face pale and blank as a snowdrift. When she turns again, it is restored. She unpins her *chignon* and drapes it over a stand on the dressing table. She shakes her black hair loose until it tumbles to her shoulders. She begins to undo the fastenings of her tea gown then stops.

'Perhaps you'd like to do this for me?'

His fingers quiver as he fumbles with endless ribbons, but eventually waves of chiffon and silk flutter to the floor. The shedding of the last pretence.

'There now. That wasn't so difficult, was it?'

Rose stands before him in her chemise, the shape of the woman brazenly clear. For an instant she becomes the American girl, Mrs Langtry, Georgie's postcards and all the other women whose bodies he has thought about in the darkness. But this woman is real; he can smell her. Somehow he finds the courage to lift the chemise over her head. The promise of her breasts was not a trick; they are full and heavy and tilt a little upwards at the nipples. Her hips curve outwards like a cello. The flesh of her body is even whiter than her arms. How odd the triangle of hair without a cock and balls hanging below it, the orifice more terrifying for being hidden away. He knows he is comparing her body with that of a boy, but he does not find it wanting, some pale comparison. It is simply another country and he wants to go there.

Rose reaches up and kisses him lightly. Her tongue darts between his lips but only for a second before it is gone again. Later, he will not remember her skilful removal of his cream linen suit, his shirt, his cravat, his undergarments.

'My my, what a handsome laddie.'

He will not remember any embarrassment or moving from the middle of the floor onto the pillows of silk and satin. He will only remember melting into Rose's flesh, with kisses, at first gentle but which acquire an ever increasing urgency. He need not have worried about hanging the holy medals. There is no problem there.

The smile on Rose's face does not falter; it merely changes from moment to moment. In the beginning, it is patient, tolerant, maternal even. Then a wash of surprise floods over it. He is entranced by her breasts, in awe of them. She cups them in her hands and offers him the pinkish-red tips. Her long, white legs tighten round his back and draw him in. The orifice, the mystical cunt, is not frightening at all. All holes are the same in the dark, the red-headed boy had said, but he is wrong. It feels altogether different from the forceful intrusion necessary against the hard angularity of the male; this is a gentler thing entirely: a warm, welcoming place. He enters it with exhilaration and inhabits it with unrestrained joy.

But now Rose's smile changes again. Now there is a flash of panic in it. She begins to make little cries and he wonders if he should stop. He imagines they are cries of regret, of shame about what she has been forced to do, but then he realises they are of a different kind. Perhaps there was a line which Rose did not intend to cross and he has pulled her over it.

The realisation brings the feeling so blessedly familiar to him now. As he fills Rose, he fills himself. He is Eddy. Nobody more, nobody less. He is not a man who has to bear two names. He has no family, no duty to the world. He is simply a man who is desired and wanted. He can do this. It is just another country and he is at home here too.

Rose does not linger on the sweat-damp sheets. The smile is much more fragile now; it flickers and almost goes out. He can tell she no longer wants to look at him. He lies and watches as she cleans herself at a pitcher and bowl. He does not want to move. He is enjoying the smell of her on his skin and the sticky evidence of victory on his cock. He would like to tell her how much this means to him but he is not sure it would be welcome.

It is stifling in the room now. He asks her to raise the blinds a little and open the window for some air. From the garden comes the sound of yelping and barking, then the voice of his brother cries out.

'Bravo! Bravo!'

They both laugh and it is genuine again now. It is back to the way they were before they came into this rose-filled room.

He, too, has been a good boy today, he tells himself. He, too, has learned a new trick. Except, of course, that it is not a trick. It is an instinct, natural and true. It is a part of him now, just as much as the other thing.

'I've done it!' shouts Georgie as they return to the garden. 'Watch this.'

He throws the ball. The puppy fetches and drops it at his feet. Georgie is triumphant too. He never likes to be beaten. He calls on Rose to come and look. He throws the ball again and again, his cheeks flushed with pleasure. It is as if he has forgotten what has been done here today, as if it is of no consequence compared with the taming of the little dog.

Soon Georgie declares that they must leave. Eddy kisses Rose's long, white hand. Would she really like to sketch him or was she merely being polite. 'Not at all,' she says. He tells her that he would like to come again soon.

'Jolly good,' says Georgie. 'Give Rose a bit of company when I'm on the ocean wave.'

In the cab, neither of them speaks. They are crawling round Berkeley Square before Georgie slaps Eddy's knee.

'Well then?' he says. 'A pleasant afternoon?'

'Very pleasant. Thank you.'

They both look out of their opposite windows. Couples are strolling under the plane trees in the square. Eddy wonders how many of them will soon be doing what he has just done. He shuts out the thought. He does not like to think that it is a vulgar, commonplace thing.

'Rose thought well of you,' says Georgie.

'I am glad. She's a charming girl.'

'No, I mean that she was quite impressed with you, if you take my meaning.'

The blood flies to Eddy's cheeks. He does not answer, but he is not displeased.

'In fact, she couldn't believe you'd not done it before,' says Georgie. 'Like a duck to water, as she put it.'

Eddy manages a small laugh.

'Have you been holding back on your baby brother?' asks Georgie.

Eddy glances at him quickly. His brother is looking at him now. He tries to stop the truth appearing in his eyes but is not sure he succeeds.

'Perhaps you're not so bad at telling fibs.' says Georgie.

He lies again on crumpled sheets. The window is wide open. It is impossible to sleep. The bells chime out from the towers of the city. Eight hours since Eddy fucked a woman. Nine hours. Ten.

He hears Georgie snoring in the room next door. If any dreams appear to his brother, they will be of a puppy fetching a ball. He will not be troubled by anything else. Eddy pictures Rose in her bed, the little dog at her feet. Those sheets will have been stripped by now and left for the attention of the absent maid with the sick mother. The beautiful body will be shrouded in crisp, fresh linen, all evidence of him washed from the room and from her flesh. Today she was made to do a thing she did not want to do, but which she did to please someone for whom she cares, loves perhaps. That was noble of her and ignoble of his brother, even though Georgie meant well, as he always does. Until Eddy reached the little house, it had not occurred to him that the woman would mind one way or the other. He is ashamed of that now.

He is also ashamed of something else. Today he hardly thought of Jem at all. That had been his greatest fear, so he had determined to banish Jem from his mind just as, for the last half-year, Jem seems to have banished him. The letters become ever shorter, mere notes of pleasant nothingness. Eddy tries to read between the lines but finds nothing there either. The letters are dead things. There is no heart to them. Today, though, in the little house, he had not imagined the banishment would be so easy. Jem did not pull him back as he followed Rose along the narrow hallway. Jem did not stand by the bed watching them as her legs parted. Jem's features did not impose themselves on hers as Eddy spent his seed. Not at all, in fact.

A small ache of betrayal gnaws at him but it is not strong enough to spoil the immensity of his joy. If he can make love to a woman, might he not also be able to love one? When the time comes, might he not achieve a life that was more than just a performance, an inescapable sham? It would never be the life of which he so often fantasises, that life which it seems the world would never allow. But might it not, nevertheless, have its own riches, its own beauty and truth? He tells himself he must not hurry. Sleepy Eddy never hurries. He is famous for it. He must take things one step at a time.

The pictures of the afternoon flick through his mind. He wraps his body round the bolster and humps it until he spends again. The bells in the towers strike out. Eleven hours since the world shifted on its axis and, after a long, lonely winter, let some warmth shine down upon him. But when at last he tumbles into sleep, it is not Rose whose face appears. Eleven hours late, the god strolls once again along the avenue of pleached limes.

CHAPTER XII

1887. Aldershot.

'Use your bollocks while you can,' the colonel is fond of saying. 'You never know when some damn Afghan will try to shoot them off.'

He has been a soldier for two years now. It is a monotonous life. For six miserable months, he rises at dawn to trot round the riding school, rain and wind in his face, itching like hell in a hideous, tight stable jacket. Every morning he longs for his comfy little bed at Trinity, listening to the bells and the footsteps hurrying along the cloisters. It is not the discipline he minds; after three years on the *Bacchante* he is used to that. It is the utter stultifying boredom. The camp is a godforsaken place, the town even worse. The drills are endless. The noise of bloody trumpets at every moment of the day. The colonel is a lunatic.

Luckily, his companions in the barracks are a good sort, on the whole. In the beginning, it feels just like his first day at college. He knows that everyone will soon find him out. And, of course, they do but, as before, they have tried to make him welcome and he is grateful for that. But dinners in the mess are not like those in the turreted rooms. Here there is little talk either of the great wide world or the intricate matters of the mind. Beyond the military manuals, there are few books on the shelves. The Misses Brontë are not the sort of ladies who would be welcome here. At the piano, nobody is going to sing *Voi Che Sapete*, only the crudest ditties from the music hall.

Here they must live in a tiny kingdom inside boundaries which cannot be scaled. A kingdom ruled by regulations and timetables, decorated with the tattered flags of ancient conflicts and haunted by the spirits of heroes and martyrs. A kingdom that smells of the tack room and leather polish. The citizens of the mess are oddly indistinguishable from each other; it is a race of unpolluted blood.

Their duties done, they give themselves to pleasure. After all, who knows when they might be called to march out and impose their will on some distant corner of the globe. Some of them might never come back. So it is only right that every service should be provided for their happiness and *esprit de corps*. Those citizens of Aldershot who earn their living by doing so regard it as a patriotic duty to supply the public houses, the cockfights, the bare-knuckle fighting, the brothels and all the other diversions that cling to the outskirts of the tiny kingdom like limpets to a rock.

At first, his comrades make the same presumption Georgie did, so he is soon lured to the necessary places to be made a man of. But the pleasure he took with Rose has been repeated count-less times now, both with her and many others. He suspects his new companions were surprised by his eagerness to join them.

It does not take him long to discover who amongst them are the masters of the revels and oh, what revelry has been enjoyed.

Nor is it long before he stumbles on another master of the revels, a different species entirely. This creature is not to be found in the mess, but in the tack room. His style is not of bullish *braggadocio*; it is altogether quieter, almost silent in fact. His language is that of nods and winks, of innocent words that hold other meanings, of notes passed on scraps of paper torn from army ledgers. Eddy does not seek him out; they find each other as it is inevitable that they will.

One sultry afternoon, a mere glance does it. He decides to take a canter but his horse limps before they even leave the stable yard. The head groom on duty is a small, wiry, middle-aged man with crinkly grey hair, an unshaven face and an accent from somewhere in the north.

'Mark will look after it for you, sir,' he says. 'He has a magic touch, does Mark. The beasts all love him.'

It is true. When Mark bends down to grasp its hoof, there is no resistance. But Mark is stripped to the waist in this sticky weather, his breeches cling to the twin mounds of his arse, a rivulet of sweat oozing between them. Eddy's eyes stay on him for a second too long.

'A good strong lad, our Mark,' the wiry man says, rubbing his forefinger across his stubbled chin. 'There's no mount he can't handle.'

'He certainly seems very fit.'

'A shy lad too, though he's often said how honoured he'd feel to be presented to you, sir.'

Eddy says that he will return in half an hour. His heart is pounding.

His first trip to the house in St John's Wood changed everything and nothing. It certainly did not flush away that other part of him which he had prayed to God it might. But God did not answer this particular prayer. Eddy wonders if that was because he was a little ashamed of making it anyway.

When he goes back, the horse is ready; a sliver of glass had been trapped in the shoe. Somebody will swing for that. Mark has his shirt on now, his hair is combed, his face newly scrubbed. Eddy can smell the soap. But Mark seems not at all shy. His face is open and cheery, his gaze and his handshake firm.

'And where do you come from?' Eddy asks.

'I'm a Brummie, if it please you, sir. That's Birmingham, sir.'

'I believe it was in Birmingham that Mr Watt invented the steam engine, wasn't it?' Dalton's teaching still rescues him from time to time.

'I think it were, sir.'

'Excellent chap,' replies Eddy. 'Excellent.'

'Perhaps Mark should ride out with you a short way, sir,' says the wiry man, 'just to be certain the animal is sure-footed now. Perhaps over to the big wood and back.'

And so it begins. And when it is done, they sit against the fat trunk of an elm and smoke a cigarette. Mark rejects the Turkish ones and rolls his own rough tobacco.

'Is there some other small gift you might like?' Eddy asks. 'Perhaps a few guineas for the public house tonight?'

But Mark looks a little hurt.

'It's been an honour to spend time with you, sir. And to spend with you too.'

Now he heaves with laughter, pleased by his simple joke. Eddy would love to be able to laugh like that. It is the laugh of a comfortable soul.

But that evening it is the cockfight Mark goes to and, by chance, so does Eddy. They are separated by the circle of bloody sawdust; each with his own companions, his own tribe. They catch each other's eyes amid the shouting, the swearing, the squawking and the flying feathers. Eddy would like to go round the circle and greet him, but he knows that is no more possible than waltzing on the moon.

Yet are they not all soldiers together? Life is short, death may come for them any day. Afghanistan still rumbles. Who knows what lies ahead? Use your bollocks while you can, the lunatic colonel had said. Through the hazy weeks of summer, the skylarks wheel in song-flight, almost loud enough to drown the stamps of the boots on the parade-ground. Let us make hay while the sun shines.

*

1887. London. The Golden Jubilee.

There is certainly something about a soldier. For a moment, he thinks his man might weep.

'If I may say so, sir,' he whispers, as if they were in church, 'I have never been more proud to dress you than I am today.'

Eddy admits that it really is quite sensational. Even if he was hardly made to be a soldier, there is no doubt he was made to look like one and no uniform is more spectacular than that of the Tenth Hussars. How awful it would have been to have ended up in some other regiment and languished in an inferior rig-out. He gives way to the pompous thought that this finery has long been waiting for him to come and wear it. Clothes may well make the man but surely the reverse is true also.

'Since Beau Brummell himself was a member of the regiment, can anyone else have looked this fine?' says his man. 'Since the Battle of the Alma, has any Hussar cut such a dash?'

Nothing mars the sharp, lean line of Eddy's tunic, embroidered with ribs of gold braid, the epaulettes broadening his shoulders to a perfect proportion against his waist. His tight white breeches are well filled too, though he wishes his thighs were sturdier; such is the price for disliking football and rugby. And the moustache has come into its own at last. At first it was a dispiriting thing, a plant that refused to blossom, but now it is a vigorous and manly growth, curled at the ends and waxed so hard that even the Norfolk winds cannot upset it. His Papa and Georgie, with their coarse, careless beards, decry its elegance and precision, but Eddy would not be seen dead with a beard. Nobody remotely fashionable has one these days; they are relics of a bygone age.

His man rubs a piece of gauze across the brass buttons and the pummel of the sword. Together they consider the image in the mirror.

'Are you ready, sir?' he asks.

Eddy says that he is and takes a deep breath. His man crowns him with the busby of black sable and ostrich feathers, the fur brushed and polished until you can see your face in it.

'A great day in the history of our country, sir,' his man says.

'Nothing like it in living memory. And you at the very heart of it.'

In the procession to the abbey, Eddy and Georgie are to ride behind Grandmama's landau. They have been appointed as her closest guardians. It is an awesome honour. She will have hundreds of other protectors, but her grandsons will be the front line. Should danger arise, it will be down to them to save her, to be like human shields. In Grandmama's lifetime, there have already been eight such attempts and it is only a few years since the poor ruler of Russia was blown to smithereens. But he must block out such thoughts. Today he must strive to be what he appears to be. Albert Victor must ride out.

'Oh, my two handsome darlings,' cries Alix at the sight of her boys, though it is Eddy on whom her eyes fasten.

Even Bertie's mouth, half-open to bark his annoyance that they are one minute late, closes again. For two years now, he has drummed into Eddy how vital it is that he should succeed as a soldier.

'Universities are all very well but something more grounded, more manly is expected,' he says. 'Brains and brawn. The Empire demands both.'

Oh dear. Of course Eddy knows he will not truly succeed as a soldier and it is only a matter of time before his Papa realises it. But for today at least, he is playing the part and today the play is all.

What Alix calls 'our little tribe' has invaded the city, though it is not little at all. There are hundreds of them, flushed from their coverts by the clapping of Grandmama's hands. Eddy can no more remember their names than the dates of those damned battles. So many of them look alike too; the eyes, the noses, the chins, the certainty. Grandmama has sent her blood coursing along every river in Europe, rushing across borders, through valleys and mountain passes, over wide, deserted lowlands into every sea, north and south, east and west, that laps against the Continent. Few of them are much to admire, though Eddy thinks the cousins from Hesse have some beauty. Both Alicky and her brother, Ernie, are alluring things; the girl especially, though only just. He wonders if, when she grows a little more, Alicky might do. He may decide to fall in love with her. What a shame he cannot have them both.

From his horse, he looks down on his Grandmama. How harmless and fragile she looks, embalmed in her black dress and white lace bonnet. Even today she has refused to be majestic.

'They will see me as they like to picture me,' she says. And of course she is right. In such matters, she always is.

In the landau, she is almost motionless; the smallest of waves, the slightest of smiles, giving no more than crumbs from the cake. Bertie and Alix sit opposite, giving everything. Bertie grinning like he's just had a winner at Epsom. Alix blowing kisses to the children held aloft in Sunday-suited arms. Restraint and abandon. The perfect mixture. Something for everyone.

It is hot. The noise is fearsome. Eddy's mount is restless. The horse has never seen crowds so large before, perched ten deep on tiers of scaffolding, bearing down upon his fragile head of feathered plumes. As Eddy struggles to control him, he is suddenly grateful for those cold dark mornings on the parade ground. His Papa's eye is on him. Damn you, he thinks, I will do this. And he does.

They are supposed to look straight ahead, never from side to side. But there is a sudden eruption above him. On a high balcony, a gang of young men are whooping and cheering, champagne bottles in their fists. Their checked suits are too loud, their body movements too extravagant, their huzzahs too feminine to be mistaken for anything other than what they are. He realises it is him they are calling and whistling at.

'Isn't he beautiful?'

'Love the uniform, dearie.'

'And what a big stallion he's riding!'

Bertie turns away in distaste. Alix, deaf to it all, gives them a special wave. Eddy hopes his burning cheeks will be put down to the sunshine.

'I thought men like that shot themselves,' says Georgie above the din. 'If they don't, they bloody well should. You look rather flushed. For God's sake, don't faint on us.'

For a minute or two, Eddy believes that he might. The sweat trickles down from under his busby, clouding his eyes until he is forced to wipe it away. The horse is still nervous. Huge sausages of dung plop out onto the street. The crowd laughs and holds its nose. It is hardly an unfamiliar odour, but today with the heat and the noise and the humanity, it curdles his stomach.

Now, as they turn into the square outside the abbey, he looks into the crowd again and sees the face. He only notices it because the big head of tousled hair is quite still, not turning left and right like all the others. It gazes straight at him and it saves him.

'Jem Stephen is here,' he says to his brother. 'My old tutor at Cambridge. Remember him? Just there on the right.'

Georgie does not reply, does not turn his head. Georgie always does things by the book.

They are moving quite quickly now, but Eddy peers backwards into the forest of faces. He does not care if his Papa sees or not. For a moment he loses Jem, then finds him again. Jem is not cheering or waving. He just watches calmly, with the faintest of smiles. Eddy thinks he sees pride in the eyes. Does he imagine it? Jem is his friend, or was once. Like Rose is his friend. And Harry and Patrick and silly O.B. Like Mark in the stable yard is his friend. All those good people who are not of their 'little tribe', who do not carry names which can be found on a map. And Eddy stops feeling faint. He straightens his back and sits high in the saddle. And soon the horse quietens down, tosses the plumes on his head and trots on into the morning sun.

The landau stops at the gates of the abbey. It is his task to help Grandmama down. When her tiny feet are safely on dry land, Albert Victor performs his deepest bow and kisses the fat old hand. The smile which, in these last few minutes, he has struggled to keep buttoned under his tunic, now swells and bursts out on his face. It is a smile stored away for two years, that he thought he might never use again. Assuming it can be for no one else but herself, Grandmama at last allows the mask to crack, the dimples to appear. The roar might be heard on the Great Wall of China.

Mr Inslip seems embarrassed. It is obvious at once. Always so unruffled, even in the face of the most shameful misbehaviour, he is ruffled tonight and no mistake. His cheeks, usually the colour of a lightly cooked steak, have gone as pale as the summer moon in the sticky sky outside. Old Silas, the ancient man employed to open the unremarkable door of this unremarkable house off Portland Place, has been similarly disturbed by the sight of Eddy on the doorstep, hat drawn well down over his eyes. He is asked, most graciously, if he would wait in Mr Inslip's small study while Old Silas goes to fetch his master.

Eddy waits and wonders what he is doing here. Since yesterday, battered at every moment by wave upon wave of faces blowsy with joy, he has only wanted to focus on one: the face that did not turn to left or right, did not yell and cheer, but merely gave a proud little smile. But was it pride in the smile? Was it just indifference? Was it just a trick of the light? And why had he been there at all? For the same reason as the rest of the crowd? Or something of greater significance? All last night, all today, he pursues the possibilities in his mind, like a dog chasing its tail. What should he do? Anything? In the end, he thinks he will go dotty. In the end, he does what he had schemed to do this evening, once the latest grand dinner had ended, once his Papa and Mama had withdrawn and the gas was turned down. He creeps out into Pall Mall, an art at which he is now expert, finds a hansom, comes here.

'We were not expecting to be honoured by your presence this week, sir,' Mr Inslip says, a little out of breath.

Mr Inslip's sentences always come slowly from his mouth, as if he has run his tongue over every word, savouring each one to make sure it is completely appropriate.

'There must be many calls on your time during these splendid days,' he says.

'I rather need a brief escape from it all,' says Eddy.

'Indeed, it must all be most stressful.'

'You seem a little stressed yourself tonight, Mr Inslip. Is it the heat?'

It is another warm night and the city is irritable. It knows it will not be able to sleep and is already cross at the thought of it. The streets, still *en fete*, bristle with flared tempers. From the shadows of the hansom he hails in Pall Mall, he sees a dozen drunken conflicts; the fights of the poor, the fisticuffs of the prosperous.

'Truth to tell, sir, you find us in the middle of a small celebration of our own this evening. In honour of the great event.'

'Oh dear, a family affair? Not open to members of the club?'

'Oh no, sir, you'll find several familiar faces here tonight,' replies Mr Inslip. 'But we are celebrating in our usual light-hearted way. Fancy dress. That sort of thing. But I fear that you might not be amused, or indeed even take offence, which would distress me greatly.'

'I've never failed to be amused in your house, Mr Inslip,' he says truthfully, not least by his host's wondrously apposite name. 'Lead on. I insist.'

Mr Inslip's features do an odd little dance that settles into a nervous smile. As he is escorted up the staircase, the usual excitement stretches and wakes in Eddy's body.

The drawing room is an imposing chamber. Despite the heat, the tall windows are shuttered and barred. From the pavement outside, no chink of light will be visible. The other residents of this respectable terrace by Portland Place will suffer no sight or sound of impropriety. Neither the purity of their souls nor the value of their properties, evidence in bricks and mortar of their status and success, will be besmirched by the presence of The Hundred Guineas Club.

Anyway, it is a most select establishment; the price of admission revealed in its name. The drawing room is as richly furnished as its members are accustomed to in their own houses or in the smoky retreats of St James's. The walls are hung with many mirrors in flamboyant gilded frames. Between the mirrors, shallow recesses are sculpted into the walls, each one sheltering a velvet couch and a small table laden with every desirable refreshment. Tall vases of scented roses struggle against the tobacco smoke. The creamy-yellow haze of candle-light makes the place feel even warmer. As always, someone is playing jolly tunes on the piano. There are about ten other gentlemen present. He knows three or four of them; one used to go to O.B.'s Sunday evenings. They are all a little tipsy, a little dishevelled, too, but that is to be expected.

'Where are the ladies this evening, Mr Inslip?'

'They have briefly retired to the other room, sir.'

'Do beg them to join us. We must have some beauty to gaze upon.'

As usual, the big negro footman brings him a glass of champagne, bows low and flutters his long lashes. Such a wicked boy. The other guests greet Eddy correctly, but it is clear they are *un peu distrait* to see him, though he cannot imagine why. On every visit to Mr Inslip's house, he has tried to be just one of the chaps. It is hardly a place for ceremony after all.

The door to the other room opens and Mr Inslip returns. Behind him, like a string of ducklings, eight or nine of them, come the ladies. The ladies of The Hundred Guineas Club are always young and pretty, a delight to the eye. They always wear hair pieces of the highest quality, move gracefully in gowns of satin and silk. They converse politely and demurely, they flutter their fans in a multitude of meanings. Tonight, though, they are all dressed identically and in a very different style. Tonight, the rainbow of satins and silks has been replaced by thundering black bombazine. The towering chignons are hidden under little caps of white lace. To a woman, to a man, they are all dressed up as Grandmama.

Eddy's champagne glass halts in its ascent to his mouth. And then he laughs. It erupts from him like lava. The muscles in his belly ache. It is the sort of laugh Mark in the stables laughs. It infects the rest of the gentlemen and then the ladies themselves. Soon the room pulsates with it.

Mr Inslip dabs his brow with his handkerchief, claps his hands and orders a quadrille. The pianist strikes up the tune and then, in the infinite reflections of the mirrors, Eddy sees countless dancing Grandmamas. The smoke and the candle-light fragment their own features and persuade him it is indeed Grandmama who is twirling before his very eyes.

A waltz is played. He is invited by the prettiest of the ladies to take to the floor.

'Will Albert dance with Victoria?' she asks.

She is a beautiful creature with high-winged cheekbones and skin like a nectarine. As he recalls, by day she is a guard on the underground railway, but by night she emerges from the depths and transforms herself into a dazzling apparition called Angelica. She is currently Mr Inslip's star attraction and Eddy has enjoyed her several times before. Tonight, the comedy of her costume does not quench the desire she arouses in him. It is indeed odd to be waltzing with Grandmama, something he has done on so many occasions, and to know that under the black bombazine and the frilly drawers is a magnificent arse and a sturdy prick.

Eddy and Angelica start the dance, then the other couples join them until, once again, the room is filled with swirling Grandmamas. Mr Inslip was wrong to worry about causing him offence. He finds himself almost moved by the spectacle. It is indeed what Mr Inslip said that it was. A tribute, however strange. It is no more than fancy dress after all. An elaborate concealment of the truth. Just as it was when Eddy rode through the streets behind the landau and everybody cheered. And then the Mary-Anns on the balcony saw him and were not fooled for an instant.

There is more champagne, more dancing. The room gets ever hotter until one of the young ladies swoons. She is laid out on a couch, her bodice unhooked, her stays loosened, her false breasts untied; turned from a queen to a commoner with a chest as hairy as an ape's. A rear window is cautiously opened, just a little, or else we shall all expire.

But the heat of the evening accelerates the usual progression of a soiree at Mr Inslip's. The dancing becomes too exhausting, the couches too inviting. At first, Eddy goes on laughing to see a Grandmama sitting on a gentleman's knee sipping champagne and giggling as his hands rove over the black bombazine, pushing up the petticoats to reveal the stockings and garters that cling to muscular calves. When the ladies abandon the language of the drawing room and replace it with the language of the farmyard, he does not flinch or tut-tut. After all, Angelica is nestled on his own lap, the ribbons from her white lace cap tickling as she nibbles on his ear. And then, earlier than usual, the great tradition of Mr Inslip's soirees begins. The candles are snuffed out, the room cast into darkness. Grandmama no longer presides, the Lord of Misrule is sovereign now.

Angelica unbuttons him. As she begins her work on his member, she fumbles in her drawers to release her own. Oh the fun of it, the delirium even. Who cares if this delicious being is a woman or a man? What is the problem? Eddy's confusions are no longer a trial to him; he has learned to embrace them, to abandon himself to this wondrous melting together of the flesh. For the last two years it has been his greatest escape. Who cares who he is or what he is, who or what the others are? Nobody here for sure. People who want nothing, expect nothing. These are the companions he has come to crave.

Angelica has bagged the couch nearest to the open window. The summer moon pokes in and, for once, the regulation is broken and the room is not entirely dark. For once, it is possible to see the writhings and couplings in the other corners. The scent of the roses and the cigars is now mixed in with other odours. He begins to feel a little queasy. But Angelica's tongue is in his mouth now. He can taste his juices on her lips. It is one of her tricks for exciting him. She whispers wicked things into his ear. He can feel her stubble grazing his chin.

'Christ, it's hot,' she says.

She reaches inside her bodice and pulls out the false breasts. She throws them onto the floor, where they lie abandoned; like two flesh-coloured molehills which have surfaced through the carpet.

The white lace cap has come a little loose with her exertions and hangs lopsided on her wig. Now she leans over the back of the couch and pulls up the black bombazine, the petticoats and the drawers. She slaps her splendid buttocks. They quiver in the moonlight.

'Fuck me, Albert!' she says and giggles so much that the arse cheeks quiver even more.

It is now that he sees their reflection in the mirror. And suddenly it seems a terrible tableau. For a moment he is frozen in the horror of it, then he dashes for the window, throws it open and vomits down into the garden. Some cat below screeches and howls; a dog begins to bark. He stumbles across the room, buttoning himself as he goes, searching for the door to the staircase. In the gloom he cannot find it. Like a blind man, he runs his hands over the walls and the pictures. Suddenly it is thrown open for him by the big negro footman, naked now, his cock bouncing in the air before him.

'Leaving us so early, sir? Did our young ladies not please you tonight?'

'No. Tonight they did not please me.'

Eddy teeters past him, down the staircase. But the front door is locked and bolted. He is not accustomed to opening front doors and has to shout for Old Silas. The ancient takes an age to appear; his cravat undone, his eyes bleary, his breath rank with brandy. Eddy's throat is raw with vomit, the smells of Angelica still in his nostrils. He longs to get out of here but Old Silas takes forever with the locks and the bolts. When the door swings open, a big man is standing on the step, his fist raised ready to knock.

'I never thought to find you here,' says Jem Stephen.

'Neither did I,' says Eddy.

They stand as still and silent as figures in one of his Grandmama's tedious theatrical tableaux. Old Silas sways nervously, holding on to the big brass doorknob.

'The door must be closed again quickly,' he says. 'It is Mr Inslip's strictest rule.'

'I saw you in the crowd. Yesterday,' says Eddy at last.

'I saw you on the shitting horse,' says Jem.

Standing in the doorway, the heat of the city night slumping against his face, every inch of Eddy begins to shake.

Jem Stephen takes a pace forward, stretches out his hand. Four summers ago, in the cramped bedroom of the Bachelor's Cottage, the books had lain scattered like a pyre round Eddy's ankles.

'Other worlds, Eddy,' Jem had said that night.

As he trembles like a jelly on Mr Inslip's well-worn doormat, Eddy thinks back to those other worlds. How they came to be discovered so joyously then were lost again.

Jem still stands, the blue eyes steady, the big hand reaching out.

CHAPTER XIII

1887. London.

It was a windmill that hit him. A windmill no less. Almost a year ago now.

'*Trust Jem Stephen to be so melodramatic,*' Harry writes in reply to Eddy's telegram. '*The rest of us would have been clouted by the branch of a tree, but Jem has to go one better. Perhaps he was going to tilt at it, engage it in an existential debate.*'

The truth is more prosaic. It seems he rode up the hillock on which the windmill stood merely to admire the view across frosted Suffolk fields. But then the wind whirled up a tornado of dead leaves, his horse shied and he was cracked on the skull by the descending vane. The doctors declared that it looked much worse than it was. No fuss, no fuss, said Jem to the chums. No need to tell everyone. No need to tell Eddy.

But soon it is clear that the doctors are wrong. It is worse, far worse than it looks. Harry writes that those brief bouts of melancholia, which they once considered so Byronic, are longer and deeper than before. For days on end, he takes to his bed, pushes them all away. Yet, if anything, the opposite mood is more unsettling, when Jem is flying high on the magic carpet of his latest inspiration for a glorious future. But the magic carpet is a flimsy, threadbare thing. He tumbles off it with increasing regularity.

'*The fall can happen in a single moment, like a cloud crossing the sun,*' writes Harry. '*I felt you should know all this before you arrive at our little reunion. In case it's one of the bad days.*'

Eddy has been invited to many of these reunions. Harry and O.B. never cease to suggest luncheons, dinners, balls, but it is ever harder for him to maintain the connection. His dull soldier's life keeps him moving and when in town he is expected to do much more than before. Grandmama is getting old, says his Papa, and he cannot do everything himself. Eddy must buckle down, learn the ropes, do his bit in the family business.

But at the foot of Mr Inslip's steps, as Eddy still shakes and gulps for fresh air in the fetid night, this latest reunion, at Harry's house on the river, becomes the trivial topic of their conversation. At this moment, nothing beyond the trivial is possible between them.

'Do say you'll come,' says Jem, as he hands Eddy into a hansom.

'I will come.'

And right after breakfast Eddy telegraphs to Harry. The reply arrives the next day and it changes everything.

At first, he is torn between misery and joy. Misery at the injury and the suffering. Why on earth did Jem not want him told? He would have dropped everything, found the best doctors, nothing would have been too much trouble. But it is joy that wins the struggle. Now everything is explained. Jem had simply been too unwell to stay in touch. No wonder his letters had become such flimsy, occasional things. And really, that command to not let Eddy know, what was that if not an act of selflessness and caring? How much more evidence could there be of Jem's unaltered affection? Oh, how brave and strong and true he is.

The smile that gushed from Eddy outside the abbey occupies his face again and refuses to leave. But in Pall Mall nobody notices. Grandmama's celebrations are still going on, the foreign relatives still roost in every corner of the house. This week, an ecstatic expression, whether real or assumed, is obligatory. And anyway, dear Eddy is always smiling.

After dinner, he sits in the drawing room as they chatter round him. He answers when he is spoken to, but he is not really there. He is in far distant places, where anything is possible, anything permissible.

His gaze ambles round the room until it happens to descend on Mama's little trinket box. Encrusted with emeralds and diamonds, it is fashioned in the shape of a windmill. He has seen it a thousand times before but now, as a breeze sneaks in from the summer night and spins the bejewelled vanes, Eddy stares and stares until he is forced to close his eyes for fear they might reveal him.

Jem snores softly, a magazine spread open across his chest, legs spilling over the cradle of the hammock. He is too big for it, as he is for so many things.

He has planned it this way; that Eddy should come to him

alone in the garden. He does not want their meeting to be in the presence of all the others, as if he, Jem, were just one of the crowd. He does not mean to fall asleep, but last night he was plagued by those stygian dreams he suffers now, those rivers of darkness that carry him into places his mind does not want to go.

When he opens his eyes, he forgets where he is. He feels a flare of panic, but then sees his visitor. His body struggles to free itself from the clutches of the hammock. The magazine flutters to the ground; the pages skittering over Harry's flower-beds. They chase and collect them together, laughter covering the awkwardness.

'You're thinner these days,' Jem says at last.

'And you are not.'

'Is the regiment working you too hard? I know you don't like hard work.'

'They most certainly are.'

'And are you happy?'

It is the question Jem aches to know the answer to, had not intended to ask. He notices it slip out of his mouth in the way these things do of late; those questions he should not really put, those remarks he should not make. He hears himself do it with an odd detachment, as if he were listening to somebody else.

He kicks himself. How stupid, when he had already known the answer. In the doorway of Mr Inslip's house, as Eddy had quivered like an aspen, it had been achingly clear. At that moment on the steps, to all his other troubles, Jem Stephen had added a wrenching sense of shame. How, two summers ago, could he have turned and walked away? What rationale, seemingly sensible, imperative even, could have made him commit such an act against his own humanity? What barrister, as he was now however risibly supposed to be, could build any defence for it? He certainly couldn't himself; no wonder his practice seemed to have failed at the starting gate. He had let his head rule his heart. And now, in all these frightening new ways, his head seemed to be letting him down. What hubris is there? he thinks.

'Are you?' asks Eddy now.

'What?'

'Happy?'

'Oh gosh, yes!' says Jem, waving the pages of the magazine. 'This is my new venture. It's a literary periodical. *The Reflector*. I brought this copy for you. I'd so like to hear what you think.'

Eddy flicks through the pages, makes the necessary noises.

'But what about the law?'

'Oh I do that too, but this is where my heart really lies. O.B. has contributed a piece. And Harry too. Might you honour us with a short article?'

'I, write?' Don't be silly. You know I hardly even read.'

Jem feels it like a kick in the guts.

'So in the long run I did no better than old Dalton?' he says, fumbling for the matches to light his pipe. 'I'd hoped to have given you that at least.'

A silence falls in the garden of the tall, lean house at Hammersmith. Harry has christened it 'The Chummery', its main purpose the pleasure and recreation of his many friends, old and new. Eddy is welcomed with bows, cheers, decorous slaps on the back. O.B. even prostrates himself as if Eddy were the King of Siam.

'You were a golden crop, my dears,' sighs O.B. into his

glass of sherry. 'It's a ghost of a place since you all went down. The current lot are bank managers to a man. I search for just one shining boy, but in vain. In vain, my dears.'

There is a jolly lunch. Jem tries to pretend that time has stood still, that the cloisters and the quad are right outside the window as they always used to be. But it is not the foppish Cam that saunters past the window, but the great bullish Thames; not the courteous town of ivory towers, but the vast roistering canvas of the capital, upon which Harry and the others have begun to paint their lives. Jem tries to deny to himself the awful truth that he is no longer their focus, the king of their court. They had always questioned him, argued back against his pronouncements; he would have tolerated nothing less. But now they argue with more vigour, they are more stubborn, sometimes almost insolent. Now he must struggle to maintain his authority, to dominate as he always did. Jem may have got fatter, but in this alien landscape he has shrunk while the others have grown. Behind the usual smokescreen of pipes and cigarettes, he feels himself dissolve a little, his edges blur. Suddenly he can stand it no longer. He leaps up, reimposes his presence on the room.

'Come on, Eddy, let's go and look at your new bridge. Harry, you will lend us your little boat.'

But the late summer sun has gone in now, the blue sky has turned an odd whitey-grey as if mould were growing on it. Eddy, the old sea dog, doubts the wisdom of a trip in Harry's little boat, but Jem half-drags him from the house to where the boat is tied. The chums line the drawing room balcony. As Jem pulls away from the bank, O.B. begins to sing *Hearts of Oak* and everyone takes it up.

Despite the chubbiness, Jem is as strong as ever. The breeze is behind them, and as he rows down towards the bridge it feels like they are flying. He can see Eddy relax and begin to enjoy it. Still they must talk of inconsequential things, of harmless memories shared, like two old friends reunited. Then Eddy says how pleased he had been to see him in the crowd, how it had saved him from being sick all over Grandmama's head.

'I just wanted to have a look at you, to see how you were these days.'

'I didn't think you gave me much thought any more,' says Eddy, pretending to watch a family of ducks paddling against the tide. The *paterfamilias* is plumed, chest out, pompous as Bertie. 'I get more letters from my tailor than I do from you.'

'It was my job to help you grow wings, then to let you go,' says Jem, flinching at his own hypocrisy. Letting Eddy go. Ha!

'Well, I've missed your company,' says Eddy, still contemplating the ducks.

Jem does not reply, cannot reply. He feels it coming and knows he cannot stop it. All the strength of his body is powerless against it. All it takes is the wrong word, the wrong inflection even. Words have always been his joy, his companions, his armoury. Now he is fearful of them, of what they can do to him. He takes an endless breath, tries to stop the thing dragging him under.

'They'll be itching to marry you off soon, I shouldn't wonder,' he manages to smile. 'Has any regal maiden captured you yet?'

Eddy mentions his German cousin, pretty Alicky from Hesse. She is still rather young, but she is sweet and they all think she would do very well.

'You do not answer the question,' laughs Jem.

'No, she has not captured me, but I might have to try to allow her to.'

'Has anybody else?' asks Jem.

The sharp breeze scudding off the water does nothing to cool the sweat running down his face. Their eyes meet. Another question that should not be asked, but whose meaning cannot be mistaken.

'No, nobody else,' replies Eddy. 'I learned some years ago to disengage my heart from my body. But my body has given me a lot of happiness.'

'You didn't look very happy at Mr Inslip's the other night. It distressed me greatly.'

Again, Eddy does not answer. The wind is strengthening now and specks of rain are threaded through it. Eddy the sailor suggests that they turn round quickly or even make for the bank.

'But look, here's your great new bridge!' Jem shouts. 'I came to watch you open it. I come to see you perform your duties whenever I can.'

'Do you really? If only you'd let me know.'

'Oh no, that wouldn't have done at all. What's your old tutor amongst all that mayoral regalia and ladies in grand hats and feather boas? Just a face in the crowd; that's old Jem Stephen these days.'

At last, Jem manages to twist the boat round, but the wind is against them now and the going is hard. Eddy offers to take the other oar but Jem will not allow it. They have covered no more than a dozen yards when he loses the struggle with himself. The fall comes, as Harry warned, in a moment. The big man crumples up, like a string puppet thrown into a corner.

He lets go of the oars to cover his face with his hands. Eddy catches them just in time before the wind wrenches them from the rowlocks.

'Jem, what the hell's the matter?'

'I am nothing. I am a zero. A great useless zero.'

Eddy cannot pat him on the back, take his hand or put an arm round the heaving shoulders. He must row or they are in trouble. He can only comfort with words. He tells Jem what a wonderful teacher he is. What a difference Jem has made to so many people. How his friendship and guidance have illuminated their lives, how they all love him.

The river is broad here, the current strong. The rain finally explodes from the clouds and in a minute they are drenched. Eddy does not have the strength to get them back to the house, he can only try for the nearest bank. Jem does not seem to notice the rain. He speaks again, from behind the big hands still cupped over his face.

'I'd always hoped I might help you in your public work.'

'I haven't forgotten.'

'I still dream of that, you know.'

'It would mean a lot to me, but you said it yourself, you're not the man for the golden chains and the feather boas. Your gifts don't lie there. When the proper time comes, I'm sure I will need you then. One day.'

Eddy fights to row the boat towards the bank but Jem does not offer to help him. Instead, he trails the big hand into the churning grey water and watches it roar between his fingers.

'It would be so easy, wouldn't it? One awful minute perhaps, but then all done.'

Jem's tears come again. He cannot tell where his tears end

and the raindrops begin. Now he sees that Eddy is weeping too. Eddy gets them to the bank, pulls Jem off the boat onto the muddy ground. They are half-drowned rats squelching up towards the towpath.

'Where are we going, Eddy, you and I?'

'I don't know, Jem.'

Eddy half-carries him back towards the house. Suddenly Jem stops and laughs.

'And I've got the clap.'

'Me too,' says Eddy.

Harry and the others have been looking out for them. They come running. There is fright in Harry's eyes. They dry Jem and put him to bed. They will watch over him tonight, Harry says, as they do so often now. Eddy does not stop shivering until he has drained the second brandy.

'Goodness, Mr Stephen, we all get a bit downhearted,' he says. 'When my lady wife proposes a visit to her mother in Cheltenham, my heart sinks to my boots and sulks there for a week. But it passes.'

Jem perches on an elegant chair which is much too small for him. The edges of his buttocks hang in mid-air. He is uncomfortable in every way.

Eddy has done what he vowed to do as he downed the second brandy in Harry's drawing room above the river. Discreetly, he asks someone who asks someone else who provides a name and an address. It takes almost a month to persuade Jem to go.

It is a grand room in Wimpole Street. The eminent doctor sits behind a walnut desk large enough for table tennis. He is an avuncular man; snowy hair above a florid face, jowls that ripple when he talks. His voice is soothing as honey and lemon. Above him, a blazing chandelier hangs like a sun, as if to assure his patients that illumination of whatever darkness assails them will soon be forthcoming.

Jem has already lain on the couch behind the screen, has been poked and prodded. He has had his balls squeezed. He has pissed and passed a stool for perusal. The scar on his skull, the legacy of the windmill, has been examined and been declared a first-rate piece of work.

'So these melancholias of yours, Mr Stephen. Like mine, they pass too, do they not?'

'Oh, yes,' says Jem. 'On some days I could conquer the world.'

'Well, there you are then,' beams the doctor. 'Melancholia is just part of the ebb and flow of our short existence on earth. On their gloomy days, some of our greatest artists, writers and poets have produced their most remarkable works. But soon they desert the dreary desk and they're out playing cricket. Why, Mr Dickens himself went to the music hall in the evening after he wrote *The Death of Little Nell*. I know because I was with him. It perked him up in no time.'

'But sometimes the only place I want to be is bed,' says Jem. 'I want to sleep forever.'

'Mr Stephen, your reputation as an athlete precedes you to these rooms. My own dear son recalls you well from Eton. He venerates you still. Big Jem Stephen, how I wish I were like him, he used to say. But you have gone a little bit to seed, Mr Stephen. Your body is used to vigorous activity; when it does not get it, it gets rather cross. You need to awaken it again, that's all.'

'So you don't think I'm mad then?'

The eyebrows rise up and almost disappear into the snowy hair. The jowls wobble with merriment.

'Good heavens, no. You're not thinking of assassinating Mr Gladstone, are you?'

'Only for his sense of fashion.'

The doctor slaps the red-leather top of the desk; the jowls dance again.

'There you are, you see, a sense of humour. Excellent. It is the best medicine I can prescribe you.'

'And if it doesn't work?'

'Then turn to God, Mr Stephen,' he says, removing his smile for a moment. 'There is more comfort to be found in Him than in any set of rooms in Wimpole Street. He is the only true physician of the spirit.'

The doctor rises, comes round the great desk and extends his hand. Jem is dismissed.

'So it's just chin-up then?' he asks.

'My dear sir, in your case, we are contemplating a plurality of chin,' says the doctor, the smile in place again. 'So let us aim to remove some of this weight, restore you to the athlete you used to be and get that chin back to being a singular entity.'

When he walks out into Wimpole Street, he suddenly thinks his legs may buckle. Those tree trunks that made him Keeper of The Wall become like saplings in a gale. He clings to the railing outside the doctor's rooms. A little girl bowling a hoop stares at him until her mother pulls her away. A policeman asks if he is unwell. He looks up into the sooty November sky. He wonders, he the great unbeliever, if some deity might indeed come to his aid, because it seems that nobody else can. But the sky does not answer him back. His eyes sweep along the length of the street. Perhaps behind one of the smart black doors is someone who might understand, explain, help. But how would he ever find him? The search might take a lifetime.

When he is able to let go of the spear-tipped railing, the blood trickles out between his fingers. He can see through the tall windows into the splendid room. The jolly doctor is shutting up shop for the day, a servant heaving him into his greatcoat and topper. The gas is lowered in the blazing chandelier until the light gutters and dies.

CHAPTER XIV

1888. London.

Under the wrinkles and the lines, the pockmarks of youth and the liverish stains of age, the judge's displeasure bubbles quietly. The nerve that slumbers in the fleshy bag below his left eye is twitching. This evening is far from the event he had wanted.

Jem sees the twitch; they all do. They all know the contours of that face as well as their own. Long ago, the judge's wife and children learned to read it like a barometer. Tonight, a skim of a smile is there because the occasion demands it, but it is the usual flaccid thing. It will not blossom into a sudden grin, no teeth will be shown, no head flung back, no eyes dance. Judge Stephen's smile will nourish nobody. It never has.

Jem feels a stab of satisfaction that, for once, his father must suppress himself. And in his own house too, at his own table. There can be no explosion tonight. At least, he prays not. These days, his father's temperament is scarcely less erratic than his own.

Yet the judge should be delighted. It is indeed a coup of sorts. He has Albert Victor seated on his right, talking to him with the greatest deference and amiability. Invitations have been issued before, but they have always been graciously declined. So it is a surprise when a letter arrives, wondering if it might be possible for Sir James and Lady Stephen to receive him for tea or perhaps even dinner, should they have an unoccupied evening. But the letter also requests that no fuss is made; their guest would prefer a quiet dinner with the family. He would so like to meet, at long last, his dear old tutor's parents and siblings without pomp or ceremony.

'Without pomp or ceremony?' rails the judge. 'What's the bloody point of *that*?'

His wife takes the tiny bottle from the tray, shakes three drops into a small glass of water, pats his shoulder as he drinks it. It is important that he be kept calm. There must not be another stroke.

'Your father wants a glittering occasion,' she whispers to Jem, 'filled with his most distinguished friends and, in particular, his enemies. So they may then go forth and spread the word about the glory of the Stephens.'

But tonight, the dining table at De Vere Gardens is hardly a quarter full. They are huddled together in the centre; two long fingers of deserted walnut stretch out on either side, lost in the shadows beyond the reach of the candlelight. At first, there is a stiff gavotte of questions and answers; enquiries into the health of Eddy's grandmother, his parents, his brothers and sisters, his horses and his dogs. Eddy responds with his patient sweetness.

'I want to know all about you too, if I may?' he says and, somewhat to their surprise, they hear themselves telling him.

By the time of the entree, the table is a warm and easy place. There has not been so much careless chatter round it for many a long day. Even the judge relaxes his grip, allows his wife and his children to speak. Jem wonders if his father is learning things about them he never knew, had never troubled to ask.

Jem has been nervous about tonight. Eddy had invited himself without informing him. What does it mean? He does not know what Eddy wants, or if he wants anything at all. Does anybody want anything of Jem Stephen anymore? Certainly not the literary public it seems; after a few months of frantically flapping its wings, *The Reflector* has come crashing to the ground in a bloody mess of debt and bruised feelings. Jem is no longer sure what he has to give to the world, to this family, to anyone.

'How proud your parents must be of you, sir,' the judge is saying. 'The army is a noble life. Almost as noble as the law.'

'It doesn't seem so noble on a freezing morning in a stable yard covered in the mess of horses,' replies Eddy. 'Begging your pardon, ma'am.'

'But it teaches you discipline, unselfishness and concern for the needs of those round you. My son James here might benefit from a spell in a regiment.'

'Dear old Jem in the army?' Eddy laughs. 'Oh no, he's far too clever for that.'

Jem sees the nerve beneath his father's eye wake up again.

'You think so, sir? Sadly, it seems he is far too clever for anything,' replies the judge, the smile quite vanished. 'Too clever for the law, the great enterprise of this family. Too clever for this doomed periodical which was supposed to take the world by storm and make the giants of literature quake in their boots at the arrival of a new Colossus. It seems, in fact, that he lives in a stratosphere all on his own, a planet of pure cleverness. Or do I really mean stupidity?'

Sometimes Jem wonders if this is all for show. If it is a mere performance as the disappointed parent and if, secretly, his father is pleased that his golden son is drifting into eclipse and that he himself will go on unchallenged as the greatest of the Stephens, his title never toppled. But, if so, it is a performance worthy of Irving. The venom in his father's eyes spills out over the table, spreads like a stain among the plates, the glasses, the cutlery, the candlesticks. His mother and his siblings look at their plates. Only Eddy does not look away.

'With respect, sir, the idea that Jem Stephen has one stupid bone in his body would be greeted with laughter in every college in Cambridge University.'

'That's as maybe, sir,' replies the judge, 'but I'm more concerned with his performance in the university of life. That's the one which matters in the end.'

'For those of us who have remarkable parents, like you, sir, like my own, too, it's an almost impossible thing to come after them and live up to their achievements. We poor sons of great men need time. Jem Stephen has not even begun to make his mark on the world.'

In the split second that Jem remembers the scene, Eddy remembers it too and repays his debt.

'Whatever our failings, it is surely wise not to chaff us for them but to celebrate the best in us. Jem has already enriched the lives of so many people, including my own. I am proud to call him my friend.'

Eddy waits for a reply but nothing comes. So he smiles, raises his glass, begins to sing.

For he's jolly good fellow...

But it is not the raucous anthem in the hall of Trinity on the day of Bertie's visit. Eddy sings softly, not much above a whisper, never taking his eyes from Jem. It is a love song that he offers.

Jem's mother and siblings are unsure of the protocol involved when Albert Victor breaks into song. It is outside their experience. Do they join in? Perhaps best not to. But they applaud gently when he has finished. What a delightful voice he has. Surely he has been trained by a professional from Covent Garden. There is a pianoforte in the drawing room; might he honour them with another? But, please, a longer piece this time.

Only the judge does not applaud. He is leaning back in his chair gazing at Eddy.

'A passionate encomium,' he says.

The judge always chooses his words with the forensic precision of the legal mind. And for all his faults, he is a sophisticated man. He has travelled the world; few aspects of the human condition are a closed book to him. In the choice of an adjective, Jem sees that his father sees too.

But there will be no more songs tonight. Eddy rises, begs to be excused for leaving so early but he must be back with his regiment at the crack of dawn. May he visit them again? He has so enjoyed meeting dear old Jem's family. On the doorstep, he kisses Lady Stephen's hand, clasps it for longer than is necessary until tears prick at her eyes.

As the cab trots away towards Kensington Road, the judge

turns on his heel without a word and vanishes behind the fat oak door of his study. He is not seen again for the rest of the evening.

It is well past midnight when Jem is lying in bed, the gas turned out, reading by the light of a candle. His father enters, clad only in dressing gown and nightcap, a sight Jem has never seen in all his life. The judge does not take a chair but sits on the end of the bed. Jem is astonished. Such intimacies have never been extended before.

'I am unable to sleep,' says the judge. 'I have been going over this evening in my mind.'

'It seemed to go well, Papa, did it not?'

'It revealed something I had not previously understood. The strength of the affection between you and our guest.'

Jem feels his heart race. This close, in the deadened night, his father must surely hear it. Christ, what comes now? But suddenly the judge seems to sag into the bed.

'I cannot carry the baton much longer.'

'Papa?'

'I am not as I used to be. The doctors flutter round me, making reassuring squeaks, but I know better. I have long stood at the top of a hill but now the earth is moving under me and soon I will slide. The name of Stephen will slide too, back into the anonymity from which it came. Unless...'

The judge stands up again, paces the floor. The room is becoming chill; Jem sees him shiver. His father pokes at the dying embers of the fire. How frail he looks. Then, in an instant, the frailty is gone. Poker in hand, the judge rushes back to his son. He grasps him by the nightshirt, pulls him half-off the bed. He thrusts his face into Jem's. His eyes are wide and wild. Jem can smell the staleness of his breath.

'Can you not see that this connection is your last chance to make something of yourself? I thought it had been lost to you after Cambridge, but this evening I can see that it has not. Not yet. For God's sake, find a way of using it. He is not a clever man but, despite what I said at the table, *you* are. Make yourself indispensable. I don't care how you do it. Give him anything he wants.'

Jem's mother is in the doorway, candle in her hand, her red-gold hair streaming like plumage down her back.

'Let Jem go, my dear. Let him go.'

The judge allows Jem to fall back against his pillows. Without taking his eyes from his son, the judge reaches out to his wife, his hand flailing in the air.

'Let's go back to bed,' she says. 'I will give you some of your nice drops and you will sleep like a babe until morning.'

She wraps her arm round his shoulder, kisses his cheek, guides his shuffling steps out of the room. In the doorway, the judge stops and turns his head.

'Jem...'

'Yes, Papa?'

'Give him anything he wants.'

'But I am like your priest, sir,' says the tailor. 'Your secrets are safe with me. I would sooner have my tongue torn out than reveal them to vulgar comment.'

'Nevertheless,' says Jem, 'please do as I request.'

'Sir, my tape measure is an old and trusted friend. It never lies to me. It confides that your waist has, most impertinently to be sure, enlarged itself to thirty-eight inches and that's that.'

'I don't doubt its veracity, but you will kindly make all

my new trousers to the thirty-six inches which I have been in the past.'

'But you'll scarce be able to breathe, sir,' says the tailor.

'By the time my new suits are ready, my waist will have returned to its original dimensions.'

'In a fortnight, sir?'

'A morning run round the park should do it.'

'Quite a long run, I should think, sir.'

'Ah, but you see, from now on, I have determined that all things are possible.'

He strides down Savile Row to the top of the Burlington Arcade. Round the portico, the usual swarm of Mary-Anns hovers for their prey. Those who know him, and they are not a few, smile and wave. For once he does not blush and scuttle on. Today he does not care who might see. Today he has only good feelings towards his fellow man. He acknowledges their greetings, enquires after their health.

'I'd be better with your big prick up my arse,' says one.

He smiles, slips the boy a guinea and tells him to treat the others to supper tonight. Rough-hewn compliments rain down on him as he disappears into the shiny tunnel of the shops, those little jewel boxes of temptation to which he so often succumbs. On impulse, he goes into a barber's.

'There you are, sir,' says the man on finishing his task. 'Five years younger, if I may be so bold. Not that a young gent like yourself need worry about such things.'

But it is true. He does look younger. He has let his hair grow dishevelled of late as compensation for its undoubted thinning on his crown. Now he looks neat and tidy. Indeed, his whole face looks tidier. His eyes seem brighter, his mouth set in an upward curve, the gossamer lines which have begun to crinkle his skin hardly visible.

In an umbrella shop, a splendid Malacca cane with the head of a snake beckons him from the window. Is he mature enough yet for a cane? Might it not negate the rejuvenation of the barber's craft? But golly, how elegant it would look with any of the five suits he has just ordered in Savile Row. But no, it is rather expensive and he has already spent enough for one day. Poor dear Mama. She is always so understanding about his debts, so generous with that small inheritance from her aunt, the one the judge knows nothing about. But what an excellent cane it is. And after all, he really must have something right now, this very day, something tangible, something to prop up his new exhilarating sense of being.

At the end of the arcade, Jem and the Malacca cane emerge into Piccadilly. The sky is a hesitant blue; confused perhaps by a seeming change of season. Some stray wind from warmer climes has lost its way and flown north to scour the city clean of its fogs and filth. The thunder of the iron-clad wheels and the stink of the horse dung seem less oppressive today; there is a lightness in the air. He can even catch the perfumes of the women heading towards Fortnum's.

Women have always been strange creatures to him; apart from his mother and sisters, they remain as exotic and unknowable as some tribe from a distant planet. The idea of intimacy with one, of either body or mind, is quite beyond his usually unfettered imagination. Still, in the sunshine, he must admit they are pretty on the eye, like winter butterflies floating along the street. He goes into Hatchards and buys a book for his mother, the silly romantic stuff in which she likes to lose herself. He does so love to see her smile.

He strides through St James's towards the park. He passes Marlborough House, looks up at the window which Eddy has pointed out as his bedroom. Of course Jem has never been admitted to that part of the mansion, though it is a room he often imagines. But Eddy is in Yorkshire with his regiment. The room will be quite empty; perhaps there are dust sheets over the bed and the furniture. Still, he waves up at the window as if his friend were smiling down.

On the Embankment, a low sun glances on the breezy, crinkled water. He walks as far as London Bridge. It will do him good, he thinks, the start of his new regimen. Now he can see the tall-masted ships at the wharves and the jetties, the coal barges, like black beetles, being dragged along by the tugs. The gulls are circling above The Pool, half-crazed by the smells from the boats going into Billingsgate. He has loved this scene since he was a boy; the wild excitement of people embarking for the unknown, for the mystery of other worlds far away from De Vere Gardens, Kensington. How brave they are, he always thought. Should he, too, have sought his future in another land; Australia, the Americas? Some fresh, merciful country, where he might have shaken them all off and found some sort of rebirth.

Suddenly hungry, he stops to buy apples from a coster-monger. He had no breakfast this morning; he had not felt like eating.

'There you are, sir. Round and juicy as a whore's breasts,' says the young man with a wink.

Between the flat cap and the spotted neckerchief is a flat, open face. They grin at each other, two lads joined in the cheery bond of carnality. We do not look unalike you and me,

Jem decides. He imagines a life anaesthetised by simplicity, with no cares greater than the quality of each morning's fruit in Spitalfields Market. Perhaps, he thinks, it is that simplicity for which he must search, like some Holy Grail. Perhaps, if he is to survive, he must try to be a costermonger in his soul.

He wanders away from the river. The great blackened shape of the cathedral, sinister on dark days, looks quite benign under the scrubbed sky. He munches his apples as he walks. His mother would be horrified. Such vulgarity to eat in the street. Jem laughs out loud.

'That's right, my friend,' says a tramp, sprawled on a bench, his ragged arms wrapped round a dirty terrier. 'You've got to laugh, ain't ya? Otherwise, you'd go stark, staring bonkers.'

It is the same prescription he was given in Wimpole Street. But he knows it is a facile one, weak as a fraying rope. Now he knows that the only possible cure is a purpose in life, a purpose of crystal clear simplicity, simple as the selling of apples.

He cannot believe the change that has come upon him in just a few hours. Was it only this morning that life had seemed unsupportable? As usual, he had taken the underground to Temple, trudged up to Lincoln's Inn and climbed the worn stone stairs to his chambers. The Clerk was already buzzing round, his arms full of briefs, a black-suited Father Christmas.

'Anything for me?' asks Jem.

'Not so far, sir.' The Clerk is a kindly man, but he does not meet Jem's eye. 'But it's early yet. This could be your lucky day.'

Jem sits at his empty desk underneath the fat black beam from which the barrister who failed to save his client from the gallows hanged himself. He tries to write a poem, another damn poem, but the words come as sluggishly as treacle from a tin. He cannot cleanse his mind of his father, as the judge shuffled out of his bedroom last night.

'Give him anything he wants.'

As the door had closed, he had stared blindly at the spot where his father had stood. He had thought he might be sick. Now, at his empty desk, it rises in him again. He had imagined he had long since judged the judge, understood what made him function. Until now, he had disliked him, despised him even, though aware that most of the men of their tribe were cut from the same cloth. But until now he had not abhorred him. For it seems that, in truth, his father is a reckless gambler, willing to risk dragging the name of Stephen into the eternal mire on the chance of some greater glory. Oh the hypocrisy of it. It is as if Jem has encountered a stranger.

For all his life, he has considered himself hardly worthy of his father's notice. Why otherwise would his parents have set sail for India and left him to face such emptiness? But now it comes to him that he is not cut from his father's cloth and that he does not want to be. Surely that must mean something. Something good, valuable even. And if, in the end, he loses the battle with himself; if, on some dark day, the worms inside his head finally consume him, then maybe something of that good might be left behind, a commemoration of all which had once been fine in him.

In an instant, under the shadow of the beam, he suddenly sees what he must do. He sees the way forward. St Paul himself could not have asked for clearer guidance. It is so simple. He must give himself to Eddy in every way except the one his father had implied. He must transfuse into Eddy everything that is still strong and clear in himself.

He remembers the helpless, drunken face on the steps of Mr Inslip's house, the frightened face pulling on the oars to try to reach the river bank. But, above all, he sees the dozy, smiling face that appeared from under the hat on that sunny morning in the avenue of pleached limes. Dear Eddy, so gentle and meek. Dear Eddy, who so needs a friend. Jem had tried to be that at Cambridge, but it had gone wrong, gone flying off down that different, dangerous alleyway. Well now he must try again, so much harder this time and with no thought of himself. If he can do that, if he can remake Eddy in the best of Jem's own image, then whatever happens in the end to Jem Stephen, all will not have been lost. In Eddy, Jem Stephen will go on being. And one day, isn't Eddy going to reign over a quarter of the world? What greater legacy could anyone hope for?

He makes a silent vow to himself. And when it has been made, his tired mind is like the sky outside the window in Lincoln's Inn. It is washed clean of doubt. It knows, quite simply, what it has to do. And the joy of the thing is indescribable.

He leaves the chambers and walks out into the streets of London, into the promise of some sort of future, however short or long it might be. He breathes it in, fills his lungs with it, feels the warmth of it on his face. He buys the five expensive suits, the Malacca cane. He watches the light shine on the wintry waters of the river. He buys the juicy apples from the costermonger and bites into them as deeply as he can.

He stops by the cathedral. He has not been inside since he was a boy. Like all those who live in London, he inhabits a different city from those who merely visit. Anyway, unbeliever that he is, why would he? But now he does and he almost chokes on the beauty of it. He thinks about how often he has mocked the believers, those fools who seek some sort of eternal existence, that intellectual peasantry so far beneath him and those with whom he keeps company. But even if the whole thing is false, what a support it must be. And is it not support that he has been seeking for so long and in vain? It was the jolly doctor's alternative prescription after all.

'He is a true physician of the soul,' the man had said.

For an hour or more, Jem Stephen sits in the nave and stares into the eyes of God. He tells himself he is doing no more than that. For now, anyway. It is merely a social introduction, the exchange of calling cards.

Then he climbs the spirals that twist upwards into the abyss. He climbs as high as he can go, up the vertiginous wooden stairs, scarcely more than ladders, that wriggle between the inner and the outer domes, until he comes out into the sky. The city rolls out below him. The steeples and the towers, the regiments of cranes and the masts of the tall-ships. The serpent of the river, the skein of the streets. And everywhere the chimneys, ten million smoking heartbeats. But way up here, above the smoke, under the blue canopy, the breeze roars into his face and fills him with new life.

For a moment, as he holds tightly to the gilded rail, one of the worms is at his shoulder again. It would be so easy, it says. Jem flings out an arm, pushes it away.

'Not today!' he shouts above the wind. 'Not yet.'

Anyway, he thinks, even if I were to clamber over the rail, no harm could come to me. I would not, could not, fall. Today I would simply fly. As if I were on a magic carpet.

CHAPTER XV

1888. London.

Apart from the crackle of the fire and the pounding of Eddy's childish heart, there was silence in the room. The fingers of butter-soaked toast rested on the stripes of Bertie's trousers. He threw his calves forward. The race began.

'Eddy, your runner is not moving. It has scarcely moved at all.'

'Yes, Papa. Sorry, Papa.'

'What exactly were you apologising for?' asks Jem now.

'I don't know,' replies Eddy. 'Being slow, I suppose.'

'But it's the toast that was being slow, not you,' says Jem.

'Yes, but I should have chosen a better piece. After all, Papa did order us to choose our runner carefully. For flexibility and endurance.'

'And how on earth were you going to do that unless, at the age of seven, you had a degree in physics or, indeed, in bakery?'

'But just look at Georgie's piece and Toria's and little

Maudie's. They were all flying down Papa's trouser leg.'

'It was just luck.'

'So why did I never seem to have any? Why was I always the last in everything?'

'That's your imagination, nothing more. It's the false picture of yourself you've created in your head and now believe to be true. Anyway, there are more important things than a buttered-toast race.'

'That wasn't how it felt to me.'

'But that's how it *should* feel to you. How it should feel to you from now on, whenever your mind goes back to it.'

Georgie's toast reached Bertie's shoe. He whooped with pleasure.

'Well done, Georgie!' said Bertie.' 'Poor old Eddy, not even as good as the girls.'

'Useless cunt,' said Georgie.

Eddy feels the old tears prick at his eyes again, but he will not let them fall.

'I so wanted to please Papa. Just for once,' he says.

'You couldn't please someone who didn't wish to be pleased,' says Jem, 'who only wanted to find fault.'

'But why? Why did he want to treat me so?'

'The answer lies in him, not in you. Perhaps we will come to talk about that another day.'

'Useless cunt,' says Georgie once more.

Eddy puts his hands over his ears, but Jem pulls them away, almost shouts at him.

'You're not the cunt, *they* are!'

He pats the back of Eddy's hand, speaks softly again.

'You must find no fault in yourself, no inadequacy.'

Eddy tries to smile. He wonders how long it will take for him to manage that.

'But you're allowed to feel anger,' says Jem.

'Yes?' says Eddy.

'How would you like to express it?'

Eddy blushes, looks at the floor.'

'I'd like to ram those fingers of toast up their arses.'

'Good, but the toast might be too flaccid to achieve that. Why not just shove them down their stupid throats?'

Eddy gazes on the sight on his Papa and Georgie spreadeagled on the sofa, their eyes bulbous with surprise, the golden goo running down their shaggy beards.

'There you are,' says Jem. 'How does that feel?'

'Wonderful,' says Eddy. 'Quite wonderful.'

They need to find a place of their own and they do. It is not spoken of, or acknowledged, as such, but that is what it becomes. How appropriate, thinks Eddy, that it should be an ice rink.

He tells Jem the circumstances of his birth. His Mama repeats the tale so often that he feels as if he had been perched on her lap in the sharp, chill light, not deep inside her belly in the warm darkness. Alix wrapped in sables, being pushed in a sledge-chair out onto the glassy face of Virginia Water. Bertie playing hockey, trying to impress her with his skill. A band plays on the shore, the breath of the musicians hazing the brass of their cornets and flutes. It is the first young flowering of their marriage. Then, without warning, Eddy begins to kick hard. But he is not expected for another two months and nothing is prepared. By the time the January moon rises over the frozen water, he is wrapped in the length of flannel a pageboy runs to fetch from the draper in Windsor.

'Perhaps I was angry with her for taking me out in the cold for so long,' says Eddy now. 'If so, my plan went dreadfully wrong. Instead of being allowed to hibernate until spring, I was rudely expelled at once. To this day, as you know, I do so hate the cold.'

Jem lights his pipe, stares out across the maelstrom of figures on the rink.

'You were born eight weeks early? I didn't know that.'

'Does it matter?'

'I don't know that either but I've heard that it might. That it might explain certain difficulties later on.'

'Oh well,' says Eddy. 'Not much I can do about it now, is there? Come on, I'm supposed to be teaching you to skate.'

Jem groans, knocks out his pipe and lets himself be dragged back onto the ice. But the Keeper of The Wall, the bull who can charge his way through any obstacle, is not a graceful creature. His asset is sheer strength, not delicacy or coordination. He staggers and stumbles, crashes into the railing, loses his bowler, falls on his big arse, sweats and curses.

Eddy is always there to catch him, to wrap an arm round him, to hold him up or go tumbling down with him in a tangle of arms and legs. The ice rink had been Eddy's idea, the skating lessons a notion that had come to him. A way of touching each other, of feeling Jem's breath on his face and smelling the scent of him. Innocently too. In public. Hiding in plain sight. They are not the only pairings who have chosen this trysting place. The rink at Knightsbridge has a certain reputation.

Jem always laughs as he struggles back to his feet. Yet

Eddy notices how fast Jem extricates himself from his grasp, how he veers away and teeters off towards his next fall. Eddy notices it, but sweeps it away into a distant corner of his mind, where it cannot mar the joy he feels in the time they spend together.

Now, whenever Eddy can get away from his regiment and come to town, they will meet. Sometimes in a cafe or a public house but, more often than not, here among the swirling couples and the mists that rise off the ice like the breath of some mammoth entombed below the surface. They swap their two old armchairs in Trinity for one of the benches that rise in tiers above the rink. They find a distant corner, sip their cups of negus and try to rebuild that which had been broken between them.

In the beginning, Jem chatters as he always did, about some new book he has read or some old book he thinks Eddy might care to peruse. But that does not last long. Soon, Eddy is aware that Jem is no longer pushing stories into him, but pulling them out. At Trinity, Jem had never asked questions about Eddy's existence before they knew each other. It would not have been appropriate, seemly even, given the disparity of their positions. But now he does. Now he asks Eddy everything. Now Jem listens while Eddy talks. He says nothing until Eddy finishes the tale. Then, like a listener who is not sure he has heard quite correctly, he will ask little questions. Whatever the tale, the questions are usually much the same.

'What makes you think that is the truth of the situation?' he asks. 'Might it not be possible to look at it this way instead?'

At first, Eddy finds it hard; he is not used to talking about himself. Nobody has bothered to ask these questions before.

Now it is strange to him, like trying to speak in some foreign tongue. He feels a sense of invasion, of a door roughly broken open but, in time, he begins to like the air that blows in.

Now and again a telegram arrives on the morning of their meeting. Jem cannot come that day after all. Apologies and excuses are made. Eddy chooses to believe the excuses. He tries not to worry about the truth of it, tries not to imagine the magic carpet tumbling from the sky.

On one such day, he even goes to the rink alone, just to feel the comfort that it gives him. Somebody careers into him and engages him in conversation. The man is young, black-eyed and handsome; an infantryman in the Grenadiers. He would love to be in the cavalry, he says. They talk about horseflesh and it is not long before the infantryman is talking in a softer voice and using the language of the stable.

'Can I buy you a cup of negus, sir? Or perhaps you'd like to drink something a bit thicker?'

Eddy is stirred; it is months now since he has had either man or woman; not since the night he fled Mr Inslip's house. But the soldier's eyes are hooded; hard and dead as lumps of coal. Eddy shivers from head to toe, wishes him well and spins away into the mist.

For a few hours, he worries that the place might now be tainted in his mind. But he will stick to the vow he has made. He will no longer give himself. Not pointlessly at least. Not without the best of him being there too, looking over his shoulder, whispering in his ear...

'Yes, this is good, this is right. I will grow from this.'

And then Jem returns. Never mentions his absence of the previous week. They sit on their distant bench on the top tier, drinking their mulled wine. Jem asks more questions. Eddy tells more tales. He talks of the morning when the *Bacchante* had sailed into Gibraltar. The Governor's launch swaying towards the gangway of the ship; the Governor at the prow, his face fat and ruby-red, his sword glinting in the sun.

'All these people bowing and scraping to me. Smiling fake smiles, never showing me their true faces. It will always be like this, won't it? All my life.'

And now he tells Jem about the baby kangaroo. The awful impulse he had felt to set it free forever. How he had suppressed that urge and how, Eddy having failed him, the poor creature had clawed its own way from the cage. How Eddy had pretended to mourn but had rejoiced in his heart.

'You will only be in a prison if you choose to make it so,' says Jem.

'But there will never be an end to it. The bowing, the scraping, the false smiles.'

'If you refuse to see the bars, they will not be there. Just walk out through the bars, go towards those smiles and make them real. Allow them to give something back to you, something to enrich and nourish you. That's all you have to do.'

'How the hell do I do that?'

'They've all come to see Albert Victor. Give them Eddy instead.'

'Why would they want *Eddy*?'

'Because Eddy is an estimable man.'

'Ha! They wouldn't think that if they really knew me. If they knew the things I've done or the thoughts I think in the middle of the night. They'd tear down the flags and the bunting pretty damn quick.'

'I repeat, Eddy is an estimable man,' says Jem. 'So give them Eddy. Or at least a bit of him.'

'I don't know how to do that.'

'You can learn. I will help you.'

Jem's big hand reaches out for Eddy's, grips it tightly.

'You do not need to be a prisoner, nor do you need to drown. I will not allow that to be your story.'

'Come on, let's skate,' says Eddy after a while.

'No, my back aches today. Let me just watch you,' replies Jem.

Eddy goes onto the ice. Apart from a passable performance in hockey and tennis, he is not a sportsman. But he is good at this. He always has been. On the little lake at home in Norfolk, he far outshines his fat father and his lumpen brother. Now, for Jem, he glides and spins and twirls. He becomes a creature of the ice and the mist. It is as if he has never trodden on the dull, solid earth, never moved in any other sphere.

'You're a gazelle,' says Jem, when Eddy climbs back up to their bench. 'A gazelle in a bowler hat.'

Jem laughs his usual great laugh. They buy two more mugs of negus. Eddy sits and drinks and feels the warmth pouring into him.

CHAPTER XVI

Spring 1889. London.

The little villa with the green door looks exactly the same, lolling in the pale sun in its suburban road. Rose and Eddy sit out in the garden as they did on his first visit. That is now three summers ago. The garden is more mature now, so is the Labrador puppy, so is Rose.

Not that she is any less pretty; quite the opposite. But her face has lost its girlish plumpness; the cheekbones are sharper, the eyes a little narrower as if they had seen things they would have preferred not to and are on guard against witnessing more. There are even a few silver threads among the raven-black tresses. But the smile, though it seems to come less quickly now, still shines with the light of a good soul.

He has travelled to St John's Wood countless times since his first nervous visit, though the nature of these changed quite quickly. At first, they always retired to Rose's bedroom and repeated the sweaty congress of before. But slowly, without comment or fuss or offence, this became rarer and then extinct.

In time, Rose transforms into a sort of fourth sister, though of course she is not at all like them. She already has a pet dog, she does not require another.

And so they drink cordial among the flowerbeds and tell each other of the things that have been happening to them and of the things that have not. Rose listens, gently strokes his hair.

He turns to Rose because perhaps it is only she who can understand. She, too, has been disappointed in love. This fact is crystal clear. Mr Sherlock Holmes would instantly pounce on the carpetbag of clues; the flaking of the green paint on the door, the silver threads in the raven hair, the fervour with which she embraces the dog. And Rose is in love still. Maybe, like Eddy's mother, this is to be her tragedy.

Georgie seldom comes now, to this nest which he created and from which he is flown. When not at sea, he is either at home in Norfolk or enjoying fresher pleasures. He brags to Eddy of a new girl in Southsea; a real ripper, he says. It is the phrase he once used of Rose.

'When he does come, it's just for those wee tricks of mine, the ones by which I first captured him,' she says. 'That's all that's left of us now. The wee tricks. I am just a whore again. The lover I had is gone.'

As if she scarcely cares, Rose asks about Georgie; where he goes, for whom he plants gardens and buys puppy dogs. Eddy says he has no idea, but he can see she feels the lie and that she is grateful for it.

'How daft can it be,' she says, 'for a woman like me to have thought of love?'

'Or for a man like me?'

'In our respective professions, perhaps it is a distant dream.

Perhaps we may only think of arrangements.'

'But I don't want such an arrangement.'

He says it so loudly that he frightens the dog and sends it trotting off to a corner of the garden.

She hushes him, pours another glass of cordial. It is only Rose to whom he has ever spoken of his confusions, although it was hardly necessary. From the first moments of their coupling, she had known he was no novice. Did she not suggest as much to Georgie? It was only after a while that the truth of it dawned on her.

'Any man who could take a woman's arse so expertly was no stranger to the art of buggery'.

She had laughed as she said this, while his face had burned. But then, the miraculous thing occurs. He realises that she does not care. She is not repelled, she does not see him in any different light.

'Nothing that is human disgusts me,' she says, 'unless it is heartless and cruel.'

Over time, there is hardly anything he does not confess to her, nowhere in his history that he does not lead her. He takes her into the turreted rooms of Trinity, the underground station at South Kensington, the bar of The Alhambra, the moonlit alleys of the park, The Hundred Guineas Club. He introduces her to many people, most just in passing, but to others again and again.

Most of all, he wants her to know Jem, to admire him as he does, to understand what Jem means to him. And soon he can see that she does. Eventually, he even tells her about the note pushed under his door at Trinity. For the first time, he breaks the seal of the confessional; he repeats the precious words aloud to another person. It is to Rose he rushes with the news that Jem has reappeared in his life, a saviour in top hat and evening cloak on Mr Inslip's doorstep. And today, it is to her that he finally bursts out, lances the boil that has been swelling up since that night.

'Why will he not love me as I need him to do? Tell me, please.'

'Oh dearie me, I don't know,' she says. 'But he must have his reasons. And if he cares for you, as you say he does, they must be loving reasons. I think you should trust in that, however hard it is.'

The Labrador returns to them and she feeds it a biscuit.

'Of course, you could always just ask him.'

'Oh no. No, never. He has not been too well in recent times. I must treat him with great delicacy. I mustn't upset or fluster him or he may run away from me again.'

'Then, as I say, you must trust him. Accept things as they are. Find joy in what comes to you, not in what you may never find. That's what I have had to learn. And whatever happens, we must try to live in a state of grace with it.'

She laughs out loud and crunches into a ginger biscuit.

'Now is that not rich coming from a wee whore like me, who fell from it so long ago?'

'Why did you fall, Rose?'

Over the three summers, over the glasses of cordial and cups of tea, even in the crumpled sheets of their earliest meetings, he had never dared to ask this question.

'It's just the hoary old tale you read in the penny dreadfuls. Good girl falls in love, finds herself with child, her man deserts her, her family drive her from their door.'

'And where's the child now?'

'Oh the bairn died. Did I not tell you it was a right penny dreadful?'

In the spring garden, they sit in silence. Rose watches the dog still chewing on its biscuit. Sparrows have gathered, hoping for a titbit. Eddy stares at his shoes, noticing how the overgrown grass has smudged the leather.

'Can you and I ever be in a state of grace, Rose?'

'Why do you think we can't be?'

'The things we've done. The things of which God would not approve.'

'Och now, I'm not sure God's as black as He's painted. I'm not sure He's this stone-hearted old misery they thunder about from the pulpits. Anyway, what did you or I ever do except search for kindness?'

The dog nudges up against her skirts. She coos at it, stroking its shiny head. Then she leans back and stares at Eddy, her hand above her eyes to block out the sun.

'I think I might be able to sketch you now. When you first came, I knew I couldn't capture you because I didn't see you clearly. But now I think I can.'

So they go inside to a colder light, into the little sitting room with the upright piano, the bookcases, the sketches on the walls of the family who shun her. And she sets to work, peering hard at him, harder even than Jem does. He is supposed to have his gaze fixed on a vase of tulips, but he steals glances at her and in her eyes is an expression unfamiliar to him. He feels laid bare to some sort of appraisal. He wonders why he does not feel uncomfortable, but he does not.

When the thing is done, it is quite unlike the other images

made of him. No soldier's uniform, no smart suit, no collars and cuffs. It is merely a head, floating in space, disconnected. He is nobody and everybody. He does not recognise himself.

'Aye,' says Rose, standing back and squinting at the paper. 'I think that you're there.'

'What is it you see, Rose?'

'Just you,' she says. 'That's all I was looking for.'

They smile at each other in the little sitting room and then the smile is invaded by something else. It is something he needs. The touch and feel and smell of the act. That sense of blazing presence which it has always given him. He has deprived himself of it for far too long as he waited for the thing which has not come.

He feels no guilt as he slides into Rose's outstretched arms, into her bed, into her body. As he spends inside her, he cries out like a banshee. For a moment, his chest heaves so much he can hardly breathe. For a moment, he thinks he might die.

From the sweaty pillow, her hair fanned out across the brocaded silk, Rose stares up at him.

'You're one of those who needs this,' she says. 'Some men do. Some women too. You must accept that also. You must make your arrangements.'

They stand at the green door. The dog licks his hand in the hope of a walk. Rose embraces him; a sister once more. He promises to come back soon, not to desert her for so long. He notices the fading paint again, asks if there is anything she needs. She shoos him away.

'But who knows?' she calls after him. 'One day everything might come to us. Tearing round the corner like a bairn on roller skates to knock us flat. Until then, we must be brave.'

She pulls the dog into her, stoops and kisses its head.
'At least *you* still have your friend,' she says.

The door flies open, slams against the wall. The curtains are torn back, the blind flies towards the pelmet. A rolled copy of *The Times* whacks his arse. He jolts out of his oblivion. Oh God.

'Morning!' shouts the judge. It is not a greeting but a piece of information.

Jem does not want to get up. Not now. Not this morning. Perhaps not even this week. His big body, still getting bigger despite his attempts at exercise, feels like some felled giant in a Germanic fairy tale. But then he remembers what stands in his diary, circled in red like a little beacon. However bad he feels, he must get up today. There can be no doubt about that, no falling back, no losing sight of the purpose. He must rise, and slowly, easing himself up by clinging onto the bedside table, he does.

His mother comes with him to the front door, takes his bowler and briefcase from the maid, offers them as if she is handing him the keys to the kingdom. She kisses his cheek and squeezes his arm. She calls out as he reaches the pavement and wishes him a happy day. He is blessed in his mother. He knows that. She did not want to leave him and sail to a foreign land. It was that bastard who made her do it.

But all dark thoughts must be blocked today; for the next few hours at least. This is an important occasion for Eddy, so Jem must be there. He has put on one of his new suits; the trousers so tight he thinks his belly might explode. Instead of taking the underground railway towards the misery of his chambers, he takes it to the East End, that other London, that strange city that clings to his own like some filthy barnacle. A new hospital ward is to be opened. Eddy's Mama, its patroness, has a cold and Eddy must stand in for her.

Jem will slide himself into the throng, well back, but close enough so that Eddy can find him. It is always the same now; Jem in the crowd. As he was outside the abbey, as he was for the opening of the great bridge at Hammersmith, as he is now at every charity bazaar, boys' club, public library and dockyard extension. Whenever Eddy must be Albert Victor, Jem will be within his sight. He does not wave or cheer; he merely stands there, head held high, shoulders broad, the hint of a smile on his lips. At the end of it, he will just melt away. A letter will be sent by the next post. What was good, what might be improved upon. But never criticism, only praise for the effort that has been made.

Yesterday they went to a bench high up on Primrose Hill and worked on the speech. Jem had written a rough draft and Eddy read it aloud to the dog walkers and the courting couples. When a line did not ring true from him, it was changed. Jem put in a little humour; a joke about Eddy's swollen ankle when he recently fell from his horse in the field. If only he had been hunting the fox along Whitechapel Road, Eddy would say. It is not much of a joke, but nothing pleases a crowd more than being permitted to laugh. Like furniture in a room, they rearranged the words and the sentences until he could inhabit them and feel at home.

In front of the hospital, on a platform decked in flags and flowers, Eddy listens to the greetings of the mayor and the venerable doctors. Jem sees Eddy's eyes sweep across the herd of people, to and fro, backwards and forwards. Often it takes some time, but then Eddy's expression will ease, his shoulders relax, he will uncurl himself a little. Jem loves that moment, holds it close to himself, feeds on it for days.

But today Eddy starts at a disadvantage. The crowd has come to see their beloved Alix; anyone else is a disappointment. But at least he has Alix's beauty; when he stands to speak, graphic invitations are called out from young women in the crowd. The venerable doctors and their wives flinch and pretend they have not heard, but this is the East End after all. This is where people expect to die young, so they might as well say what they think.

Eddy blushes, but the speech is competent. A few sentences are lost on the wind; his voice is still too light and must be made stronger, but there is progress. When Eddy tells the joke, he forgets to put the smile into his voice so they are not sure whether it is a joke or not. But then he puts it on his face instead and they all laugh; a corner of the curtain lifts and they can see him. When he has cut the ribbon and turns to enter the hospital, he lifts his top hat to them and smiles again. And now they cheer.

In the morning, before Jem has time to post his critique, a letter comes. Quite a memorable day, writes Eddy. He had been taken to see Merrick, the Elephant Man, who is given shelter in the hospital. He worries that he might show revulsion but his Mama has already met Merrick and shaken his hideous hand; now she even sends him a card at Christmas. How can Eddy refuse?

The sight of the poor soul is quite disgusting; a nightmare in human flesh. Eddy says he will dream of it for weeks. There is an unpleasant odour from the warts that pock the man's rough lumpy skin and his speech is hard to follow, but the doctor who looks after him has come to understand it and can translate. The nurses here have been kind to Merrick, affectionate even, and he has blossomed under their care. There are no mirrors in his little basement room. There is a small courtyard with flowers and plants in pots where he can take the air and not be seen. But oh, what a sad and dreadful life he has had; exhibited like an animal, reviled and rejected. And yet the Elephant Man is courteous, charming even; really a pretty decent sort of chap.

'He hobbled up to me,' writes Eddy in the letters they exchange over the next few days. 'He shook my hand firmly, looked me straight in the eye and said, "I am pleased to meet you. I have the honour to be acquainted with your dear mother. I am Joseph Merrick."'

'Amazing,' Jem writes back.

'He has no doubt at all about himself,' replies Eddy. 'Given what God in His wisdom has made him suffer, isn't that extraordinary? He has no doubt at all.'

'Extraordinary,' says Jem.

If he needs to run, he will be able to. He could find his way out even in the dark.

He has known the park since he was a child. The nursemaids would bring him and Georgie to sail their boats. He had always loved the ducks too; though bloody Dalton had made him learn all their stupid Latin names. That had spoiled things a bit, but then Dalton spoiled so much. And, on their rare Sundays in town, Papa and Mama would stroll here to let the people see them; their own ducklings lined up behind them in a row, confirmation of the success of their union and of the reliance that could be placed on their dynasty. So yes, he knows the paths of St James's like a blind man. Darkness does not terrify him here, even if it should.

There is some lighting, of course, on the paths at least. The nervous can cling to the row of dim gas lamps, like Theseus's ball of string, as they enter the labyrinth. Despite his familiarity with the place, tonight Eddy is among them. It is nearly two years now since he stood on Mr Inslip's steps, two whole years since he abandoned the thing which dear Rose tells him he needs and should have. So here he is again, making his arrangements.

His bowler is tilted down, his astrakhan collar raised round his neck like a ruff, the smoke from his Turkish cigarette clouding his face. But the disguise is not foolproof.

'I thought it was you,' says a voice behind him. 'I remember the smell of those cigarettes. The walk too. How is life treating you?'

At once he knows the face, though it takes him half a minute to place it. The red-headed boy from King's. The one with the long wicked legs that used to wrap themselves so tightly round his back. But in this light, the blazing hair is a commonplace brown, the face is a little older and there is strain in it; a sort of weariness he does not remember from before. The boy is no longer a boy.

Eddy allows himself to be pulled off the path into the refuge of the fat rhododendrons that line the edge of the lake. For a while, they converse as if they have bumped into each other in a Pall Mall club or in the Royal Enclosure.

'Did you marry that girl you spoke of?' asks Eddy. 'The heiress?'

'Buck-tooth Betty?' he replies. 'Oh yes. Our estates now live in connubial bliss, so everyone is happy. I have done my duty.'

'Children?'

'Two. Girls, unfortunately, as I dreaded. Both as hideous as their mother. Nobody will marry them except for money, so history will repeat itself. I am imprisoned in a hellhole of ugliness. Sometimes I can't bear it, I really can't.'

'So you still take your pleasures as you said you would.'

'Indeed. And I assume by your august presence that you do too. This is our fate, you see.'

'Is it? I suppose it is.'

From the shrubs and trees round them, noises come. Noises of exhortation, encouragement, raw red pleasure. The redhead smiles, reaches out and runs a thin finger along Eddy's jaw.

'For old times' sake?'

The boy who is no longer a boy pulls down his trousers and wraps his arms round a tree. As Eddy enters his arse, he is surprised to discover that he remembers it, the shape, the feel, the pulse of it, like one remembers a wine not tasted for a long time then discovered again. Suddenly the rage rises up and engulfs him. He pistons into the redhead as fast and hard as he can go. He knows he must be causing pain but he does not care. The boy pants heavily, cries out, clings to the tree as if it is a life raft, his only chance of survival. He turns his head round, his eyes wide.

'By Christ!' he says, 'why didn't you tell me you liked it like this?'

Eddy wants to run now. Just like he ran from the room at

Mr Inslip's house, down the stairs and towards the front door. But tonight he does not run. He just pulls his cock out of the redhead, does up his buttons and turns away towards the pale light on the pathway. The redhead calls after him, begs him to return.

When he reaches the edge of the park, he stops. Even at this hour, The Mall is full of hansoms, taking people home from the theatres and the restaurants or to the last train at Victoria. On this warm evening, many have chosen to walk instead. There are faces all round him. He scans them one by one but tonight there is nobody there.

CHAPTER XVII

Autumn 1889. Venice.

He is bewitched by the magic of it. Not one of his Grandmama's countless paintings has prepared him for the shock. Every sense electric. Colour and light, marble and stone, water and air; all thrown together in a sublime canvas, almost absurd in its perfection. Even Georgie is impressed. After all, it is a city of boats.

The high windows of his room are open to the balcony. It is October but the evenings are quite warm. Below, people are still out in gondolas. He hears laughter, silly singing, the occasional shout of 'God Save The Queen!' He knows it would be wise to go to bed. The banquet was an orgy of grandeur but interminable; the speeches of the ancient fossils translated by a snail of an interpreter. His Papa's brief sentences of reply in their own lingo, learned like a parrot, send them into paroxysms of joy; it is like The Second Coming. This is what Bertie loves; when they treat him as a king in all but name. He cannot wait. Eddy has begun to realise that now.

Yet, tonight his father is distracted. All of them can see it.

'Perhaps it's a telegram from your grandmother,' says Alix as they go down the staircase of the palazzo. 'The sort that shrinks your Papa to the size of Tom Thumb.'

They laugh together, as they have always done. His mother does not change, does not seem to age, although the deafness is worse. As he has grown taller, she has grown shorter, like Alice in Wonderland, but his perspective on her is otherwise unaltered. There is nobody with whom he feels easier, more unafraid. Whatever she may have done to him, to all of them, in the pain of her abandonment, at least he owes her that.

'Mama, you are a vision,' he shouts.

'I'm just a deaf old Danish woman,' she replies.

At dinner, she seduces them all with nothing more than dazzling smiles and gracious inclinations of her head. It is the only seduction she has ever permitted herself; no breath of scandal has ever clouded her saintly name. Sometimes Eddy wonders what is going on inside that silent skull. Maybe it is like living in a church, hearing only the faintest noises from the outside world. But she gives no sign of isolation; she is the sun in splendour. She is still Bertie's greatest asset and he is wise enough to know it.

Those near her at the table have been warned to talk loudly and soon Eddy's head splits from the noise, from the heat of a thousand candles, from the perfumes of painted women and the sweat of nervous, overdressed men. Several times he catches Bertie's eye on him. On such occasions, his father will often send a small, quick smile, an encouragement to do his best. But tonight he does not smile. Yet the look is not the one his children know so well; the distant rumbling before the storm. This gaze is uneasy, troubled, fearful even. When Eddy returns it, his Papa looks away.

He is usually careful how much he drinks. But tonight, with the heat and the noise and the fear of something to come, he takes a little more than he should. So yes, it would be wise to go to bed but a stroll would be just the thing. Besides, it is not terribly late and earlier he had passed a small open door leading directly to the narrow street along the side of the palazzo. Surely nobody would notice if he crept through it. It cannot be far through the maze of alleyways to the great piazza with the cathedral and the tower. And this afternoon, on their tour, he noticed a little park on the waterfront. Such places are usually fruitful but, if not, no matter.

He does not send for his man. He abandons his evening clothes on the bed and puts on a simple suit of cream linen and a matching soft hat. But at the very moment he reaches for the door of his room, a knocking batters it from the other side. It is Papa's servant; his father wishes to see him at once. The servant emphasises the final word. There is no time to change back. Damn and blast.

In his sitting room, Bertie is belching a cigar out into the night. From the canal there is a shout of 'good old Wales'. Bertie waves down with his usual grace.

'Why are you dressed like that?'

'More comfortable in this climate, Papa.'

'If you're thinking of popping out later, think again.'

'Just a breath of air, Papa.'

'As you do in London? Do you imagine I've never seen you from my window slipping out for a breath of air long after midnight?'

'And I you, Papa.'

'I am not a man who slips out of anywhere. I stride out. Perhaps that's the difference between us.'

Eddy is ordered to sit. There is distressing news from home and it is necessary to acquaint him of it.

There is sweat on Bertie's brow. His smoke wafts out of the window and is whisked away on the warm breeze. The brocaded edging of the curtains ripples like the waters of the canal. He pours two brandies from a decanter, gives one to Eddy then returns to the window, his shoulders squared, a wall between them.

'Your Mama weeps and wails at the thought of her little angel going off to India for six months,' he says. 'I do not. I rejoice in it.'

'Thank you, Papa. I'll do my best there.' Eddy knows from the first sip that the brandy is a bad idea.

'You misunderstand me. I rejoice because I no longer know what's to be done with you. And it relieves me of the problem, for a while at least.'

'I'm sorry to be a problem to you, Papa.'

'It is four years now since you left Cambridge. I really believed you had begun to grow up there and make something of yourself. But you certainly haven't made much of a soldier, have you?'

Oh well, it is finally said. He has waited for it coming and of course it is true. He just about passes muster, scrapes through the exams. Younger men are promoted over him; his only small elevations are awarded to avoid embarrassment.

'Indeed, I'm no Wellington, Papa.'

'But what are you? Eh? Can you tell me that?'

Bertie spins round and looks at him again with the same expression Eddy saw at dinner. He is certain now that it is fear in his father's eyes and feels it transmit into his own belly. Eddy swallows more of the brandy.

'The moment you return from India, you must be found a wife. If Alicky of Hesse doesn't want you, somebody will. Your marriage is long overdue. It will steady you.'

The brandy makes Eddy bold but it is mixed with that old wild anger. There is talk that Bertie has a new attachment; it is written on Mama's dear face when she thinks nobody is watching.

'It has hardly steadied you, Papa.'

'Damn your insolence. Are you drunk?'

Eddy's anger dissolves as quickly as it came and a sadness rolls across him. It should not be like this. He rises too and looks out over the canal. The night is beautiful, a few gondolas still on the water, the flaring torches on the walls of the palazzo sprinkling them with red-gold light.

'When the *Bacchante* broke its rudder in the South Atlantic and you drifted towards the polar wastes, you came close to disaster, did you not?' asks Bertie.

'Indeed, Papa. Though in our ignorance we didn't realise it at the time.'

'I suggest that you're in exactly the same position again. Dangerously near catastrophe. And not just for yourself this time, but catastrophe for us all.'

Bertie goes to a desk and unlocks a drawer. A telegram is slammed into Eddy's hand. He is ordered to read it.

It is from one of his father's people in London. Trouble brews. The Master of the Horse has been frequenting a house of ill repute. A house where telegraph boys supplement the stingy earnings offered by the Post Office. Eddy's name is being mentioned as his occasional companion.

His head swims. Christ. His great fear, silent inside him for so long, now rises to face him, shouting in tight black lettering. At Cambridge, where the brotherhood of Plato was tolerated, his adventures had risked no judgement. In the army, he had been protected by the brotherhood of the regiment; the blood-bonding of those who might be about to die. In the backwaters of London, he could pass largely unrecognised; only the images of his Grandmama and his parents were instantly known to the man on the omnibus. He had tricked himself into feeling invio-late, whilst knowing that discovery walked in his shadow. Now it had leapt ahead of him into the light and turned to confront him.

It is some time before Bertie speaks up, his voice low and hoarse.

'Well, have you been to this place with Arthur Somerset? This Cleveland Street?'

'The name is not familiar, Papa,' he replies truthfully.

'It is somewhere north of Oxford Street. Have you been?'

Eddy will never know what makes him answer as he does now. No doubt it is partly the brandy, but there is something else too. It is not anger. Is it relief that the mask is finally ripped off and that now he can breathe? Or is it just weariness?

'I cannot remember.'

'What do you mean by that?'

'I mean what I say, Papa. I cannot remember.'

'Are you telling me it is *possible*?' His father speaks so quietly that Eddy can scarcely hear him; the last word no more than a whisper.

'I am sure your own pleasures have led you into some rather exotic places, Papa.'

'But never places of this unspeakable, filthy kind!' Bertie's voice soars in volume until it explodes into such a long racking cough that Eddy fears it might consume him. Spittle speckles Bertie's beard; his face turns radish red. It is a full minute before he can speak again.

'You are my beloved son and I ask you for the last time. Have you been to this... this establishment?'

Eddy feels the floor move under his feet. He puts the glass carefully down on a table and his hands into his pockets. He gives a long sigh and a short shrug of his shoulders.

'I cannot remember, Papa.'

'Dear God.'

Eddy leaves his father's presence without permission. No voice is raised to stop him. He walks along the corridor to his own room. He throws his jacket on the bed. He looks down onto the silver-black canal. It is wide and turbulent here, where it begins to escape the corset of the palazzos and spills out into the lagoon. The bell of the fat white church opposite strikes twelve.

Jem's words come back to him from the day on the river when Eddy struggled to keep them both above water. Only one awful minute, then all done. All done.

They sail from Venice and come to Athens. Here, both opulence and decay are different creatures. While Venice keeps you at arm's length, pushing you back in order to be admired with some perspective, this place pulls you right into its rough, sticky embrace. The breath of *La Serenissima* may not always have been sweet, but the breath of Athens can skin your nostrils.

They have all come for a wedding. Another of his endless cousins. Sophie, he thinks. Not a beauty, but so few of them are. From his room above the harbour, he watches the pretty lights that cobweb the rigging of the ships. The fleets have come from every point of the compass. It is a gathering of the clans and no mistake.

The night is hot. His mother's boudoir is next door to his, the windows thrown open.

At first it is not words he hears, but weeping. The sobs rack in his Mama's throat. Then his father's voice, loudly, as is necessary in their family. Strangers, hearing the volume, often imagine they are fighting when they are only discussing the quality of a turbot. But now it is indeed an argument. In his twenty-six years, Eddy has never heard one such before and it is a shock. Tightened faces, fractured conversation, Alix riding off alone for hours, all these they are used to, but never once the open rupture of an argument. As he realises what it is about, he begins to sweat even more.

'Oh my God, I'd rather he were dead,' wails his mother.

'Shall I give him a pistol then? Like poor Rudolf? Shall we have another Mayerling?'

'God forgive me, I didn't mean that,' she says, gulping for air between the sobs. 'But perhaps if you had been a bit more of a presence in his life...'

'Or if you had mollycoddled him a bit less. Not always had him clinging to your petticoats as if he were one of the girls. And that, it now appears, is what my son and heir, the heir to everything in fact, turns out to be.'

Another wave of weeping crashes through Eddy's window.

'I raised our children on my own, Bertie. Sliding buttered toast down your trousers once a fortnight doesn't make you a father.'

'You held him too tightly, Alix.'

'I needed someone to hold when my husband was far from my bed.'

There is a long silence now.

'Well, thank heavens my other son has turned out fine. No sign of that with Georgie, is there?' he lobs the words at her.

'Eddy is your creation, my dear. Yours alone.'

'But he has always been such a kind and dutiful boy.'

'And also, it would seem, he is a...' says Bertie. 'Christ almighty, what's to be done?'

'I may not be what you consider a woman of the world,' she says, 'but I'm not the innocent you think me. Your own sister's husband has a certain reputation; your nephew in Hesse as well. Surely these things can be kept private, can be contained.'

'Well, God knows if I can contain this. This matter is not private; it is public. The telegrams from London come daily and always worse. Let's just hope there is a carpet big enough to sweep it all under.'

'We must marry him at once,' she says, 'the moment he returns from India. Perhaps that might be some sort of cure.'

'I've no idea about that, but it must certainly be done.'

'Oh why did this happen to us? Why, Bertie?'

'I suspect neither of us really knows that, my dear. You should try to get some sleep.'

'Sleep?' she says.

The voices sag now, the anger gone. The words stop. Eddy

hears a door close. It is not long before there is another bout of weeping. It goes on and on until he has to put the pillow over his ears.

In the church, he and Georgie must hold the crown above their cousin's head. It is damned heavy and they must stand for ages like dummies in a shop window. Whenever he glances at his Mama, her eyes are fixed on Georgie. It is as if she no longer sees him.

'Oh my God, I'd rather he were dead,' she said.

Dear Jem,

I write from the boat taking me to India. There is a dreadful scandal at home and my name is mentioned in connection with it. Papa knows all about me now, if you take my meaning. Jem, what on earth should I do? I am going mad with worry. Please write back to me (do not telegraph). I have never needed your strength and guidance so much. Tell me what to do.

CHAPTER XVIII

Summer 1890. Scotland.

'Fly, my little lovebirds, fly!' cries Alix.

It would not surprise him if she had bridled the horse herself, polished the pony-trap until it shone, made the sandwiches and packed them neatly into the basket with her own fair hands. It is as if she is in the grip of a fever.

Last night, the idea came to her when they were all in the garden before dinner. For once, the weather was glorious. The hills that loured over the valley were tinged purple and gold as the sun slid away. Eddy and Helene were strolling back up from the river when she bustled towards them, clapping her hands.

'You must both go to Grandmama. Why didn't I think of it before? You must go tomorrow and get her on your side.'

He flinches at the thought of it, but he sees that Helene does not. She and his Mama clasp each other as if, in this one simple notion, a magic wand is waved and all difficulties dissolve. The sisters barge in with a chorus of approval at the brilliance of the strategy. The five women chirrup and coo and plot and plan. He is aware of not being consulted, but he does not care. He lets himself be carried along on the bubbling tide of their hopefulness. Alicky of Hesse may not want him, silly thing, but now darling Eddy has found a girl who loves him, who wants to marry him. Oh joy unconfined.

He is scarcely back from six long months in India when his life is changed in a sentence. It is a sentence giggled and spluttered from behind three identical fans.

'We've missed you dreadfully,' says Louise in her shy, awkward way.

'Indeed we have,' says Toria.

'Not as much as *somebody* we know,' adds little Maudie.

Three pairs of eyes swivel to a corner of the ballroom where a dark-haired girl is surrounded by young men and making them laugh. She is as tall as all of them and taller than several. Her nose is a little too long, just like his Mama's, in fact, but when she laughs, as she does all the time, the deficiency vanishes and she is quite lovely. Since her family was sent out of France a few years ago, Eddy has met her several times, even flirted with her in a careless way and exchanged a *billet-doux*. But it is a while since he has seen her and she is suddenly a woman.

'Helene?'

'She absolutely adores you, you know.'

'No, I didn't know. How do *you* know?'

'We wormed it out of her while you were away.'

'She goes soppy at every mention of your name,' says Toria with a snort.

And now the sentence, the echoing sentence, comes.

'She says she has always loved you,' says little Maudie.

The three of them stop gushing and go quiet. Frivolity is unsuitable for such a momentous statement. They look down at the marble floor and make little sighs, as if they had been transported from a ballroom into a cathedral.

'Helene says she felt it like a bolt of lightning,' says Louise. 'She called it a *coup de foudre*. 'Well, she's French after all.'

'Anyway, she's yours if you want her,' says Toria, as if she were talking about a horse.

'You must go and dance with her at once,' says Louise.

'Her card will be full by now,' Eddy replies. 'Look at those chaps all round her.'

'Bet you she'll tear it into tiny pieces,' says little Maudie.

And so he does. And they dance three polkas. And, ha ha, she sweeps him off his feet. She is funny and jolly and kind. She is like sunshine on his arm. They look good together. He can tell that from the faces of those who watch them. Illuminated by that bolt of lightning, that *coup de foudre*, he suddenly pictures her on his arm forever.

Seeing green shoots, the sisters nourish and water. As the summer meanders on, Princess Helene d'Orléans and Prince Albert Victor dance in many ballrooms, walk through many gardens, take tea on many lawns. The sisters do not allow them to be overcrowded; wherever they dance or walk or sit, several feet of space miraculously appear between them and everyone else. Eddy would find it rather embarrassing if it were not all so pleasant, so easy. He sits back and lets them arrange it all.

But Helene is not abashed. She is unshackled by concern about the opinions of others. He can see that in her eyes. They are odd eyes for such a pretty face. It is as if she had not liked the ones God had given her and had substituted them for those of a tigress. Yet when they turn onto Eddy, a subtle change comes over them. A gentleness appears. It is impossible to miss. It is this tiny alteration that persuades him that she really does love him and that he would be a very great fool not to love her in return. And he convinces himself that he must do so. For everyone's sake.

What a stroke of luck. Just when he must find a girl, the girl finds him. She can only be a gift from God. And to be in love with her too? Not just another sort of arrangement? Who would have thought it possible? At home in Norfolk, he even goes to their little cosy church, the place where he has spoken to God all his life, and goes down on his knees at the altar to give thanks. He says it out loud to make quite sure he is heard. What have I done to deserve this? he asks. The other question he asks, he asks silently. The question that wakes him in the small hours of the morning. Is it really possible to love two people at once?

Today, by the shining pony-trap, Alix kisses Helene on both cheeks and almost bundles her aboard. When it is Eddy's turn to be kissed, his mother grips his arm. The fevered smile slips from her face. She looks right into him, in the way she had done all his life, the way he thinks she has been avoiding since the day he came home. Now, at last, it happens. But it is something like panic that he sees.

'Eddy, you must get Grandmama on your side. She has a loving heart; she will listen. She is the only one who can overcome the problem.'

'I will try, Mama.'

'You must succeed,' Alix whispers. 'We have to make this happen. We have to.'

She slaps the horse on the rump.

'Fly my little lovebirds, fly.'

Through the long, Indian months, he expects the sky to fall at any moment. Some maharajah or other gives him a parakeet as a pet. It is trained to repeat, endlessly, only one phrase.

'*Be of good cheer,*' it says. '*Be of good cheer.*'

In the privacy of his vast and sumptuous tent, each buff-brown telegram that is passed to him trembles like a leaf in his hand. He is a child, cowering in the nursery in disgrace, waiting for the thrashing that he knows must come.

In public, he is a deity. In this land where even the humblest of his race are venerated, Eddy is showered with rose petals that stick in the brilliantine of his hair. The princes of a civilisation far older than his own bow down before him. He rides on elephants caparisoned in jewels through streets crammed with ragged people who have walked miles, barefoot, to see him. He is required to chase the buffalo, stalk the tiger, stick the pig, shoot the snipe. He must review regiments, open libraries, plant trees and inspect colonies of the lepers. In this, it is no different from the grind at home, except it so much hotter, so much more exhausting. He has prickly heat in his crotch and seems to shit ten times a day.

By night, he views the Taj Mahal, crosses the lake at Udaipur by the light of a thousand torches, watches the Nautch girls dance to delirious drums. The women, even those of his own tribe, throw themselves at him like the rose petals. Whatever pleasure he might want will be brought to him at the snap of his fingers.

And sometimes, despite everything, he snaps them. There seem to be no judgements here.

Whenever he must stand and speak, he tries to remember the tricks he has been taught on Primrose Hill, but he knows he is not performing well. Pointlessly, he searches for the face in the crowd. But he will only give them Albert Victor now; he dare not risk any glimpse of Eddy.

It is only the letters that come from the tall lean house in De Vere Gardens that bring him any comfort. They advise calmness, self-control and fortitude of spirit. They bring him silly gossip and fond greetings from Harry and O.B. and the other chums. They say how much he is missed on the bench above the ice rink and on the brow of Primrose Hill. But sometimes they are darker; they write of the nature of scandal, of how capricious the world is in its declaration of what is scandalous and what is not. And how a loving God, if He does by some small chance exist, might have a very different opinion. But in every letter, the same commandment is laid down for him.

'*Remember that Eddy is an estimable man.*'

He reads the letters again and again. But it is the telegram with his Papa's emblem upon it for which he really waits. It is well into a fresh new year before it comes at last.

'*The unfortunate business has been dealt with. We will never mention it again.*'

When he reads the words, his knees give under him and he collapses onto a couch. The parakeet screeches and flies from its perch out of the tent; the tiny bells tied round its neck like a peal of celebration.

So the sky is not to fall. How absurd, he tells himself, to

have gone through all this when he is far from certain he is guilty of the thing. But this possibility of innocence is of no real account. He is guilty of the thing that matters. And now, at home, they all know it.

He writes at once to De Vere Gardens; he even purloins the exact words of his father's message. When the reply comes, it is just as short.

'*Marry. Marry quickly. But keep your soul to yourself.*'

They have not gone far before Helene opens the picnic basket. She thrusts a sandwich under his nose but he cannot eat it.

'Why so nervous, *mon ange?*' she asks.

The ten miles to Grandmama are bumpy and bits of ham and tomato fall onto the napkin spread across her lap. She laughs every time there is a jolt, but then she laughs all the time, the laughter of a comfortable soul. In Helene's world, everything is benign. For each one of her nineteen years, she has never doubted for a second that all things must come to her. She expects nothing less. The fact that their summer is threatened by a black cloud the size of Lochnagar does not trouble her. It will lift soon. Aren't they on their way now to arrange that? The sky is blue, the river sparkles, the salmon are jumping. What is there to be nervous about?

'All will be well, *mon ange*,' she says, squeezing his hand, baffled by his anxiety.

Their fingers carry the simple little rings they have exchanged. They are engaged now. Unofficially, secretly, but engaged nonetheless. He planned the whole thing. A walk up in the hills. They straggle behind the sisters. In his finest kilt, he goes down on one bare knee. He asks and she accepts.

He releases a great whoop. A deer panics and crashes away through the heather. The sisters bustle back towards them; wild embraces, tears of joy, delirium. He finds there is sheep dung on his knee. It is a good omen, says his new fiancée. Such foulness usually repels him but he finds he is laughing too. Already, she is letting in the light, blowing away the darkness.

Now in the pony-trap, on the rocky road to Grandmama, the sun glints on the little rings. It is impossible not to feel that God looks down on them kindly and that they will indeed prevail. Soon Grandmama's granite walls rear up before them. A ridiculous house, Bertie grunts, whenever he is compelled to visit it.

'We must be serious now,' says Eddy.

'Oh how dull,' she replies.

What Helene does not know, what might give pause even to her, is that Grandmama has already spoken on this matter. There are spies everywhere. When the rumour from the ball-rooms reaches her ears, a letter arrives. On no account must he think of a Catholic. The Church would not have it. On no account must he think of the daughter of the French Pretender. The politicians would not have it. It is impossible, quite impossible. And isn't his German cousin Mossy such a nice girl. Not pretty, perhaps, but such a nice girl. To cheer him up, to win him over, she makes him a duke. Now Albert Victor is Duke of Clarence too. So many names, he thinks, so many names.

Grandmama sits in her tartan sitting room with the tartan carpets and tartan wallpaper. The dimpled smile falters when she sees Helene, but she is gracious as always. Helene is invited to inspect the pictures of the estate which line the tartan walls, some painted by the most prestigious artists, some by

Grandmama herself. Helene has the knack of knowing which are which and bowling praise at the appropriate frames. What skill to have captured a snowscape so perfectly. How on earth did Grandmama do it? And when Grandmama tells her, in excruciating detail, she listens with something like rapture. When tea is served, the old woman takes only one sip then puts down her cup.

'Well, my dears?'

He opens his mouth to speak but Helene leaps out before him, the tigress blazing from her eyes; a gently supplicating one, but a tigress nonetheless. Grandmama is told how Helene has loved him from afar for years, how no other man could ever make her happy. He is described as a paragon, a saint even. A curl of her thick dark hair escapes from its place and has to be tossed back again and again; her breast heaves with the effort of her pleading. Grandmama becomes agitated too. The little fists grip the folds of black bombazine. Eventually, she raises a hand to calm the waves.

'To change your religion would surely be a most distressing thing,' she says. 'You will upset your parents, your countrymen and also, my dear, would you not upset yourself?'

'Perhaps, but I don't care.'

'And what about upsetting God? Wouldn't you care about that?'

'But if God really is a god of love, He will understand me,' replies Helene.

Her voice cracks a little. Eddy cannot stifle the thought that, with her accent, it is most becoming. She reaches for his hand, places it against her heart.

'I would do it for him, only for him. Oh help us, pray do.'

Grandmama rises from her chair and walks over to the window. They all stand awkwardly in a pool of silence.

'What are you looking at, Grandmama?'

'Your dear Grandpapa planned every tree and shrub and flowerbed out there. We used to joke about hobbling round it together when we were old.'

She sighs like a bird tired after flight. Helene goes and sinks to her knees before the black bombazine.

'You are a woman who has known passion, I think. You have known what it is like to be consumed with love for a man. To feel your heart race at the sight of him and to yearn for his arms round you. It is the same with us.'

Eddy is aghast, but Grandmama is not. All trace of the tigress gone, Helene weeps softly now. The old woman raises her up.

'It will be most difficult. You must have patience.'

As they leave the room, she calls after them.

'I ache to say yes to you. I want you to know that. And your Grandpapa does too.'

In the pony-trap, Helene does not laugh or joke or tease or say a single word. For the first time this summer, she is silent as a nun. She slips her arm through his and leans her dark head on his shoulder. They have almost reached Braemar when he cuts into the dozy rhythm of the horse's hooves.

'Did you mean the things you said about me?'

'Did you doubt them?' she asks, not lifting her head from his shoulder.

'It has always been wise for me to doubt words like that.'

She turns her face up to his.

'Well, I am here now so you need doubt no more.'

He slides his arm round her and holds her close against him.

He feels her gentle breathing and adjusts his own so that they breathe together. He realises that only once before has he done this with another human being. In the middle of a snow-covered quadrangle with the moonlight in his face and the smell of port in his nostrils. Now, as then, it is a magical thing.

He vows that this very evening, while everyone is out by the banks of the river, he will hide away and write the letter that must be written. For weeks now, it has been composed in his head. It is drafted many times; words scored out then reinstated, paragraphs rearranged. He puts all of himself into it. He almost knows it by heart now; it should not take long to commit it to black and white. And when it is done, he will go out to the garden. He will take her hand and they will watch the salmon jumping from the water in the pale rays of the sinking sun.

CHAPTER XIX

Autumn 1890. Scotland.

Last night, the idea came to him. It was as if a blindfold had been ripped from his eyes and he saw the solution, shining bright as a new-minted guinea. There would be a great fuss of course, a splendid agonising, but in the end it would solve everyone's problem. He would be happy and everyone else relieved. Why did he not think of it before?

Since they went in the pony-trap to plead with Grandmama, great boulders have been rolled onto their path. The telegraph wires burn. Advice is sought on every side. The politicians scurry about, lost in a maze of anxieties, groping for a possible route towards pleasing the little woman in black. If the girl converts, they bleat, the Catholics will despise it, the Protestants not believe in it. After all, she might still try to infect the children; you know what these people are like. And The Pretender's daughter? Good grief. France would be furious and we cannot have that, not these days. Oh that boy has always been a headache.

In the end, the telegraph wires burn in vain. The deliberations of the statesmen and the churchmen are swept away, like leaves against a broom, by the simple authority of a parent over his child. The Pretender will not allow his daughter to convert and that is that. And it is six years before, under the law of her country, she can do as she pleases. Six gaping, unimaginable years. And if she does not convert, there is no hope for them. Not even Grandmama has the power to storm that battlement.

Helene returns to the south. They write every day; the lines of her letters rigid with the shock that her devoted father has at last denied her something. Here, their gloomy Highland tower becomes even darker. Alix and the sisters mope and fret; like Helene, they are unable to believe that they cannot have what they have decided to want. Bertie avoids Eddy's eye.

But then, as he brushes his teeth, the idea comes. Although it is very late, he goes straight to his father.

'Don't be ridiculous. How could you suggest such a thing?'

'Do you remember, Papa, when I was a boy, the day I tried to climb on Grandpapa's tomb?'

'Who could forget?'

'Do you recall what you said to me outside, by the little bridge that crosses the stream?'

'No.'

'You asked me if I would be up to the mark. Well I'm not, am I? I never have been. Don't deny you still don't think so.'

Bertie strides up and down his bedroom, muttering and spluttering, the racing papers still in his hand.

'But it is the role for which God has chosen you,' he says.

'It's the same for me. How can you wish to abdicate your birthright?'

'If the rightful son isn't up to running the business, then give the job to the son who is. That's what would happen with any other family in the land, so why not ours? Think about it, Papa.'

There is a plate of carved chicken by the bed, in case Bertie is hungry in the night. He takes it to a chair by the fire and begins to devour it. As he chews, he glances up from time to time. Eddy sees his father's eyes change as the notion flutters round his mind then begins to nest. Eddy does not need to be told what his thoughts are.

'The perfect solution, Papa. In every possible way.'

The juices from a chicken leg dribble into Bertie's beard, like streams running through a forest. He is staring into the fire.

'Just go to bed, Eddy. Go to bed.'

*

Autumn 1890. Marlborough House, London.

The sentries stop him at the gates. He is panting heavily, his hair all over the place, his trouser bottoms wet from treading in a puddle as he leapt off the bus. No doubt I look like an anarchist, he thinks.

They send for the Scots ghillie who controls entry to the house. The ghillie remembers Jem's face and leads him into the vestibule. Jem says he must see Eddy on a matter of the greatest urgency.

'I'm no' sure that he is yet risen, sir,' he says.

The man disappears inside the house. Jem sits on a long, low stool, drums his fingers on the studded green leather, tries to breathe more slowly.

'A footman has been sent up to enquire, sir. If you'd kindly wait here, I'll have tea brought to you.'

Jem gets to his feet, towers over the ghillie; the Keeper of The Wall a match for any Highlander.

'Tea? I have no time for tea,' he says.

He pushes past him into the Saloon, two storeys high, lined with vast paintings of the victory at Blenheim. A young footman in a powdered wig blocks his path.

'I must see the prince at once,' he says again.

'Well, Mr Stephen, an unexpected pleasure,' calls Bertie, as he crosses the Saloon in search of his breakfast. 'We have seen so little of you lately. I'm sure my son will see you shortly, though he is, as you well know, a fastidious dresser and an extremely slow one. You may well need to stay for lunch.'

'There is no time for that, sir. Forgive me, but I must see him now, right this minute.'

Jem makes a scruffy bow, walks a few steps backwards then turns and half-runs towards the staircase.

'Are you quite well, Mr Stephen?' Bertie calls after him.

The footman is unsure whether to pursue, looking to Bertie for orders. But he just shrugs and goes to find his devilled kidneys and scrambled eggs, his bacon and sausages, his toast with honey. He has a filly running at Newmarket this afternoon and she took a blow to her fetlock yesterday. He can think of nothing else.

Jem has never been upstairs before, but he knows the

rough position of Eddy's rooms. He powers along the upper corridor, cutting through housemaids in their lace caps like the bow of a ship through frothing waves. He guesses the door, flings it open, panting on the threshold, his face the colour of Saint-Émilion.

Eddy stands at the shaving mirror, submerged in clouds of soap.

'Good grief, Jem.'

'Your letter came this morning,' says Jem. 'What on earth do you think you're about? Set aside your rights to marry the Catholic girl? You can't do that.'

'I think you'll find that I can,' replies Eddy.

'But it's unheard of, unthinkable.'

'I've thought of little else for days now, Jem.'

'Your grandmother would never allow it.'

'I know her rather better than you do.'

Silence falls between them. Jem glares at him, searching his face to see if Eddy can possibly be serious. It feels a long way from the bench above the ice rink.

Jem turns on his heel and strides to the window, throwing it open as if a blast of sharp, cool air might bring Eddy to his senses. Autumn is tightening its grip; now the mornings nip a little. Across the park, he can see the towers of the abbey. He grabs Eddy's arm and drags him towards the view.

'Look. There. That is where you must go one day. Will you turn your back on it for some unsuitable woman?'

'*You* were the one who urged me to marry,' says Eddy. 'When I first wrote to you about Helene, you said how pleased you were. Was that not true?'

'Yes, of course you must marry. But not at any price.

Certainly not at *this* price.'

They stare at each other, the red face and the white. How absurd they must look, Jem thinks. Eddy lights a cigarette; his hand is shaking. Jem wishes he were carrying his pipe.

'For heaven's sake, Eddy, give the girl up.'

'Never.'

'Let them find you some plain German Protestant and take your pleasures elsewhere.'

'And keep my soul to myself? Isn't that what you recommended? Well, I don't want that sort of loneliness. I'd rather like to share my soul with someone. Wouldn't you?'

'If you walk away from your birthright, everything I've tried to do will be wasted. All my work with you, all my hopes for you. Wasted. I've never asked anything of you, but I ask this.'

'But supposing I've stumbled on real and lasting happiness? How could that be a waste? For you, maybe, but not for me. Christ, something really good comes to me and all people do is to put obstacles in my way.'

Eddy wipes the shaving soap from his face and throws the wet flannel across the room. It hits a wall and slithers downwards; a frothy blob on the wallpaper.

'So you love this girl then?' Jem asks.

'Yes,' says Eddy. 'I think so. I want to.'

Jem walks towards the open door. Eddy calls after him.

'You do not understand what this means to me. You do not live in my skin.'

'But that's exactly what I do,' says Jem. 'Always will do.'

He goes out of the room, past the housemaids, down the great staircase. His legs feel like lead. He apologises to the ghillie for his rudeness. In St James's Street, he finds he does not have enough money to take a bus or underground train to De Vere Gardens. He sets out on the long walk back towards his bed.

When Eddy enters the dining room, Bertie looks up from the racing papers.

'Is Mr Stephen quite well?' he asks again, between mouthfuls of kipper.

*

Autumn 1890. Sussex.

Jem can sleep easy in his bed. Eddy's grand gesture comes to nothing, blown away on the autumn breeze.

'Oh don't be silly, Eddy!'

They huddle in secret at the house of a friend. The Pretender, such a pleasant man he had always thought, has now forbidden their meeting; hardening his heart against them until it is as stony as that of an Old Testament prophet. It is a fine October day. They sit on a swing seat beside a tennis court. The lawn is consumed beneath a blazing carpet of fallen Virginia creeper; it reminds him of the rose petals they threw in India.

'Wouldn't it be wonderful to run away and live somewhere quiet like this?' he asks. 'Just the two of us. Hidden from the world.'

She gives a little smile but does not answer. And then he tells her what he has decided to do. But she is not thrilled as he expected; like Jem, she is appalled. She leaps up as if stung by a dying bee.

'Oh don't be silly, Eddy!'

It is the first time she has ever said anything remotely unkind. In a moment, the smile returns to her lips, but the lips are a little tighter now and the eyes have altered. The softness in them, that proof of her love, is there as usual but now there is something else. Something he does not recognise, does not quite like. She sits down again, takes his hand in hers, speaks softly now.

'Now *mon ange*, no more of such nonsense,' she says. '*Je vous en prie.*'

'But I don't bloody want it!' he replies. 'I don't want to be Albert Victor. Why does nobody seem able to grasp that?'

Helene does not reply. It is as if she has not heard him. He sees her shiver. It suddenly feels chilly. Soon the swing seat will be locked inside the summer house, the tennis nets rolled up and stored away. From round a corner of the house comes a burst of laughter, the chatter of their friends, the noise of a banjo and singing out of tune. Helene smiles, drops his hand and runs towards the sound. Now he is not sure that she would care to exist alone with him, where nobody else would ever see her.

And, in the end, she runs off and leaves him again. It is her Catholic God, not Eddy, who wins her at the last.

Like Hamlet's father, poison is poured into her pretty ear as she dozes. What a dreadful thing to abandon your religion, they tell her. Criminal even. Your soul damned forever. The letter comes to tell him of her change of mind. He sits in his room, the folded white paper lying open on the carpet, like a deep, bloodless wound. They must plead with his Grandmama again, she writes. The stupid law must be changed. Surely they live in the modern world. It is two whole centuries since the Battle of The Boyne. But he will not go to Grandmama again. He knows it is useless. The battlement can never be breached. It is armed to the teeth by implacable people, waving their tattered banners of ancient hatreds.

Then the letter comes that is written from Dover. She is about to board the ship. If her own father will not help, perhaps the Holy Father will; a dispensation so that their children can be brought up in his religion, not hers. Surely that might persuade the enemy to inch open the gates? Eddy is not hopeful, though his heart soars at this new proof of love. She has not abandoned him after all.

'Such a long flight for a little lovebird,' sighs Alix. 'All the way to Rome.'

Bertie, nagged to distraction by his womenfolk, calls for the carriage and goes to visit The Pretender. He appeals to him to sanction his daughter's conversion; perhaps that would persuade her to conquer her conscience.

'A heavenly crown is of greater worth than any other,' says The Pretender. 'No child of mine will sell her soul for such a reason.'

'Pompous old fool,' says Bertie. Then a dreadful notion slithers into Eddy's mind. Has The Pretender heard something? A murmur on the wind? A note discreetly passed? Has poison been poured into his ear too, of a much more lethal kind? After all, he is famously ambitious for his daughters. One is already in place to reign over the Portuguese and that is a trifling empire compared with this one. So has he heard something? Dear God, Eddy had never thought of that.

Retreating to Norfolk, they sit and wait for news from

Rome. Alix and the sisters watch him constantly, while pretending that nothing is the matter. They play cheery tunes on the piano. His hand is squeezed until he thinks it might drop off. Every night, posies are waiting on his pillow. Eventually, he throws the bloody flowers into the dark stairwell, as if into the grave of all his hopes.

The telegram is brought when he and Georgie are out in the coverts. The Holy Father will not help them.

'I'm going to lose her, Georgie!' he cries, the pain bursting out before he can prevent it.

His brother takes Eddy's gun and hands it to the loader. He seizes Eddy's arm, steers him away. Such things must not be seen.

'Let's go home,' says Georgie.

But more than one message has been sent from Rome. As they cross the parterre, the tall windows of the drawing room fly open and the sisters rush forth. He is covered in tears and protestations of love, but it is not their love he wants. He sees his mother standing in the window, but then she turns and vanishes back into the shadows of the house. It is the first time in his life that she does not rush to comfort him when he needs her.

Dinner is a drear affair, the subject not mentioned. They talk of domestic things, but even these are gloomy; the tenant farmer who has lost a leg in a threshing machine; the old dog, adored since childhood, who must be put down. The girls want him to play whist. He is surprisingly good at whist and they know he will beat them, but he will only sit in a corner, lost in his smoke.

But then he is summoned to Papa's study. Today telegrams

plague them like measles. Yet another lies open on the table, but this one has not come from Rome. Bertie leans back in his chair and rubs his eyes. He suddenly looks quite old.

'When the news came earlier, I sent one more appeal to her father but his answer has just arrived. I believe the game is lost.'

Eddy cannot think of a reply so he only nods.

'I'm very sorry indeed,' says Bertie. 'I had great hopes of it. We all did.'

He pushes himself out of his chair and throws another log on the fire. The action sets him coughing; his face swelling like a bursting plum.

Eddy says goodnight and turns for the door. But now he defies his father's edict. The question can no longer be imprisoned in his head.

'Do you think The Pretender might have been told of anything against me?'

'I have no means of knowing.'

Bertie throws the telegram into the flames. Together they watch it burn.

He must have heard, Eddy decides. He must have heard something.

CHAPTER XX

Spring 1891. London.

Today he flies.

When he rises from the underground railway, he feels like running along the street. The sun is in his eyes, the apple blossom is coming out, a workman paints a shop-front virgin white. There seems to be light everywhere. Tonight he might try to write a poem about it.

How pretty St John's Wood is. It reminds him of the back streets of his beloved Cambridge. Sweet little houses in gently curving avenues. Not proud and unbending like the regimented mansions of De Vere Gardens. A place made for ordinary people to live, love and be happy. And is the air not fresher too? Lungfuls of promise for a fresh new day.

He is wearing one of his splendid new suits. Over the last month or two, when he has been feeling somewhat better, he has returned to his exercise regimen. The waistband is not such agony as it once was. He has had his hair trimmed again; the barber in Burlington Arcade is right to insist that it makes him look younger. He is thirty-two now. Good heavens. Nearly middle-aged. But today he feels almost a boy once more.

Of course, he is a trifle nervous but what young man would not be? He has even put a rosebud in his buttonhole and hopes she will notice his tiny compliment. How good of Eddy to arrange this on his behalf. So typically generous, so loving. It seems there is nothing Eddy cannot arrange; the most eminent doctors, the occasional loan when coffers are low and now this, this extraordinary moment in his life.

When he finds the villa with the green door, he stops across the street, half-hides himself in the shade of an aspen. His heart is thumping and he feels the sweat in his armpits and between his big legs. Perhaps he should have walked a bit slower. He breathes gently, quietens himself.

'It's going to be fine,' he says to a squirrel perched on a garden wall. 'I have to do this thing. For her, if not for me.'

He closes his eyes for a moment so he can see her better. What a spiffing girl his fiancée is. At least that is how he likes to think of her now. Nothing formal has been agreed as yet, the big question has not been put to her, but he is sure an understanding exists between them. In looks, she is hardly in the league of Mrs Langtry, but he would not have wanted that anyway. She sits on the outer fringes of his family; a sort of honorary cousin. She hovers in the shadow of her mother; a quiet little thing though not demure. He has known her for years, then suddenly, for no reason he can think of, she comes into focus. She has a sharp brain too; the other day she corrected him on a quotation from Ovid. He was being pompous, trying to impress. It served him right. But then she smiled and made a remark almost worthy of O.B. Suddenly, he thought this one might do.

Hunched in a corner of the drawing room, the judge had noticed.

'Pursue her. Win her,' he said later. 'Perhaps she can triumph where the rest of us have failed.'

Jem thinks about those words. Could this be some sort of salvation? Both a way forward and a way back to where he once was. A lifting of the curse even. Is that credible?

He ponders over telling Eddy. How singular that both of them should find a girl at much the same time. He hesitates as it is so soon after Eddy's own hopes are finally dashed. But he wants Eddy's approval, his permission even. So one day, on the bench above the ice rink, he speaks of it. Eddy says nothing for a moment, studies the hooks and eyes on his ice skates. Then he clinks their mugs of negus together and gives his blessing as selflessly as Jem had known he would. Soon Eddy goes off and skates alone for a while.

'Do you enjoy it with a woman?' Eddy had asked later.

'I don't know,' says Jem.

'Heavens, don't you think it might be sensible to find out before you go any further?'

Now, in St John's Wood, the green door opens and a raven-haired woman peers out. She catches sight of him, smiles and beckons. He crosses the road.

'Jem?' she asks. 'How nice. Come away in.'

As Eddy had said, she is a pleasant soul. He likes her at once. She shows him round her garden, he throws a ball for her Labrador. She lets him see some of her sketches which are really rather good. She can even hold a passable conversation about the poetry of Robert Burns. His nervousness fades, his spirits rise. It is going to be fine, he says again to himself, just as he had said to the squirrel.

Two hours later, he sits alone in Rose's bedroom in a small satin-covered armchair. When he had entered, it had been bright and sunny, but the sun has shifted and now it is quite dark. He nurses a cup of tea, but cannot touch the plate of biscuits she has brought him. He has been sitting like this for half an hour now. Despite the tea, he can still taste his vomit in his throat.

He tries not to look at the bed, the scene of his humiliation. It was when he first saw it, the covers pulled back, the pillows of brocaded silk all plumped up, that his stomach began to tighten, his tongue stuck to the roof of his mouth. And, when she begins to remove the layers of her clothing, unwrapping herself bit by bit like a birthday present, he knows for certain he is going to fail. He had not known it was possible to feel such physical revulsion, such visceral disgust for another human being and he is ashamed of that.

It is almost worse that she is so kind, so infinitely patient, a woman able to talk about Turner. If only he had gone to some whore in St Giles, where the woman would have lain yawning, keeping an eye on the clock or counting the cobwebs on the ceiling while he struggled. There he could just have slammed the money on the table and fled. But this is different.

'We'll just take our time, shall we?' she says. 'There's no need to hurry.'

Rose tries every one of her tricks but it is no good. He cannot believe that the cowering thing between his legs is the same prick that has effortlessly rogered so many arses. And then, in quiet desperation, she puts her tongue in his mouth and wraps it round his own. He is consumed with horror; the awful claustrophobia of it. He really thinks he is going to choke, to die even. Will he ever leave this bed, this room, this house? And when she takes his hand and pushes his finger deep between her legs, he vomits. He tries to pull away but the first spurt of it goes into her mouth and over her face. The rest splatters the bed and the carpet. By the time he finds the pitcher, there is little left to spew.

Rose cries out and hurries from the room. She is gone for some time but when she returns her face is clean and calm. She smells of lavender-water and carries a tray of tea and biscuits.

'Just come out when you're ready,' she says.

He catches sight of himself in the glass of her dressing table. Where is the Keeper of The Wall now? Where is Hector, son of Priam, as O. B. described him once long ago? What sort of creature is this?

The Labrador finds its way into the bedroom. It stretches out beside him, its muzzle on his naked foot. He gives it one of the biscuits, strokes its smooth, broad back. In the next half an hour, it saves him.

In the narrow hallway, he tries to make some sort of apology but Rose just puts her finger to her lips. She pats him on the shoulder, then walks him out to find a hansom and sees him inside it. She waves from the green-painted door, then it is closed. It is raining lightly now. How small and mean these streets look, he decides; provincial even. Why did he ever think it pretty? It is not a place he will ever return to.

In the cab, he ponders how Eddy can enjoy such pleasures.

When, long ago and a little drunk, Eddy first admitted it, Jem could scarcely credit it. At the time, he was aware of a vague resentment too. Why should such versatility be denied to him? And in such a crude mechanical business too. If Jem Stephen can write poetry, speak in Latin and discuss the great issues of the day, surely, if he so chooses, he can stick his member into any hole, be it man, woman or sheep. Though never tested until today, it is a belief he has clung to and now it is shattered.

On its way to De Vere Gardens, the cab passes the house where his sweet cousin lives. He imagines her behind one of the windows reading Ovid or Plato, playing a little Chopin or at some other such accomplishment. How adorable she is; what wonderful companions they could be. But then he pictures her naked, lying against brocaded pillows, that awful thing between her legs from which his spirit shrinks and withers. In the twilight of the cab, his gorge rises again.

He puts his head out of the window to find some air. He watches his cousin's house recede into the distance until it is a tiny speck, then it vanishes completely.

*

Spring 1891. Marlborough House.

'You gave me a hell of a scare, you know,' says Georgie.

'Yes, I must have done. I'm so sorry,' replies Eddy.

'Didn't you think what it would mean for me, you bastard?' says Georgie.

'To be honest, I didn't. I don't think I was thinking very clearly.'

They are strolling along the paths that wind through the shrubs at the edge of the garden. This means they do not have to look at each other directly. These days there is a wisp of shyness between them which was not there in childhood. Sprat and Herring do not meet so often now; a few weeks in a year perhaps, though they write from time to time.

Georgie is tanned as an old barrel and the beard is bushier than ever. Eddy thinks his brother even rougher than he used to be. He swears quite dreadfully now, even in front of their Mama, so it is a blessing she scarcely hears it. The sisters find it rather thrilling; this bellowing bull crashing into their porcelain world. But still Eddy feels that when his brother went back to sea it was like losing a piece of himself. Not a day passes that Eddy does not think of him, hoping he is happy in his distant life.

'Jesus Christ, I don't want the bloody thing!' says Georgie.

'My words exactly. But it seems I'm stuck with it.'

'Yes, I know. I'm sorry.'

'Well, maybe the whole kerfuffle was a blessing in the end. I discovered that it wasn't just me she wanted, it was the bloody thing too.'

'Perhaps you misjudge her.'

They reach the hidden corner which Alix has sanctified as the last resting place of her countless dogs and cats. A crescent of dwarf tombstones pushing up from the earth. They sit on a bench and light their cigarettes.

'I told her I'd gladly give up the whole show,' says Eddy, 'and we could vanish into some private place. And a change came over her. Like a veil. I saw then I wasn't enough for her. Well, who can blame her?'

Georgie does not reply.

'Anyway, she will be all right. She has the gift of it. I'll soon become a photograph in a frame. Helene will sail on through the ballrooms until she reaches the destiny she is certain awaits her.'

'Hard luck, old chap. Did you really love the girl?'

'I certainly believed I did. But I'm beginning to wonder if that was only because they all insisted she loved me. Was I so desperate to please Mama and the sisters that I imagined it? Is that possible? Maybe it was just some sort of delirium.'

One of Alix's yapping dogs appears and begins to claw at the grave of a predecessor. Georgie lobs a stone, sends it yelping into the bushes.

'You're not the only one who's lost a girl, you know,' says Georgie. 'And for the same damn reason too.'

Eddy is ashamed. Absorbed in himself, he has forgotten the parallel. He has forgotten Julie, the last Catholic girl who drifted into their orbit. Sweet Julie. She knew how to handle Georgie, how to pull the thorn from the lion's paw. He was always gentler when Julie was there.

'I'm sorry, Georgie.'

'It won't be long before they force some ghastly hags on us both, you know.'

'I know.'

'For God's sake, Eddy, make sure you have the life of a man before you have the life of a puppet.'

'Make my arrangements? That's what everyone says.'

'Make some memories to warm you when you're old.'

'And the women they force on us?' asks Eddy. 'Do we not have to think of them at all?'

'They will be of our tribe; they will know the rules of the game.'

'I'm not sure our Mama did, are you?'

'Let's not talk of that Eddy. Not ever.'

'Oh to hell with it all!' says Eddy. 'Tell me some of your filthy sailor's jokes. The filthier the better.'

And so they smoke and laugh and, for a while, it seems like they have never been parted. They talk of the *Bacchante* and the great storm that damaged the rudder and sent them drifting towards Antarctica. They talk of Dalton and his young wife and child and how impossible it is to picture Dalton actually fucking. They roll up their sleeves and show each other the dragon tattoos they had done in Japan. They are Sprat and Herring once more. The shyness melts. They are easy again now, sitting together in silence.

'We still write to each other,' says Eddy after a while, 'though they have forbidden us to meet any more. Helene still believes we'll find an answer and be together one day.'

'And what do you reply?'

'That I yearn for the same.'

'And do you?'

'I don't really know any more.'

'Well, I'd stop all that if I were you,' says Georgie, quite sharply. 'Nothing can come of it. Stop now. Be cruel to be to be kind.'

'But she was such fun, Georgie. Such a good chum. I could forget myself in her.'

Georgie slaps him on the back. He suggests a visit to the music hall tonight. When the brothers have vanished along the path, the yapping dog creeps back and scratches at the grave again.

'It's a small house,' says Eddy. 'Well, perhaps not small, but modest enough to only require a couple of servants. It's a splendid day and I'm sitting on a veranda looking out over a garden. The awful thing is that I've become rather stout and the hair on my head has almost gone. My moustache has vanished too, but I've got a beard. Didn't I swear I'd never have a beard?'

'You certainly did,' replies Jem. 'The antithesis of fashion, you always said.'

Again they are up on Primrose Hill. Tomorrow Eddy must open a shoe factory somewhere in the north and they are supposed to be practising his speech. Jem is usually quite fierce about these rehearsals, almost as bad as Dalton in his prime, but today he does not seem to care. Instead, they sit and smoke.

'And I'm wearing really scruffy clothes. Loose cotton trousers and a calico shirt without a collar.'

'Good God!' says Jem. 'The Empire may fall.'

'There's a pond full of ducks and moorhens. The children are playing with their boats.'

'Whose children?'

'Mine,' replies Eddy. 'Then one of them falls and scrapes his knee and somebody carries him to me. "He wants his Papa," they say. I clasp him close and feel his tiny heart thumping into me and his wet cheeks damp against my shirt. I kiss his forehead until it uncreases and his eyes are calm again. Of all the children, this is the one I love the most; the quiet one who always hangs back.'

'Sweet,' says Jem. 'So it's a little paradise, then?'

'Not completely. I've had to build a high brick wall round the garden, though it's half-hidden under honeysuckle and wisteria; I can permit no ugliness here. But I've made one stupid mistake. I left one gate in the wall, painted white, made of wrought iron. And there are people gathered there, peering in through the bars. Grandmama, Papa and Mama, Georgie and the girls, Dalton, the whole caboodle. At first they smile and wave and I wave back, but I don't let them in. Mama weeps and Papa shakes at the bars like an angry bear. They're all hurt and baffled, especially darling Mama. It's hard for me because I love them dearly, but I know I must never admit them or all is lost.'

'So it's just you and the children in this idyll, then? Plus, of course, a few servants.'

Eddy laughs.

'Oh no. I'm not alone. There's someone beside me on the veranda. We sit in two wicker chairs pulled close together. We drink iced lemonade and watch the children sail their boats. We talk of everything and nothing. We're never parted, not even for a day. And I am so unimaginably content.'

'And it's always the same, this dream?' asks Jem. 'You and Helene on the veranda.'

'No,' says Eddy. 'The dream changes, you see. Sometimes it's Helene, sometimes it's you.'

CHAPTER XXI

Summer 1891. Marlborough House.

Mossy or Missy. Missy or Mossy. Or some other cousin he has never even heard of. He has cousins like dogs have fleas. He gets them all mixed up. The pages of the *Almanac de Gotha* are sprinkled with the crumbs from his Grandmama's toast as she scours it in increasing frustration.

It has been going on for months and he is past caring. Let them sort it out. Let them choose the one they can all agree on, the one whose nationality, pedigree, religion, childbearing hips and state of sanity can be wrapped up in one pretty package of possibility. Let them tie her with a pink bow and lay her before him for his approval or, in truth, his silent acquiescence.

He comes up to town from camp. Bertie has summoned him to an interview with the solicitor tomorrow. This new trouble must be sorted out at once, his Papa says. Oh dear, and they seemed such sweet girls too, both of them. He is hurt that they are trying to injure him. He should never have written those letters though. Silly Eddy.

He is expected on the morning train but, on a whim, he travels the evening before. So he will need a *divertissement*. He might see if Harry is free to dine. He has not seen him for a few months now. Yes, it would be nice to meet dear Harry; he is a kind and good soul. They might dine at the club. Perhaps drink a bit too much. Perhaps even go for a little adventure afterwards. He has heard rumours about the underground station at Russell Square. It is amazing what burrows under the surface of the city, what gorgeous, irresistible grubs can be uncovered there.

Or he could call on Sybil. Dear sweet Sibyl. He thought he was in love with her for a while. He really did, even when he still leeched to his last hopes of Helene. Pretty Sybil laughs and flirts and dances; she carries a light within her, just like Helene. No doubt that is why she attracted him. But, of course, she would never have done. The mere sister of a very mere earl, she falls at the first fence. Still, after the long, sad winter, she brings him something of summer and he is grateful. They might go to Evan's Music Hall, to Romano's or to Kettner's; though the risk of following in his father's footsteps is of finding him at the end of them. He should hate to bump into Bertie and his 'wicked boys', nor would Bertie wish his son to see him in his other world, with his cronies and his women; that other 'family' which Eddy has resented since childhood because it had sucked so much of the joy from his own. Anyway, Harry or Sybil. One or the other. It hardly matters. It is only another evening, another few hours to be filled.

In the end, he does neither. The stupid train is delayed and he does not reach Pall Mall until nearly ten. He will dine in his room and go to bed. He is tired as usual. He feels so weak these days. Dr Fripp seems to think he may have caught some bug in India but is not certain quite what.

The Scots ghillie at the door is surprised to see him, a little flustered even, though the man tries not to show it. The footman in the powdered wig says that Papa is dining at home this evening, a small supper party, and has asked not to be disturbed. No doubt the 'wicked boys' are in conclave.

Eddy has a tray brought up to his room. He falls asleep in an armchair and when he wakes, it is almost one o'clock. The tray is gone and the gas turned down low. He wonders if Papa's guests have departed now. He looks down into the well of the staircase; the house is shadowy and silent but perhaps Papa is having a last cigar in his sitting room. Perhaps he should knock on the door and wish him goodnight, store up some good will for the interview with the solicitor. Fat chance, of course, but nothing ventured.

The door to the sitting room is concealed behind a fake bookcase lined with fake books, but a pencil line of soft yellow light underscores Bertie's hiding place. He hears the murmur of voices and taps gently but there is no answer. He taps again, then opens the door. It is not surprising he has not been heard. Hearing is the last of the five senses prevailing in the room.

His father sits on a blue leather sofa, in his evening clothes. He is indeed smoking his cigar, but squatting between his legs is a half-dressed woman, her breasts bouncing free from her unlaced corsets, her blonde curls bobbing up and down. Standing behind the sofa is another woman, her skirts gathered up to her waist, her legs wide apart. Bertie's head is thrown back, blowing puffs of smoke onto her cunt. She giggles and squeaks like a happy kitten.

Eddy is rooted to the carpet, his fingernails etching themselves into the cedarwood of the door. He has lived with these imaginings since he was old enough to picture them. But this is the fetid reality. The reality behind the crude jibes of their shipmates on the *Bacchante*, behind the tales of bathtubs filled with champagne and of a special chair built to facilitate the sexual pleasures of the obese. The reality of the silences at the breakfast table, of the days when Mama never leaves her room. The reality of his father's lifelong betrayal, not just of her but of them all.

Eddy stands in the doorway for only a moment, but it is the moment in which he knows, without the slightest tremor of doubt, that he must take a different path from the one his father lives and the one which, in his sorrow, he has been living again in the last few months. He has no idea how he might do this, only that he must. Perhaps God, in His mercy, will show the way, as Dalton so often promised that He always would.

Suddenly, Bertie lowers his head to enjoy the sight of the busy mouth between his legs. Instead, his eyes rest on the child in the doorway. His jaw falls open, the cigar hovers in the air. They hold each other's gaze. Eddy thinks he might weep for both of them, for the waste of it. But he does not. Instead, he slams the study door behind him. He slams it so hard that it ricochets open again and crashes back into the room. He grasps the handle and repeats himself. The ghillie and the powdered footmen come running. A gunshot? An anarchist bomb?

The slam echoes up the staircases, onto the landings and

along the corridors. Even when he is safely back in his room, it goes on ringing in his ears. He hopes that he will never stop hearing it. He must always try to remember the sound and the freedom it has brought him.

*

Summer 1891. Sandringham, Norfolk.

'There are no songs in old Motherdear tonight,' she says.
Last evening, when the sisters begged for tunes on the piano, she went dutifully to the stool. As usual, one of her tiny dogs leapt onto her lap, eager for a tune too. Alix shuffled her music, lifted her hands to play, then sighed and let them fall.

Eddy worries. Some change has come over her lately. Her spirit is not what it was. There is a lassitude which is alien in her; as if he has infected her with his own habitual complaint.

Now, she says she will ride out alone today.

'Would you go in my place to visit old Mrs Ashby?' she asks him. 'There is a cancer in the poor woman's breast and she will not see Christmas.'

A sudden chill shoots through him. Might such a horror explain his Mama's own new weariness? Has she decided not to share the dreadful news, to spare them her pain? Is she riding off alone to weep?

He decides to disobey. Mrs Ashby must wait. He will follow at a distance, keep watch over her, make sure she is safe. He will play Mr Sherlock Holmes; she will not even know he is there. As soon as she trots off, he rushes to the stables. He is not correctly dressed, but no matter. He follows the route he knows she will take. He moves fast because she will have streaked far ahead of him by now, but he is wrong. He takes a sharp bend in the woods and almost crashes into her. She is riding at walking pace, no more.

'I told you I would go out alone,' she says, lifting her veil. She tries to smile, but her expression is blank.

'I know, Mama, but surely you didn't really want...'

The blankness of the face knots itself into annoyance.

'How does anyone know what I really want? And, if they did, would anyone really care?'

She wheels the mare away and digs in her spurs. In seconds, she has vanished from his sight. He pursues her as fast as he can, but when Alix climbs onto her saddle, some alchemy happens. It is as if she and the beast melt together to become some mythical creature. She is certainly never happier. It is as though when she steps off the ground she leaves her sorrows flattened within her footprint. It has always been so.

When he catches her again, the mare is standing still on the beach, looking out over the German Ocean. The day is a rebuke to all sadness. The sky is a hazy white-blue, vast as a cathedral; the gulls and terns and avocets fly to and fro, feeding their chicks. The grassland jumps with butterflies; even the barren shingle has become fertile, dappled with blueweed and yellow horned poppies.

She does not greet him when he rides quietly to her side. They sit in silence as flocks of knots swoop in low over the shallow waters, their pale underwings flashing like knives as they twist and turn in the sunlight. He glances sideways at her, frightened by the blankness. Her eyes are unfocussed, as if there is nothing she wishes to be read in them.

'Mama, are you ill? Is it something serious? For God's sake, please tell your Eddy.'

Again, she tries to smile at him and now he is comforted by seeing some love in it.

'No, my darling. Don't fret. I'm as strong as this old mare and I'll live until I'm eighty.'

They slide off their saddles and onto the shingle. They walk along the beach towards the eastern horizon, leading their mounts behind them.

'Your Papa and Grandmama want to send you away again,' she says.

'Away? But where, Mama?'

'They can't agree. The telegrams go back and forth. The usual dance.'

'But it's only a year since I came back from India. Why?'

His mother stops and looks down at her riding boots, their gloss dirtied by the scruffy shingle. She drags her eyes up to his.

'Oh Eddy,' she says, brushing his cheek with the back of her hand.

Mother and son stroll along the beach where they have walked in every season of every year of his life. The sweep of the land as it meets the sea, the smells and the sounds of it are all unchanged, but they are not. They are different now.

'Nobody knows what to do with you, my darling. So many scrapes.'

'So I'm to circle the world forever like *The Flying Dutchman*?'

'Unless you can suddenly discover a clear path forward. A good and righteous one.'

'I thought that path was Helene. For a while, anyway.'

'We all did.'

They are not quite alone on the late summer beach. Pockets of people are stitched onto its vastness. They pass two small boys splashing in the shallows, the parents perching on an old log; the father smoking, the mother darning a faded shirt. Pipe and shirt are thrust aside for bows and curtseys.

Alix talks to them as if she has known them all her life and ruffles the hair of the children. When they pass on, she keeps looking back over her shoulder. The young mother pours lemonade into metal mugs; the father breaks chocolate into pieces and hides them behind his back. The shrieks of the children mix into those of the gulls.

'What a lovely family,' she says.

They walk until the beach begins to narrow and peters out into the German Ocean.

'From here, I always imagine I could paddle home to Denmark.'

'Or walk on water, Mama? Half the world believes you capable of it.'

'At this moment, I would swim there against the strongest current and the wildest wind.'

She pulls the veil down across her face.

'Eddy dear, I know what it's like to lose a love. Like you, I didn't have my love for very long, but unlike you I must pretend that I'm still in possession of it. I've always found this pretence a little trying. Lately I'm finding it almost impossible.'

Now the malaise is clear to him. He had considered the possibility, but dismissed it. After all, his Mama has lived with the others, ignored most of them yet even embraced one or two.

But the new woman is not like the others, that battalion of eager conscripts stretching back into the swamp. The new woman is demanding, dangerous even. She is not some courtesan or silly actress, safely corralled in pastures where Alix will never tread. The new woman is of the best blood and has entree to those places where Alix is used to respect and veneration. The new woman threatens Mama's dignity, the compensation which, apart from her children, has been her sustenance. It is whispered that the new woman is almost a new wife.

Poor Mama. Only since he himself has known the pleasure of women, has Eddy begun to understand what it is that she lacks. She is beautiful and kind and good, but she is not sensual. She has never grown up enough for that. The perfect figure signals no longings. The coldest cunts come from Denmark, said a shipmate on the *Bacchante* before Georgie gave him a bloody nose. Poor Mama.

'So I am going away for a while too, Eddy,' she says.

'When will you return, Mama?'

'I don't know. Of course I will return eventually. People such as us are like dogs on a very long chain. We imagine we are free but then the chain is tugged and we must face the truth.'

Again the gloved hand traces the outline of his cheek.

'Oh Eddy, did I hold you too closely? The chain too short? Right up against my skirts? That's what your Papa believes.'

He does not answer because he has none to give. His mother's hand drops away, hangs limply by her side. For the first time, for just an instant, he can see how she will look when at last she begins to grow old. She gazes up at him then grasps the pommel of her saddle.

'Now let's go and see old Mrs Ashby. We'll smile and bring her comfort, even if we cannot bring it to ourselves. That's what God wishes us to do. That's why we are here.'

As they ride back past the young family, a thought suddenly beams across her face. It is the first glimpse of her familiar self in weeks.

'Shall we get out the tea trays tonight and toboggan down the staircase? We haven't done that in ages. It would be such fun.'

CHAPTER XXII

Summer 1891. Eton and Hammersmith.

When the train from Cardiff stops at Slough, he gets off and takes the little branch line to the south. The first sight of Windsor rising from the plain enchants him as it always has; even now, even tonight when he feels the fall coming. The evening sun softens the great grey walls until they are almost golden, flickering against the windows, turning them into a hundred tiny jewels. It is Camelot, on a return ticket from the Great Western Railway.

He deposits his small suitcase in the left luggage office and walks round the skirts of the castle down towards the bridge. He knows every shop in the street, every tavern, every bump in the pavement. The old man who runs the coffee stall is still there, though even older now. Jem buys a coffee, looks for recognition in the man's face but finds none.

'Hello, Ted,' he says. 'How are you? Remember me?'

'Forgive me, sir. My memory isn't what it was.'

'Jem Stephen,' he says. 'I've bought a thousand coffees from you in days gone by.'

'Ah, yes indeed, sir,' the old man lies. 'Excuse me not knowing you at once.'

'That's all right, Ted. I expect I've changed a bit.'

'We must all change, sir. Nothing and nobody stays the same.'

He stands on the bridge and watches the couples in the rowing boats, the families strolling along the towpath. Swans crowd against the bank where children are throwing bread. How odd, he thinks, that Eddy should have fantasised of having children. Such a notion had never crossed his own mind. Well, perhaps long ago, in his own childhood, when he had taken it for granted that all the normal milestones would come to him as smoothly as to everyone else. But not since then. Oh dear, no.

A little girl in a pretty blue frock stands gazing at a swan which has swum right up to her. They stare as if each is dazzled by the other. It is a beautiful sight. Why then has he not felt the urge to perpetuate himself in this way? He wonders if, somehow, he has always known that his body would never allow him to do such a thing, that it would demand fulfilment in quite a different way. And if he hadn't known it before, he certainly does now. For the hundredth time, he sees the darkened bedroom, the rumpled bed, the kindly dog lying at his feet. He tastes the sick in his mouth.

Anyway, what need does he have of children? He made his vow long ago, on that day he climbed to the very top of St Paul's. To perpetuate himself in Eddy. Eddy who will one day be worshipped by the world. What more could he ask than that? Jem turns and looks up at the walls of Camelot. He looks at the windows of the very rooms which Eddy must know so well, behind which he sometimes lives and moves, eats and sleeps and dreams.

He is missing Eddy. They have seen so little of each other this summer. Eddy has been with his regiment to York and Ireland and Jem now trudges to the south of Wales, where the judge has found him a ghost of a job as a clerk to the assize. It is a small, rainy world of unremarkable people with unremarkable problems. He loathes every moment. It shrivels his spirit.

But still their letters come and go. Even on the darkest days when he is at the bottom of the well, he will pull himself up by the rope, inch by inch, until he reaches the daylight, until he reaches the blank piece of paper on which he must do his work. He will search deep into himself to find those thoughts and feelings that still remain strong and true. He will commit them to the blank paper, blow on the ink until the words are imperishable and send them to Eddy so that they may grow into him and nourish him forever.

It is pleasant standing on the bridge in the evening light, watching the children and the swans and the boats. But it is not the reason that made him get off the train before it reached London. He crosses to the far side of the bridge and walks up the narrow high street towards the place that once he could call his own.

It is far quieter on this side of the river; like the difference between Saturday and Sunday. It is the long vacation after all. The tuck shops, the bookshops and the outfitters are shuttered; half the houses seem asleep. When he reaches the jumble of pink-brown brick, the great school sits in eerie silence. It is hardly the maelstrom of his memory; the running, the shouting; the tailcoats flapping in the breeze. The main gates are shut but he knows ways in. It was his fiefdom after all. He wanders under the arches and round the quads. He goes into the chapel by the side door that is always left unlocked. Only a few people pass him, smile and wish him good evening; those few masters and not a few boys who are marooned here, even in the long vacation, unwanted anywhere else. But nobody stops him.

He wanders up and down staircases, along corridors, into schoolrooms. He sits for a moment at desks where he once sat. He goes into the dining hall, still heavy with the smell of boiled vegetables and burnt fat. Still nobody stops him.

Then he goes outside again and wanders through the lanes and round Fellows' Pond. It is everything he hoped for. Nothing different. The glow coming off the walls in the summer evening, as if they are smiling at him again, pleased to see him. It is like looking at a picture book, of some paradise that could not possibly be real. Another Camelot, in fact. But it is real, he knows that. Perhaps it is he now who isn't. Some sort of ghost, returning to haunt, unable to let go.

He keeps it until the last. He is torn now between yearning to see it and fearing what he might find. But when he goes, it is just the same. The Wall. The moment he lays eyes upon it, he knows he has made a terrible mistake in coming, but it is too late now. He walks the length of it, hearing the noise again, smelling the sweat, feeling the touch of the bodies, seeing the faces of the other ghosts. Jem stands before The Wall. And when his mind has looked at it too long, he covers his eyes and sinks to his knees on the blowsy grass.

'Good evening, sir. Are you all right?'

From a distance, a boy calls out to him. He struggles to his feet, wipes his eyes on his sleeve. He smiles and waves. There is a group of four or five of them, but the boy who called now comes nearer. Damn. He is a big boy, broad and ruddy.

'Did you feel a little faint, sir?'

Jem says that he did for a moment but that he is fine now. The boy looks closer at him.

'Forgive me, sir, but weren't you Big Jem Stephen?'

'No, you've made a mistake.'

'But you were, sir. I'm sure of it. 1876 wasn't it? Keeper of The Wall? I've seen your photograph in our house.'

'No, really, you're mistaken. A resemblance perhaps.'

'Well you're a lot older of course, but it is you, isn't it? Come on, don't be modest, sir. You're a hero here.'

The boy calls to his companions.

'It's Big Jem Stephen. Big Jem. Come and see.'

He has not been called by that name for nearly fifteen years. There is something in the sound of it now which tips him over, which completes the fall that has been rising all week. He grabs the boy by the lapels of his coat, lifts him off his feet and slams him up against The Wall itself. The boy stares at him with saucer eyes, begs to be put down.

'I am not who you say I am!' shouts Jem.

'Whatever you say, sir'.

Jem detects a whiff of mockery in the voice.

'I am not who you say I am!' he shouts once more.

He shakes the boy until his head bangs back against the bricks. Then the others are upon him, pulling him off. Strong as he is, he cannot defeat them. They are young and he is not. They are lean and fit and he is not. And soon he is on the ground, that forbidden place to be in the Wall Game, the position of disgrace. He thrashes and lashes out, but it is no good. Three of them sit on top of him, while the fourth runs to find a policeman.

He is Gulliver, pinned down and impotent. He lies with his face squashed against the lawn. His tears run down the blades of grass and disappear into the earth.

A policeman is found. Jem is hauled to his feet and escorted out through the quad. But then, perhaps for old times' sake, the place takes pity and offers a sliver of comfort. An elderly master appears who remembers him too. The policeman is dismissed, the boys told to pull themselves together and run along. Jem is taken into the master's sitting room, given a brandy and put to bed. The master is still in touch with Harry and a telegram is sent at once. Harry arrives just after breakfast and by afternoon Jem is asleep again in the little house in Hammersmith that looks out over the river.

Harry thinks it right to inform De Vere Gardens. But when a servant arrives in a hansom to escort Mr Stephen home, Harry sends him away with a note to the judge. Jem is not fit to travel any further, he writes; it might be best to keep him here until he is a little better. It is nervous exhaustion, nothing more. But the servant returns within the hour. The judge's own fragile state does not blind him to that of his son and what the world may say about it. He demands that Jem be woken and returned to his family and swallowed up again by the tall lean house where nobody can see him. But Harry will not have it. While the hansom waits, he goes to his writing desk.

'It seems to me that Jem has more than one family. Those of us who call him our friend love him as we would love a brother. Until this crisis passes, he is safe here with me. I will look after him and will not permit him to be removed.'

And then Harry sends another message. To the barracks of the 10th Hussars in York. He does what he has never dreamed of doing before. He sends for Eddy.

In the high bedroom of the little house by the river, Jem lies watching the sun reflect the ripples onto the ceiling. The hours and the days pass, but he has scant awareness of time. His world shrinks to this one small space; four walls hung with Chinese paper and a window curtained in cheery yellow silk. Harry comes with food and drink, coaxing him to swallow like a nurse with a baby, bringing him the good wishes of friends, chatting about this and that, never giving up although he receives no answer.

But Jem isn't really there. He is up on the ceiling. His eyes fix on the blank sheet of white plaster and see all his stories written there.

It was a big ship, bigger than any they had seen before. Well, it needs to be jolly big to take their parents all the way to India, said his older brother. In the sharp east wind, the ship pulled at its mooring ropes like a racehorse in the gate; it cannot wait to be off. Jem hated it on sight.

He could not grasp the idea of this place, India. What did it offer that home cannot? Why on earth must his Papa go there and demand that Mama goes with him? And they had all heard such terrible stories. The dreadful mutiny of the natives, when many God-fearing white women and children were slaughtered and thrown down a well. Women just like his Mama. Children just like him. He was glad he was not going to such an awful country, but would willingly have done so if he might protect Mama from such a fate. For her, he would have fought the evil mutineers until the last drop of blood in his body.

Jem and his two brothers stood in a neat line on the quayside to say farewell. They were dressed in their Sunday best. It was an occasion after all. Nanny stood quietly behind them, ready to take them home on the train to London. Soon, though, dust sheets would shroud the furniture, the shutters would be closed and the house locked up. Nanny would move on to another household, to other children. Jem and his brothers would be sent to various schools. Nanny had told him he must be brave today and not let his parents see that he was upset. He was twelve years old then; tears would be unbecoming in a young gentleman.

His brothers seemed not upset at all. They were mesmerised by the docks on Southampton Water; the soaring cranes that swung the crates of luggage through the air, the funnels belching steam, the sails and the spars. Whatever sadness his brothers may have felt, it was obliterated by the fascinations of boyhood. Jem wondered why he could not be like them.

On the train from London, his father had said nothing whatsoever; there had been no instructions, none of the usual lectures on what they must or must not do. It was as if he had abandoned responsibility, sighed in relief and no longer cared. His mother was near silent too; but quietly smiling if she caught Jem's eye. Nanny sat apart in a corner of the compartment, dabbing her eyes with a handkerchief soaked in lavender water. It was as if they were all going to a funeral.

'But why are you going, Mama?' he had asked her yet again last night.

'It is the duty I owe to your father.'

'But what about us?'

'You will be well cared for. And I will return when I can.'

'I don't understand why Papa comes first. We're still children, aren't we?'

'It is the duty God decrees for a wife,' she said again. He heard a little break in her voice and took some comfort from it, but it was not enough.

In the dockyard, his parents stood in front of him at the edge of the quay. It would be so easy, he'd thought. He was quite a strong boy now. Just one hefty shove. The quay was quite high above the water so, if his father had not drowned, the fall itself and the shock of the icy sea might have done the trick. He was so frightened by the ferocity of the urge he had begun to tremble.

'You're not going to blub as usual, are you?' his brother had sneered.

When the moment came, his mother embraced him.

'I will return,' she whispered again. 'I love you.'

'Come along, Mary,' his father had said. 'No need for all that.' His father had shaken the hands of his other children.

When it was extended to Jem, it had not been taken. His father had stared hard at him, as if trying to identify someone he did not recognise.

'Take Papa's hand, Jem,' his mother had said.

But Jem had not. He sank his eyes into the ground and would not raise them again. He did not raise them when the gangway was pulled up and the ropes, thick as a man's arm, had whiplashed the water. He did not raise them when the quayside erupted with shouting and waving and the music of a brass band. Not even to see the great ship tugged gently out into Southampton Water.

It was only when Nanny had seized his elbow and dragged him away, did he allow himself a glance out to sea. But there was nothing there except emptiness.

Now, in the little room in Hammersmith, Jem turns his face away from the story on the ceiling and buries his face in the pillow. In a minute, Harry will hurry in, murmur comfort and wipe the wetness from Jem's cheeks. He will take Jem's hand and sit there until the evening shadows lengthen over the river and the ceiling fades into the gloom.

CHAPTER XXIII

November 1891. Marlborough House.

'Christ! I feel like death,' says Georgie.

He lies prostrate in his bed, the morning tea untouched. He looks even smaller than usual, in his uniform of pyjamas, unadorned by braid or medals. His face is flushed. His head is hot and hurts like the devil. He has started a cough. He wants to know if Eddy has caught the damn thing too, if he is sharing his pain. Eddy feels ashamed to admit that he is not.

For a day or two, they do not worry and then they do. On the third day, Bertie comes into the room, takes one look and summons the clever doctors. The doctors declare that the old foe has returned, the one who has haunted their family for thirty years and mocks their place in the world with a casual viciousness. The one who carried off Grandpapa and once did near the same to Bertie. The fever. The typhoid.

Alix and the sisters leave the lazy shores of the Black Sea and hurtle back across the frontiers of Europe. Bertie hides in his smoking room, staring out of the window and listening to the hurdy-gurdy man out on the street. Eddy sits with him for a while, tries to comfort him with cheery words. His father hardly looks at him, though once Eddy catches him doing so; a long, unconscious gaze, hard as the walnut that panels the walls. Eventually, he slips away, unnoticed, under cover of smoke.

He goes to the chapel, gets down on his knees before the altar and prays to Him harder than ever before, harder even than for Helene. In return, he offers himself up. Surely it would make more sense if God spared Georgie and took him instead. He gives a long list of Georgie's virtues and his own faults. And just in case God does not in fact know everything, he enumerates his sins at length. He wonders if a thunderbolt will lance along Pall Mall, pierce the stained glass window and strike him down right away, right here at the altar. But outside the windows, he hears only the dull clatter of carriage wheels muffled inside the November fog. In the chapel, silence hangs heavy in the chilly air. He shivers. He has no idea if God is listening.

In case God does not consider him worth taking, he tries another tack. He promises that if Georgie is spared he will do anything to please Him. He will try, really try, to come up to the mark. He will stop being the cause of heartache and anxiety. Above all, without complaint, he will marry this damn girl, since that is what they all want now. He swears all this on his brother's fragile life.

When he makes to stand up, his knees do not support him and he falls on his face below the altar. Maybe God requires his total humiliation. So he tells Him that, whatever his sins and shortcomings, he has always believed in God's mercy and asks for it now. One last gambit.

He wanders out into the gardens. It is scarce a fortnight since he and Georgie last trod these paths together. That day, he sees his brother is nervous. Georgie kicks at neatly raked piles of autumn leaves, creating chaos out of order. Not his way at all.

'It's to be May of Teck,' he says.

Eddy's stomach tightens. So the arrangement has been made. He knew it would be. He was just not expecting it so soon. A bit of a shock.

'Papa asked me to tell you before he left for Waddesdon. He's sure you'll be agreeable.'

'But I hardly know her.'

'You've known her all your life.'

'I've barely spoken a bloody word to her in ten years.' Eddy hears the flutter of panic in his voice. 'Boring, swotty May of Teck? Good grief.'

'As you well know, there's a hell of a shortage at the moment. Besides, little May's grown into quite a big girl. Damn good breasts and no mistake.'

Eddy tries to smile back, to be insouciant, not to care.

'Papa gave Mama a choice,' says Georgie. 'Send you on another endless tour or marry May of Teck quickly. Naturally, Mama chose to keep Mama's boy near her.'

Eddy stops and lights a cigarette. He inhales as deeply as he can. Alix has been gone for nearly two months now. Her letters, the usual torrent of trivia, gave no hint of this. Papa's careless dereliction is no surprise, but Mama's is a fresh wound. Perhaps he is no longer the son to her that he used to be.

'I'll wager it'll be fine,' says Georgie, slapping him on the back. 'And they really are tremendous breasts.'

Eddy goes to his room. He stands by the open window as rain begins to fall. He still feels the need for air, however filthy it might be. A storm must be coming; seagulls swoop and dive round the towers, cackling at him like gossipy women. Like everybody else, did they know before he did? He writes a note to Jem. Just the bare facts of it. He cannot write of his feelings; at the moment, he has none. He is numb. May of Teck. Oh Christ.

Now, in his sickroom, Georgie's latest visitor is delirium. He is still talking about breasts. Fingers clawing at the bedclothes, he tells filthy stories and shouts sailors' profanities that shock the nurses as they hurry away with the evil-smelling green foulness. Grandmama sends telegrams almost by the hour. Bertie still sits lost in smoke. Unknown men with sweating, blackened faces heave coal into the jaws of the train pulling Alix and the sisters home.

Eddy wanders through the rooms, up and down the staircases, in and out of the gardens.

'Hear me!' he screams up into the sky.

*

December 1891. Luton Hoo, Bedfordshire.

'Do you expect good sport?' asks May of Teck.

He blushes because he has been glancing at her breasts again. Georgie was right about the breasts. They are her best feature, bursting forth from her tiny, tightened waist like blooms from a narrow vase.

She is a puzzle. Not quite pretty; not plain either. A good height for a girl, she carries herself like a soldier. Her skin is smooth, her hair a brown so light it teeters into yellow. Her nose comes close to turning upwards, but changes its mind at the last moment. Her gaze is firm, her eyes bright blue. It seems to be his fate that everyone in his life will have blue eyes. What can it mean?

He hopes his blush will be put down to the heat of these opulent rooms, kept at the temperature of a tropical plant house, too hot even for a man who hates the cold.

'I don't know the reputation of the shooting at Luton Hoo,' he replies. 'Will you be following us out for luncheon?'

'One must,' she says, screwing up the blue eyes as if at the idiocy of the question.

'You don't enjoy the shooting?'

'I'd rather stay inside and read. But you will not repeat that. The ladies here would think me most bizarre, if they don't do so already.'

They are sitting together at breakfast, at the distant end of the very long table. The others have seated themselves as far away as possible. They are marooned, shipwrecked in their situation, forced to cling to each other's sentences, however fragile they might be. The most obvious topic of conversation will not be mentioned: the fact that she has just returned from staying with his Grandmama in Scotland, where she has been evaluated with little more subtlety than if she were an Aberdeen Angus. And the fact that she has passed the greatest test of her life, with flying colours they say, and that nothing will ever be the same for her again.

At the opposite end of the table, her parents are pretending not to watch. Fat Mary bustles about, even when she is sitting down. She twists and turns on her precarious chair, chattering to both sides, but her gaze hardly leaves them. When it does, it is to keep watch on Mad Frank, to check that he is calm, not about to explode and throw his bacon and eggs over a servant.

Eddy scarcely knows May of Teck or her odd parents, but he knows all about them; their sad tale as familiar as one of Mr Hans Christian Andersen's, endlessly retold by the women of his family as a terrible warning. A tale of extravagance, financial ruin, even exile but, above all, of once-pure blood tainted forever by the morganatic marriage of Mad Frank's father. This romantic folly has banished his innocent son and daughter-in-law to the furthest borders of the family. Poor May and her three brothers are doomed to carry disappointment in their veins. She has always been a damsel in distress, but it has now been decided that Eddy shall be her knight. Her own story is to be given an ending happier than her wildest imaginings.

This morning May shows few signs of distress. She eats her buttered toast with an almost troubling composure. Eddy suspects she has practised eating it in front of a mirror until she did it perfectly. Yesterday, as the house guests gathered, he noticed how she held herself at a distance. Pulling herself back from the whirlpool of her parents, speaking only when spoken to. But she is speaking to him now, those blue eyes locked onto his.

'Does shooting never bore you? All that noise, the blood, the foul weather, the same thing all the time. Don't you ache for something new?'

He has never been asked this before, not even by himself. He will not reply that from the time he was big enough to hold a gun, he has made himself into a passable sportsman mostly to please Papa, to win the entree to his manly world. Anyway, before he can reply, May answers her own question.

'Oh well, I'm sure your father expects it of you.'

She kisses her napkin, removing invisible crumbs of toast. Under her gaze, he suddenly feels quite naked. He wonders if he is just a little frightened of her.

'We all have a duty to try to please our parents,' he hears himself say, blushing again at the spectacular irony.

'Indeed we do,' she says, 'and we must always strive to fulfil it. At times it's a little irksome though, isn't it?'

A trickle of sweat runs down inside his tweed jacket. He has galloped here to Luton Hoo on his white charger, pretending that it is a house party like any other. He has armoured himself to do what he must do. They have assured him that the damsel is more than willing to be rescued, but maybe she is not after all.

'Irksome, yes,' he replies. 'Don't you ever want to run away from it?'

'We must honour our father and our mother, even if they're not always as we might wish them to be.'

A wave of cackling breaks along the table. Fat Mary seems to be expanding with excitement, almost by the hour. May's mouth tightens. She looks down into her tea cup.

'If we don't, then the edifice begins to crumble and that is unthinkable, don't you agree?' she says. 'We must set an example in everything or people like us would have no purpose. None. And then what should we do?'

The tiniest tremor quivers on her bottom lip. It makes him suddenly bold. He tells her about the long-ago dream of riding his pony up and away into the clouds. He has never told anyone before and he is telling this odd, stiff girl.

'There are other ways of escaping, you know. For me, it's music and pictures and books. Mostly books.'

'That's what my old friend Jem recommends.'

'And do you take old Jem's advice?'

'I tried to, but it never quite worked.'

May of Teck's blue eyes are curious now.

A long pause. 'I could help you if you like.'

He asks what she is reading at the moment, hoping that he might be able to make a sensible response. But it is a book about Italian art, so he is lost.

'I like to pretend I am inside the pictures,' she says, 'walking across a cornfield in Tuscany in the sunlight or going inside the little churches and castles perched on the hillsides. Escaping, you see. Would you like to look at it?'

He tells her he would. But breakfast is over now. The guns are restless, hungry for the bite of winter air. Fat Mary waddles away from the table, her chubby fist clamped to Mad Frank's elbow, steering him to some place of greater safety. May and Eddy part at the foot of the staircase.

'Would you do something to please me?' he asks. 'You can either drag yourself out across the muddy fields to lunch with the shooters or you can say you have a headache and must stay in your room.'

'But why?'

'So you can walk across the fields of Tuscany instead.'

'You would wish me to tell a lie?' she asks.

'Yes. I would miss your company at luncheon but I would like to picture you in the sunshine.'

May of Teck laughs out loud. He has never heard her laugh before. It is a hearty, vulgar laugh, almost masculine, but she quashes it quickly and glides up the staircase in the wake of her mother's great arse.

He is pleased with himself. He feels he has been suitably poetic, romantic even. And then he realises that he meant it.

In the evening there is to be a ball. The neighbours and the county people will come. He begs his hostess's pardon and tells her that he will dine but will not dance tonight. He is a little tired. She does not enquire further; she does not need to. Her boudoir is at his disposal should he wish to rest during the evening. He will not be disturbed by anyone, she says.

He arranges for May to be brought from the ballroom at an appointed time. Half an hour before, he goes to the boudoir in order to calm himself. He hacks a route through the potted palms to reach the oasis of a little sofa. Like the rest of this bloody house, the room is sweltering; his high collar a noose round his neck.

It is a terrible dance we must dance, he thinks. Who is May of Teck? What is she? He has not felt her head resting on his shoulder, seen love for him in her blue eyes or tears for him on her cheeks. He has never matched his breathing with hers and melted away into her. But he must quash these thoughts now; there is a job to be done. Other thoughts are less easily suppressed. What does she know of him? How much has been kept from her? If she knew, would she care? He is sure that Fat Mary would not, that she would subscribe to his own Mama's belief in marriage as a cure for every fault of character. Anyway, to Fat Mary and Mad Frank, he is the knight on the white charger coming to the rescue of them all.

There are quiet voices outside the boudoir now. He feels a little sick. He runs a finger round the inside of his collar. The door opens and May pretends to be surprised to find him here.

When she squeezes in beside him on the little sofa, he senses the warmth of her, smells the light sweat drifting off her skin after the polkas. Her fringe of poodle curls is damp, the great breasts rise and fall. He tries not to look at them.

She asks about his day. He says that he shot poorly because his mind was on other matters. He hopes that this gallantry does not go unnoticed. He enquires about her own day; she did not come to luncheon with the guns after all. She smiles.

'I spent it walking in Tuscany.'

'Did that make you happy?'

'Intensely.'

He reaches out and takes her hand. Their two sticky palms glue together. May's breasts rise and fall even faster. When his voice comes out, he chokes and stumbles on the words.

'Do you think it might also make you happy to walk alongside me? To be my wife?'

May of Teck smiles again and says that it would.

So, he has done it. Eddy has done something right. As he climbs into bed, he looks again at the telegram that came this morning. It tells him that God has granted his prayer, that his darling Georgie's slight improvement was not a false dawn and that he is finally and indisputably saved. Death will not yet part Sprat and Herring. And now he has honoured his bargain.

CHAPTER XXIV

December 1891. Windsor.

He can hardly breathe. There is little enough air in the railway carriage and Fat Mary swallows most of it as she gabbles without end, fanning herself against the hot compartment. Her vast body is corrugated with waves of flesh, her chins wobbling in time with the motion of the train. Her sickly scent does not entirely mask the sweat that stains the silk of her mutton-chop sleeves. When she crashes down on the overstuffed cushions, a tiny cloud rises from the dusty velvet.

May sits, as usual, in her shadow. She says nothing at all, as there would be precious little point. She gazes out of the window as suburbia melts away into barren fields. Eddy sits opposite her; they watch each other's reflections in the glass of the window. He thinks he sees her send him a slight, secret smile; the way that lovers might. It occurs to him that this is what they are now. Just as it was with Helene, though of course this is quite a different thing. How odd. He steals another glance at her body. The travelling clothes do not entirely

Alan Robert Clark

conceal it. He pictures how she will look without them, on her back, the smell of her in his nostrils.

He feels guilty at such thoughts with her father sitting beside him. Poor Mad Frank. Usually he is pale as a ghost, his face drained of his tainted blood. But today there is some colour in his cheeks, as if his beloved daughter's change of fortune has given him the confidence to let it show.

Fat Mary rattles on about arrangements for the wedding. It is to be in late February, just over two months away. Grandmama does not believe in long engagements.

'All the crocuses and daffodils will be coming out,' she says. 'Your wedding will mark the end of winter, the beginning of spring.'

Fat Mary sighs and says it again.

'The beginning of spring.'

At Luton Hoo, when he and May returned from the boudoir to the ballroom, every head turns to them. A waltz is played and he takes her onto the floor. But the waltz is never finished. There is a sudden kerfuffle in a corner. Fat Mary has swooned with pleasure and is lying flat out on the parquet, a great whale in grey satin. Later, he is told by one of her friends that May dances again that night. Round and round her bedroom, whirling with joy, showing off the pretty ankles of which, they say, she is inordinately proud. Such abandon has never been known before.

Now his fiancée leans closer to the window, her palms spread across the glass, her eyes shining.

'I can see it from here,' she says. 'In this light, it looks like Camelot.'

294

Fat Mary does not trouble to look at the view. She gives one more contented sigh, leans back and closes her eyes. She is silent for three whole blessed minutes. Mad Frank's bony fingers drum nervously on his knees.

In the momentary peace, Eddy puts his hand in his pocket to check it is still there; the telegram that arrived this morning from Reverend Dalton. He wonders if, by touching it, he can somehow get closer.

'Jem Stephen in a very bad way. Taken forcibly into hospital. Will explain more when I see you.'

At the station, Fat Mary alights with balletic grace. She is surprisingly light on her feet. If it were dignified to do so, she might run all the way up the hill to reach Grandmama's presence. But Dalton is here to meet them. Fat Mary is pleased that the Canon of Windsor has come to acknowledge her improved status in the eyes of the world. Perhaps she thinks it improved in the eyes of God too. She has arrived at this platform many times before, but not like this. Never like this.

'Jem?' Eddy murmurs as he shakes Dalton's hand.

'We will speak at the first opportunity.'

In the carriage going up the hill, Fat Mary's sweat is even worse as she waves at the crowded pavements. He suddenly thinks he might pass out.

'Are you all right?' May of Teck asks softly. 'It is so stuffy in here.'

'I just need some air,' he lies.

They are sitting side by side now and she lays her hand on top of his on the seat. It feels odd to him because it is still the hand of a stranger. He thinks of those other strangers for whose hands he has reached in his life so far. At first, they had always seemed so strong and sure. But they were never to remain in his for long. Somehow, in time, they were always snatched back. He wonders how strong May's hand will be and for how long he will be able to retain it before, perhaps, she draws it away.

But one hand has stayed loyal, is always outstretched to him. He reaches into his pocket again and clings to the telegram.

*

November 1891. Cambridge.

'Good Lord, Mr Stephen. What is it you think you're doing?'

The window is wide open. Through it, he hurls things down into Trinity Street. He does not look to see what he is throwing. It does not matter. Anything he can lay his hands on. Folders of lecture notes. Copies of his new book of poems. Cushions. An eiderdown. A tablecloth. A lamp. His shoes. His socks. Out in the narrow street, a small crowd begins to gather, unsure whether to be amused or alarmed.

His landlady is a stout woman, round as a Bath bun. She has been kind to him while he has been renting these rooms. In recent weeks when he has not been going out, hardly eating even, she has kept a close eye on him. She has brought him soup and bread and sat patiently, coaxing him to take a little. She is a down-to-earth woman, of good farming stock, and now she is not greatly shocked by the sight of a large naked man as he propels some of her goods and chattels out onto the public highway.

'Come away from that window at once. You'll catch your death.'

'No!' he shouts. 'I am not finished yet.'

He feels the freezing air on his skin but he sweats like a pig. He is shaking from head to toe but all he wants is to rid himself of things. Stupid, pointless things. The things by which the world sets store, by which it values a man. His poetry, his academic work, his clothes even. In the end, what good have all these trappings been? What power did they have to prevent the state in which he finds himself? When he thinks, without a shadow of a doubt, that his mind is going to explode.

And he has been so happy this term, so excited by his change of fortune that he begins to believe himself saved. Coming back to Cambridge is the best thing he could have done. It was Harry and O.B. who nurtured it and made it possible. Dearest Harry. What a friend he is, nursing him with such care in the summer when he was unwell. It is Harry who tells the judge in no uncertain terms that the legal life is not for his son. Gentle Harry even bangs his fist on the table. For once, Jem's mother makes a stand too. For once, the judge listens.

O.B. arranges that Jem will return to the college, give some lectures, do some coaching. And when he does, it is as if a wand is waved. Again he strides along the Backs and through the lanes. His students are grateful to be in such a place with such a man. In the Union chamber, his arguments demolish the enemy as if he is scarcely trying. His laugh fills the public houses and O.B.'s Sunday evenings, where fresh undergraduates sit at his feet and fall in love with him. He even gathers his new poems together and publishes them to general approval. Jem Stephen flies again.

And Eddy? Back in the summer, dear Eddy was so good to him too. Leaving his regiment in York, visiting the house in Hammersmith whenever he could get away. Sitting with him and talking about the old times. Those two old chintz-covered armchairs. The night when Jem twisted his ankle in the snow and Eddy had to carry him home and they both bayed at the moon. Eddy and Harry do not give up. They carry him again until he finds his feet once more.

But then, his season changes. The Cambridge nights draw in. His golden autumn fades and the approach of winter bears down on him as it does every year. The loss of the light, the chill that enters the bones, the decay in the air. As each day gets darker, so does he. After a while, he finds that he cannot even picture the spring. In his lodgings in Trinity Street, he takes to his bed again.

'Come along, Mr Stephen,' says the landlady now. 'Be a good boy and put this on.'

He is still shaking, but her presence quietens him a little and he lets her push his arms into his old dressing gown and wrap it round him. She closes the window, leads him to the couch and makes him sit. She sits too and rubs the backs of his hands with hers. He notices how pale her face is, so different from its usual bustling pink. He wonders if she is a ghost too, dislocated and lost. She tells him to stay put while she makes a little broth to warm him up. She will only be a few minutes.

When she has gone, he stares at himself in the mirror. He cannot see himself. His face does not look right. It is not quite him; his features seem somehow disarranged, just like the room. Where is he? He gazes into it for a long moment, then tears it off the wall and sends it crashing through the window. Screams come from the street. A frightened horse whinnies. A policeman's whistle sounds.

The landlady returns, but instead of broth she brings the policeman and the doctor who lives along the street. Together they calm and comfort him. The shaking eases away. They get him into his bed. When the broth finally comes, he sees the doctor slip something into it, but he does not protest. And he wants to please her, so he drinks a little. And then he sinks into sleep.

When he wakes, two young men are there. Are they his brothers? He thinks they might be. They look down on him with strained faces, as if they are seeing something they never thought to encounter. One of the young men asks him to get up.

'Jem, we're all going off to a lovely place in the country.'

'You can have a good rest there,' says the other. 'Get you back on top form in no time.'

Now he notices, in the doorway, two other men. They do not smile or introduce themselves, which he thinks strange and rather discourteous. And it is already dark outside. The curtains are drawn. It is an odd time of day for travel. But he does not object. Let whatever happens, happen. He is quite empty. He has nothing left to give.

He allows them to put his clothes on. The landlady ties his big woolly scarf round his neck.

'Oh, Mr Stephen,' she says, as they take him out through the door. 'God bless and keep you.'

When they have all gone, she tries to tidy up a little. The cushions go back on the couch, the tablecloth onto the table. The lamp and the mirror are smashed to pieces, but no matter.

On the chimney piece there is a letter. It lies there open and she sees the crest at the top of the page. She need only nudge it with her duster to be able to read it.

'You will probably hear soon that I am to be engaged. It is forced upon me, but it might as well be this one as any other. As you know, after Helene, I no longer really care. I shall try not to dwell on my other dreams either. You will know what I mean by that. I expect it will be tricky for us to meet, at least for a while. But you are always in my thoughts. Oh well, this is it. Here I go...'

With her duster, the landlady brushes the letter from the mantel. With her foot, she kicks it into the flames of the fire.

*

December 1891. Windsor.

The child runs out and wraps himself round Eddy's legs. He is a cheerful little thing. Eddy is his godfather and his name-sake. On every visit, he brings him a few more toy soldiers. Together they are assembling the field of Waterloo on the nursery floor.

Today Little Eddy reminds him that it is almost Christmas and that one particular regiment is still undermanned. Reverend Dalton scolds his impertinence but the child is unabashed. This child does not hang back; he pushes himself forward. Eddy sees it and rejoices. He prays that Dalton will not boom his son into submission. He scoops him up into his arms and rubs their noses together. Little Eddy shrieks. They are at ease with one another.

Tea has been laid out in Dalton's small house behind the chapel. His wife is a sweet girl, young enough to be his daughter, eager to please. She is the spitting image of her pretty brother, Dalton's pet midshipman on the voyage of the *Bacchante*. For the umpteenth time, Eddy wonders why she married such a man. Dalton is neither handsome nor rich, though his position gives him status in the eyes of the world. Perhaps her spinster days were boring, but her days with Dalton can hardly be much less so. She and May of Teck sit upon the sofa and talk about weddings. Dalton's young wife is nervous, May is being gracious in the way she has been schooled to be.

Little Eddy badgers his godfather to come outside to watch him spin his hoop along the path. Dalton comes too. He pulls the house door firmly shut behind him.

'Well?' Eddy asks at once.

This is the first chance they have had to speak together in private.

'It is very grave,' he replies. 'The doctors took him to the nearest suitable place.'

'But his letters recently seemed quite rational, not at all...'

'Mad?'

'Is that the word we must use?' asks Eddy. 'Oh God. Why was I not told?'

'The family told no one. They spirited him away into that place. The shame of it, you see. It took Harry and O.B. two weeks to find out where he was.'

'What do the doctors say?'

'It's five years now since he took that awful bang to the head,' says Dalton, 'but Harry writes that they can't be certain the windmill is the culprit. It seems Mr Justice Stephen himself now displays the most erratic behaviour, so it may be some curse on the family. But whatever the cause, poor Jem's symptoms have never been worse.'

'In what way?'

Dalton pauses.

'Among other dreadful things, he urinates in his bed. *Sic transit gloria mundi.*'

Eddy feels a pulse of anger. He wants to believe he is mistaken in detecting satisfaction in Dalton's voice. It is not possible for him to hate Dalton. Perhaps he was a poor teacher, but Eddy knows his heart is good. Today, though, as the child rolls the hoop round their legs, he thinks he is finally seeing Dalton for what he always was. A little man hiding behind a booming voice. A pygmy in Jem Stephen's giant shadow.

'What can we do?' he asks. 'Should I write to him? Go and see him?'

'It might excite him. They don't want that.'

'So I do nothing? I just leave him there?'

'You pray for him.'

Since Eddy and God fulfilled their bargain to each other, he has not liked to ask for more, but he will try.

Eddy throws and catches a ball for the child. Now Dalton repeats the congratulations with which he'd welcomed them. How happy they must be. Eddy says that he is sure that happiness will come of it.

'You've done the right thing,' says Dalton. 'I'm so pleased.'

Dalton clears his throat. He tugs at the rim of his dog-collar.

Eddy has known the gesture all his life; a lecture is coming.

'I've been most worried about you for some years now. Since we finally went our separate ways.'

As Eddy keeps throwing the ball, Dalton says that he has heard things that disturbed him, things that he could not reconcile with a boy brought up to walk in the light of God.

Eddy says nothing, turns away.

'Do not imagine I knew nothing of the ways of the ship,' says Dalton softly. 'Do not imagine I was such a fool.'

This time Dalton is the one to catch the ball. He throws it as hard and as far as he can, sending the child scuttling into the distance. He seizes Eddy's elbow, pulls him round.

'This is what life must be,' he says.

Dalton's glance takes in the small house in its tidy winter garden, his child playing, his young wife and May waving out at them through the mullioned window. Dalton smiles and waves back.

'This is where real joy lies.'

'But what of those who cannot achieve that?' asks Eddy. 'For whom it means nothing.'

'There can be only loneliness, pain and sorrow.'

'They will piss in the bed? They will go mad?' Eddy thrusts the words at him.

'Do you see those two young women at the window? Both so quiet and shy?' asks Dalton. 'In truth, they are both built of iron, like our dear old ship. If we cling to them, we will be safe. If we lose our grip, even once, we will be lost.'

The child, wanting attention, becomes obstreperous. His father reaches out and grabs him, pinning down his arms and trapping him tightly. Now Dalton speaks in a voice that Eddy has never heard before. The boom is quite gone; it is another man entirely.

'This is what life must be,' he says again. 'For us.'

The teacher and the pupil stand together in the little wintry garden. After twenty years, it is their first honest moment.

As the child wriggles in his father's arms, defiant, straining to be free, Eddy feels the same emotion roar up inside him. He puts two fingers to his lips then presses them against Dalton's mouth.

Dalton's eyes fill with terror. He looks round frantically but the window of the house is empty now. He hustles Little Eddy back inside. The child kicks and cries against him, reaching out with pleading arms.

CHAPTER XXV

December 1891. Windsor.

'Have you got a cigarette?' she asks.

He is amazed. He would not have imagined May of Teck to be tainted by any sin. She seizes it like a shipwrecked sailor to a piece of flotsam.

'Thank God. I've been dying for one since we got here. Mama does not approve.'

He finds her in the Library, a place few people ever go. She is huddled on a stool by the hearth, a woolly shawl round her shoulders. Since Grandmama cannot abide the smell of burning coal, the fire is made of beech logs; a poor, wan, tease of a thing. They smoke together over the flames.

'Mmmm,' she says. 'Turkish? Nice.'

He notices how she smokes. It is not like his silly sisters, waving the damn things in the air like fairy wands. May smokes, as she laughs, almost like a man.

The weather has been vile for three long days. Rain has pounded the ground. Frozen cattle huddle under barren trees.

The puny December daylight is hardly worthy of the name. Grandmama's proud house squats under a canopy of grubby grey.

'It glowers round the towers,' says Mad Frank at breakfast. 'It glowers. Round the towers. For hours and hours.'

'Yes, dear. Thank you,' replies Fat Mary.

Inside it is scarcely more cheerful. Grandmama is not fond of gaslight, so the rooms are lit by candles, many of which soon expire from blasts through half-open windows. Even Fat Mary, blessedly padded by nature, can be seen to shiver.

'I came in search of you,' he says now to May. 'Are you hiding from me?'

'I'm hiding from everyone. I haven't singled you out.'

'You like to hide away?'

'Oh yes,' she says. 'Don't you?'

'I have a place to smoke at home in Norfolk. Up on the leads, among the chimney pots. I like the silence there.'

'You do?' she says, peering at him with those eyes of hers. 'Oh, so do I. Silence heals almost everything.'

She throws her stub into the flames and demands another at once. They smoke together without speaking, breathing in each other's presence, thinking how it feels.

'You've seemed a bit out of sorts since we got here,' May says at last. 'Have I upset you in any way?'

Of course not, he tells her, but a close friend is very ill. His old tutor.

'Jem? The one who failed to turn you into a book lover?'

'He said he wanted to show me other worlds, but I only saw things I can never have. All these characters who had choices. Everything is laid out for me.'

'And now I am laid out too?' says May.

They catch each other's eyes, then bury their embarrassment in the firelight.

'I will try to make you a good wife, Eddy,' she says. 'To be suitable for you.'

They both blush. He can only smile and nod. May rises from her stool, rubbing her shoulders against the cold. She looks up at the crusty battalions of books.

'Even if we can never really enter into those stories, maybe we can steal little bits from them, like squirrels, and use them to nourish us,' she says. 'That's what I try to do.'

'We're not like bloody squirrels,' he replies. 'We're like cripples stuck in wheelchairs. Immobilised. Only ever looking on.'

The words crackle out of him. May stares.

'Goodness, you're not stupid at all, are you?'

Her hand flies to her mouth, shocked by what has come out of it. Then a change comes over her. May of Teck stops being reserved or in anyone's shadow. Now she is as fierce as Helene ever was.

'How can you compare yourself with a cripple? When the time comes, you will have the power to do great things. It's a sacred task you are chosen to do.'

'But I'm not up to it,' he replies. 'When they told you I was stupid, didn't they say that too?'

The fury on her face is mixed with puzzlement. She glares at him for a moment, then pulls him to his feet and half-drags him from the Library.

'May, what are you doing?' he bleats. 'Where are you taking me? Stop!'

'Come!' she says.

She does not loosen her grip as they cross arctic galleries and shuttered rooms until they reach the chamber that houses Grandmama's great ivory chair. Eddy stops outside the door, digs his heels in like a fractious dog.

'I don't want to go in there,' he says.

'No, Eddy, you *shall* come.'

She throws open one of the shutters, steers him towards the chair, pushes him hard down onto the green velvet cushions. Then May of Teck, the woolly shawl round her shoulders, falls into a deep curtsey before Albert Victor, Duke of Clarence. She bows her head and does not rise.

'I know that I'm not the person you wanted, that I am a second choice, perhaps even a fourth or fifth, but I will dedicate myself to you and support you in everything. I will stand by your side and never leave you.'

She lifts her face for a reply but he does not know how to answer. Her anger has vanished and something else is there. It is a sort of pleading. It enters his mind that she might be lonely.

Behind her, in the doorway, Grandmama has materialised, in that way of hers. The two mute, bony women are in attendance, even bonier now with the passing of the years. May and Eddy leap to their feet. He stammers an apology, plumping up the cushions on the ivory chair.

'Sit down again, Eddy,' says Grandmama.

'But it is not fitting in your presence.'

'You will indulge me. Sit down.' The voice that comes from the little round body fills the room.

Eddy sits. He can hear his heart banging.

'We have seen this tableau before, have we not?' says

Grandmama. 'A very long time ago. Now let us view it a little differently. May, dear, take your place beside the chair.'

May walks onto the dais. She puts her hand lightly on his shoulder. He can feel her breath on his cheek. He glances up at her. The woolly shawl has been thrown aside, the back is ramrod straight, the eyes are on fire.

'I will stand by your side,' she whispers. 'I will never leave you.'

Grandmama says nothing, she merely absorbs them, the dumpling face unmarked by expression. He aches to flee the room, but the hand on his shoulder tightens into a vice. The rain drums against the unshuttered window.

'I came in search of you,' says Grandmama at last. 'Come, he is waiting for you.'

A carriage has been ordered. When they reach the special place, she stands before the lump of grey stone, gazing on the white figure that lies on top.

'He gives you his blessing,' she says.

She pulls their hands together then kisses their intertwined fingers. What further ceremony will now be necessary? What humble Archbishop could compete with this?

'May, we are entrusting you with more than our grandson,' she says. 'You realise that, don't you?'

May solemnly declares that she does and sinks into another of her spectacular curtseys. When Grandmama raises her up, May's eyes are full of tears.

Grandmama makes her own curtsey to the great stone.

'Before he found me, I was nothing,' she says. 'Just an ignorant girl. But he took me and made something of me. With the right heart beating beside yours, all is possible.'

Grandmama strokes the wings of one of the angels that surround the stone. She tells May of the day that dear Eddy climbed onto it, desperate to bring his Grandpapa home.

'It was then I knew that he had a good and loving soul,' she says. 'And I've never doubted it for one moment since.'

A trace of a smile lifts the sagging face. And now it strikes him. For so long he has searched people's faces for what they might know of him, but it had never occurred to him to search his Grandmama's. Surely, such things could never have reached her. Mountains would have been moved to prevent it. But now, as he looks into her smile, he is certain of it. There is nothing Grandmama does not know. And Grandmama forgives.

'Not for one single moment,' she repeats. Then the hooded eyes widen with a sudden notion. 'Will you do it again for me now?'

He no longer needs an angel to bear him up. On tiptoe, he manages to bring his face close enough to kiss the marble lips. As he pulls back, the face changes for an instant and becomes his own. He sees himself like this one day; handsome, perfect, wrapped in folds of marble, frozen in time. Might he ever be venerated? Mourned for? The idea seems absurd.

As they turn towards the door, Grandmama looks back. 'Oh how I yearn for this place,' she says. 'Please, God, it may not be long until I lie beside him again.'

In the carriage, the old woman leans against his shoulder and drifts into a doze.

'She is not what she was,' May says later, when they steal out to the soggy garden for another cigarette. 'And your father is eating himself to an early grave. We must make you ready. There may not be much time.'

Her words chill him as much as the touch of his grandfather's lips.

*

December 1891. Marlborough House.

The three white feathers shiver in the breeze. Above Pall Mall, Bertie's standard flies even in the roughest of weather and no year has been rougher than this. But, as Christmas comes, another flag flies too. The flag of truce. For now, all wars are suspended, the combatants rest and replenish their spirits.

As Bertie and Alix prayed beside Georgie's bedside, their own recovery progressed in tandem with his. Bertie's other troubles are grown less feverish too; the newspapers and the penny dreadfuls, the politicians and churchmen who revile him seem filled with seasonal forgiveness. The new woman still breathes but, for a time at least, she is banished from their minds. And, to top it all, dear Eddy has done something right at last.

Today there is a small gathering for luncheon. It is Alix's idea. Just the four parents and the engaged couple.

'We thank thee, dear Lord, for the great joy which Thou hast bestowed on both our families,' chants Mama, as she says grace.

'Amen, Amen,' echoes Fat Mary.

She begins to sniffle and Alix follows suit. Bertie's eyebrows ascend to heaven as he sticks a handkerchief under Fat Mary's chins. He cannot abide her, which is strange because, as they sit side by side devouring the food, Eddy thinks how similar they are. Not just in bulk, but in the way everyone else is required to shrivel in their presence.

The dining room is as noisy as usual. Fat Mary prattles, the dogs bark for titbits and everyone must talk loudly for poor Mama. Mad Frank says almost nothing until he finds a blond hair in his soup. He holds it up to the light, inspects the heads of the servants who wait along the wall until he spots a fair-headed man.

'Yours, perhaps?' he asks.

'Hush dear,' says Fat Mary.

Poor May. He catches her eye and then he sees it. How strange it should happen over a bowl of mulligatawny. How astonishing that it should come from shy May of Teck, the arranged girl. He is not sure if she even cares for him yet; he certainly does not fool himself that she loves him. But, in one glance, as her dotty father fusses over a hair in his soup, Eddy's life shifts and tilts, like the great plates that lie beneath the oceans. And a glance caught by pure luck. How easy it would have been to have missed it; not to have looked up at that moment. But God did not allow that to happen. He thinks how kind to him God has suddenly become. God gives him the sign in May's eyes, the spectacular discovery, telescoped down into two tiny irises, that she may be the one who needs him.

Afterwards, they walk over to St James's, to the rooms Grandmama has given them as their first home. It is a gloomy billet; the chambers are grand and bloodless, but Eddy and May are undaunted. They will fill them with new emotions;

brighter, warmer, younger feelings. Above all, within these walls they will defer to nobody. How very odd that is going to feel. May shows him samples of the wallpaper and the fabrics she has selected with a man from Maples. He agrees to it all. 'You are mistress here,' he says. She smiles like a summer afternoon.

There is no proper garden, just an echoing, neglected courtyard, but May trumpets the ideas she has for it. Little cherry trees, plants in big pots, window boxes, hanging baskets of trailing flowers, trellises of jasmine and clematis, garden chairs and tables, bright summer umbrellas, an aviary even.

'And a safe place for children to play,' he says, the words tumbling out of him. 'I hope we will have many. You'll be a good mother, May.'

She slides her arm through his and squeezes it, but does not answer. She goes to the centre of the courtyard and does a little dancing twirl. At last, he is allowed to glimpse those pretty ankles.

'Oh, Eddy, it's not perfect, but we'll make the best of it.'

'Of course we will.'

He looks round the barren courtyard. It is far from the garden of his imagination. The garden behind the high wall that keeps everyone out. Where the children sail their boats on the duck pond. Where he sits on the veranda, a little stout, a little old, with a glass of iced lemonade and another wicker chair pulled close up beside him. That garden can never be visited again, perhaps not even in dreams. This meagre place can never compare with it, but it has possibilities.

CHAPTER XXVI

December 1891. Marlborough House.

'Go if you must, but go discreetly,' Bertie says. 'May's father is eccentric enough, but a connection with a full-blown lunatic confined to an asylum is something else entirely.'

'You once told me to model myself on Jem Stephen,' he replies. 'The perfect young Englishman, you said.'

'Indeed I did and I'm truly sorry for his tragedy,' says Bertie. 'But we've had enough trouble for one year. For God's sake, let's get through what's left of it unscathed.'

'Papa, as Jem's friend, I shall walk in there with my head held high. I'm not ashamed of him in his sickness.'

Bertie studies him from behind his cigar, then looks through the frost-encrusted window onto the clattering street. The damn hurdy-gurdy man is there again, churning out Christmas carols.

'No, my boy,' he replies. 'Of course you aren't.'

Since the great slamming of the door, father and son are not the same. On that night, Eddy vowed that his father was no longer deserving of his tears and that there would be no more. He vowed that he would not go his Mama's way and pass his life mourning the fact that Bertie did not love him as he wished him to. And oddly, the chaffing has stopped now. Instead, there are smiles, feeble jokes. In the weeks since the engagement to May, his father is even paying him some attention.

But what a shame, Eddy thinks, that when the thing he has craved for so long finally comes to him, he should care so much less for it. He will never lose the scars of those thousand little cuts, but they are scabbing over now. He feels it happening. But might his heart be scabbing over too? It harbours a harshness towards his father that was not there before. He feels it now, in this moment.

'Besides, Papa, I believe you too have a friend condemned to such a place. Have you forgotten her? Are you ashamed of *her*?'

From the height of a child, Eddy sees again the breakfast table. Papa and Mama eat without a word, then Mama rises and hurries away. Newspapers no longer lie carelessly on chairs, but are hidden away. Men in dark suits, faces funeral grim, arrive and vanish into Papa's study. One night at the theatre, their Mama is cheered, while Papa is booed and hissed at by a thousand snakes. Over the years, the truth of it is dripped into the consciousness of Bertie's children as they grow up. Poor Harriet. Silly Harriet. A respectable, married woman who let herself behave most unwisely. She can only be mad, her family said; there can be no other explanation for her disgrace and our own. We must lock her safely away, out of all our sights. And so they did. And there she still lingers. And his Papa raised not a finger to help her. Out of all their sights.

The hurdy-gurdy still plays down in the street. Bertie turns back from the window and faces his son.

'In that connection,' he says, 'the shame is entirely mine.'

Bertie throws the stub of his cigar into the fire.

'Go to your friend,' he says. 'He means a great deal to you, I believe.'

'More than I can say, Papa.'

Bertie nods, pats him on the shoulder and shuffles from the room. How very singular, thinks Eddy. It has always been the other way round. For the first time in his life, he has dismissed his father.

*

December 1891. Northamptonshire.

The place is surprisingly pleasant, not at all the hellish Bedlam of nightmares. The gardens are handsome, even in midwinter. In the lobby a fire burns brightly. A tabby cat rubs herself against the nervous legs of those who dare to visit. It is peaceful too, silent as a church; no sound comes from the troubled souls absorbed by its walls.

'Today is a good day, sir,' says the doctor, a fat cheery man. 'It'll pep him up no end to see you. A real Christmas treat.'

Jem's room is large and comfortable with a view over the countryside. A fire blazes here too, though there is a chill it cannot quite defeat. He sits in a big chair, gazing into the flames. His cream shirt is open at the neck; a book lies on his knees though he is not reading it. To the untrained eye, he looks quite well. At first, he does not trouble to turn round at the unlocking of the door. Then he does.

'Eddy,' he says at last. A sort of grin cracks open the big broad face. 'Dear old Eddy.'

They clap each other on the back as they have always done, as if they were in Jem's old room at Trinity or on the bench above the ice rink. But there is a strangeness to this encounter; how could there not be? Like Stanley and Livingstone in the jungle, the awkwardness of finding an old friend in a country far distant from the one they have known together, a country they had never dreamed that either might ever visit.

Jem insists that Eddy take the chair and pulls up a stool for himself. Jem thinks of the two old armchairs, covered in chintz and ash; the bedroom door slightly ajar, the piles of books on the floor and, through the open window, the shouts and laughter from the quad. How often he thinks of that now.

'The doctor tells me you're doing jolly well,' says Eddy, 'and that you might be back in Cambridge quite soon.'

'I'm fine, really,' says Jem. 'I don't know why I'm here at all.'

Otherwise, they do not speak of the place in which they sit or how Jem came to be here. Tea is brought, and cake, but Jem touches nothing. They talk of this and that, of O.B. and Harry, of the comings and goings at Trinity and Kings, of Jem's recent book of poems.

Jem says that he is sorry not to have sent congratulations on the engagement. He is pleased that Eddy has found someone to share the load he must carry. But his face is blank as he speaks the words.

'The girl. May of Teck. What's she like?'

'She has your strength Jem.'

'Good. You won't need me anymore then,' replies Jem. 'Anyway, I don't think I have any more strength to give.'

'Nonsense,' says Eddy. 'We must get you well so you can come to my wedding.'

It is a kindly lie. Jem's presence would never now be possible. When the time approaches, an excuse will be found.

'To sit and watch you marry?' he replies. 'That would be a strange thing indeed.'

'Perhaps. But you once told me that was the way forward. For both of us.'

'It turned out that way was blocked for me,' says Jem, 'but no doubt you know of that already.'

Jem looks hard at Eddy. They have never spoken of Jem's visit to the little villa in St John's Wood and now they never will. Jem moves his glance back into the fire.

'And after the wedding?' he asks. 'What then? Will you go on as before?'

'I've vowed to myself that I will not. And to God, too.'

'If you succeed, you will be crushing part of your soul.'

'Yes, I know.'

A knock comes. A key is turned. The cheery doctor appears. Just checking all is well, he smiles. Jem leaps off the stool, throbbing with anger and advances on him.

'How dare you interrupt me when I am with a distinguished visitor!'

The impertinence of it. Does the fool have no idea who this visitor is? For a moment, he wants to strike the man but the doctor goes on smiling, talking softly until Jem feels calm again, like a teething baby being soothed with a finger. The doctor goes away and Jem sits back down, staring at the dark-stained floorboards.

'The world has changed so much in a generation, Eddy. It will change even faster from now on. You will achieve so many wonderful things.'

'Me?' Eddy smiles.

'Yes, you. The good prince.'

'I will try, Jem.'

'You must do better than that!' Jem feels the fury rise again. He springs from the stool and thunders down. 'I have failed in so much, but I cannot fail in you.'

'Jem, dear old chum, you have succeeded in countless ways. You have always been my god, remember?'

Jem wants to say so many things. Those things he has always been afraid to say, he is now afraid to leave unsaid.

'I've always wanted nothing more than to stand beside you.'

'But Jem, you don't stand beside me. You're inside me, a part of me.'

Jem reaches out and takes Eddy's hand in both of his, holding it as if it is some rare and treasured object, nervous that it might break.

'Then please don't leave me here.'

'Oh Jem, you must stay and be cared for. Just until you're well again.'

Now Jem is sure, in the tumult of his brain, of one clear thing. That Eddy will walk away from him and that it is right that he should do so. The knowledge of it cuts him like a dagger, but he knows he must be braver than he has ever been before. But there is one last thing he wants to say.

'The last night before you went down from Trinity, I slept

out in the cloisters, below your window.'

'I know. I saw you there.'

'And did you see a note I slipped under your door?'

'I saw the note.'

'Do you remember what it said?'

'I remember.'

'It was a foolish thing to write,' he says.

'No, it wasn't,' says Eddy. 'It meant the world to me.'

They stand on either side of the chimney piece like a pair of caryatids. The big hand reaches out and, for only the second time in their lives, Jem and Eddy cling to each other. Jem feels Eddy's chest rise and fall against his own. He hears their hearts beating together as if they lived in the same body. He adjusts his breathing to Eddy's so that they breathe as one.

'Say to me again the words you wrote,' Eddy whispers.

'You have my love until my last breath.'

'Then tell me why, why you would not give yourself to me wholly? I wanted that so much.'

'Because it was a thing of no consequence,' says Jem. 'And I wanted to give you something better than that, something that would last.'

'It was of consequence to me,' says Eddy.

They stand together for a long minute, until Eddy eases free and walks towards the door. The doctor has decreed that he must not stay too long. He picks up his coat and his bowler and knocks for someone to come.

'Take care of yourself. I'll come to see you again soon.'

'Happy Christmas when it comes. Wrap up warm against this infernal cold. And Eddy...'

'Yes, Jem?'

'You'll be all right now?'

'I'll be all right.'

The cheery doctor arrives again. Eddy is on the threshold when Jem strides across the room and seizes his wrist.

'Do you remember that summer morning after the last May Ball? We'd danced our socks off, but nobody wanted to go to bed?'

'And we went to the bowling green for a last cigar,' says Eddy, smiling.

'I can still smell the dew on the turf,' says Jem. 'And the swifts, ruddy great flocks of them, circling the towers and the sun coming up on the chapel. Do you really remember?'

'Yes, of course.'

'I don't think I've ever been so happy. Except for knowing you were leaving us and it would never be the same again.'

'I never wanted to leave. I wanted to stay there forever.'

'It seemed as if every possibility each one of us possessed had been captured and distilled into that one moment. As if it were a cup and we could drink from it.'

'The only time that I was truly free.'

'Long gone now,' Jem says.

'But it was magical,' replies Eddy.

Jem tightens his grip on Eddy's wrist, his long, rough fingernails stabbing into the flesh.

'Yes,' he says, his eyes dancing. 'It *was* magical.'

When the door is closed and locked, when the footsteps fade along the corridor, Jem sits back in his chair and watches the logs crackle and flake.

'Eddy's all right now,' he says aloud again and again. 'Eddy's all right.'

From the window of the train, nothing is visible as the winter afternoon descends into night. Eddy sees no houses, churches, farms; only the occasional flash of the lamps on a country station, a tiny oasis roared past too quickly to give any comfort. It seems to him as if he has left Jem on the dark side of the moon.

Eddy closes his eyes and turns his face to the wall. Now he sees an avenue of pleached limes at the zenith of a June morning. And strolling along it, his great wild head circled by the sun, there comes a distant god.

CHAPTER XXVII

Christmas & New Year 1891/2. Sandringham, Norfolk.

On Christmas Day, in the little church in the park, in the pew where he has knelt since he was old enough to kneel, Eddy gives thanks to God for all His mercies and means every word of it. He does feel at peace on earth, he does feel goodwill to all men. God and Eddy are getting along quite well again now.

And the white flag of truce still flies above their roof. It has held right through the December weeks and will surely be invincible until the tulips are in bloom. The festive season, his birthday, his wedding, will roll on, one after the other, gilded carriages in a procession of endless good cheer. Since he acquired the status of a man about to be married, his Papa has still not shouted or chaffed or found fault in anything. Bertie smiles at him over the breakfast table and asks yet again after dear May. 'What a great girl she is,' he says.

Despite the sweetness and light inside their walls, the world outside is sepulchral. It is a bastard of a winter and no mistake. By the turn of the year, their little lake is frozen solid and they skate every day. Through the half-hearted afternoons, they glide and crash and fall and laugh and, when dusk falls, a necklace of coloured lanterns is lit and negus is brought out to keep them warm. Georgie, still weak from his illness, only comes on the ice for a short while. Eddy is ashamed to be pleased that Georgie is a hippo, while he himself is a gazelle. A gazelle in a bowler hat. Alix and the girls applaud as he ducks and weaves round them.

'This winter is as bitter as the one when you were born,' she says.

The eternal story comes again. Alix in the sledge-chair being spun round on the ice. The sudden kicking. The servant boy running to buy the flannel. The grand doctors arriving too late. Grandmama's nose out of joint because she misses the gory spectacle.

'Twenty-eight years ago next week. Whoever would believe it? I was so pretty then; now I'm just an old woman.'

Everyone laughs and rolls their eyes towards the foggy heavens. But not the sisters; even when Alix is absent, they are eclipsed by the memory of her presence.

He is unlacing his skates when the message is brought. His Papa wants him at once. Despite the scarf, the Norfolk jacket, the woolly shirt, despite being in favour, the old feeling pushes into his guts. The paths across the parterres have vanished under the snow, but he has known them forever and follows them faithfully back up to the terrace, his grace on the lake turned to leaden steps.

Through the misty window of the Small Drawing Room, Bertie gestures at him to hurry inside. God, what has happened now? Eddy's new-found hopefulness is as fragile as the saplings under their blankets of snowflakes. Has May changed her mind? Has she heard something? Has some other forgotten folly risen up to haunt him? Is everything about to come crashing down?

'Read it,' says Bertie, passing him a telegram.

He takes it, has to read it twice.

'Me? Are they serious?'

'It appears that they are,' Bertie replies. 'The General says he's been observing you for quite a while and thinks you're up to the job.'

'Viceroy of Ireland? But Papa, I am not a clever man. How could I?'

'The role is ceremonial. It doesn't require genius, only good manners, a good profile and the ability to get along with all sorts. Of course, there will be much for you to learn, but you'll have May beside you and she's a formidable young lady. You will do it together.'

In his father's presence, Eddy sits down before he has been invited to do so.

'It's a job, Eddy. A direction for you. A damn sight more than I've ever had. Seize it. Don't be afraid.'

Bertie takes the cigar from between his lips and smiles. Eddy smiles too and finds that he is unable to stop. For a minute they do not speak, just beam at each other as the fire crackles and one of the old dogs snores and farts on the hearth rug.

'But I *am* rather afraid, Papa.'

'I'll do everything I can to help you. If you want me to, that is. If you don't, I'll quite understand.'

'But of course, Papa. Why wouldn't I?'

'Lately, I've felt you no longer cared what I think.'

Eddy does not answer. A denial would be pointless, and anyway he does not wish to make it. He no longer needs to slam the door; that anger has left him. He even wonders if it might be opened again, quietly, gently, just the merest crack, to let in a chink of friendship. Perhaps, in time, something more.

Can he tell Mama, Georgie and the girls? Can he telegraph May? No, says Papa, there is an etiquette to these things. They must wait until next week, until after Eddy's birthday. Bertie will go up to town and discuss it further with the men who matter.

They stand on either side of the fireplace. Suddenly, Bertie's hand reaches out.

'Shall we shake on it then?'

Eddy takes Bertie's palm. But when the shake is done, Bertie does not release him.

'Eddy, I'm fifty now,' he says, 'and when at last it's my turn, I'll be too damned old. Not enough time to achieve anything. The best of me frittered away. This is your chance not to fritter yourself. For God's sake, take it!'

'Yes, Papa.'

Still his hand is not released. They stare down at the dog on the rug. It stretches, moans, farts again. When Bertie speaks it is so quietly that Eddy can hardly hear him.

'I know I've often been rough with you,' he says. 'I just wanted you to be the perfect son in the way that I never was or could have been. So that if I mess everything up, as they all predict, then you'd be able to come after and wipe up the stain of me.'

'But why did you imagine I could be any more perfect than you?' Eddy asks.

His father shrugs his shoulders.

'All you did was to make me feel the way they made *you* feel,' says Eddy.

'Well, there you are. I mess everything up, do I not?'

Eddy pulls his father into an embrace. He cannot remember when such a thing last occurred. It is over in seconds and they go back to staring at the rug. But now Eddy determines that he will strive to open the door wide again, though it cannot be quite yet.

'The angel of death hovers over the land,' say the preachers from the pulpits. The scientists, however, do not believe the influenza has come from heaven, merely from China. Bertie wonders if they will all end up slitty-eyed.

Like Fat Mary inside her stays, the house is fit to burst. Eddy is exiled to a tiny bedroom on the east front, rabbited away down a warren of crepuscular passages. It is so small that from the bed he can reach out and touch the chimney piece. They have all gathered for his birthday, but half of them are ill. Half the kingdom is ill.

If the guests are not already prostrate, they sniffle and sneeze round the passages and staircases. In their illnesses, they are quite as repulsive as lesser mortals. Last night at dinner, Mad Frank propelled a dollop of goo right onto Alix's *crème brulée*. Dear May was mortified, but Alix had to bite into her napkin for a good minute.

'Take it back, please,' she said to the footman. 'Tell chef it is not quite *comme il faut*.'

Outside, for once, there is no wind at all, not even a whisper, which somehow makes it more depressing. With a wind, however cruel, there is at least a sense of transience, the hope of the misery blowing over, bringing something better. But for a week or more, the air has not stirred; an invisible vice gripping the fallow fields, the woods and coverts, the park, the gardens. Snow falls vertically, without flurries or flourish, bored with itself. Then the fog comes, smothering the chimney pots, slumping against the windows, sealing them in. It is a teasing, malevolent presence; allowing the occasional feeble shard of light to poke through, a moment's reprieve from the gloom, before covering them over again. The house is a planet on its own. When people manage to reach it, they come out of the mists like creatures from another world.

At the little lake, the lanterns are unlit. It has been deserted by the snifflers and the sneezers, but not by Eddy. Every morning, nourished by some new-found energy, he glides out. The scissored marks of the deserters are embalmed under the skin of fresh ice. Here, he exists alone; no other blades mark the virgin glass, no other footprints crumple the snow. He is disembodied, unconnected, floating. It does his heart good. 'Silence heals everything,' May said, and she is right, as he notices she so often is. He breathes deeply of the silence while he can. Sooner or later, the fog will lift, the snow will melt and this momentous year will properly begin. His wedding, his occupation, his life.

'I'm ready for it all, Jem,' he says into the mist one day. 'I'm ready for anything.'

But it is not long before he joins the snifflers and the sneezers. Damn and blast. The Ballroom is already being decorated for his party. Everyone, sick or well, is here; dozens more will struggle in on the night. In unknown rooms, a ventriloquist and a banjo player are practising to please him. Oh well, it cannot be helped. He will have to grin and bear it like everybody else and try not to sneeze onto anyone's dinner.

It is the day before his birthday. At breakfast, Bertie devours his customary feast, champing at the bit to get out to the coverts. 'This house is like a bloody infirmary,' he says; not that he has any experience of such places, beyond the cutting of ribbons to open them. He looks out at the fog and sighs. Eddy wonders what he is thinking, of where and of whom. But the poor man is trapped here without chance of escape, the misty fields his only freedom.

Alix rarely comes down for breakfast these days, so Eddy goes to her room to kiss her good morning. She sits at her dressing table, eyes closed, the maid brushing her hair. As he has done ever since he can remember, he takes the brush and finishes the job himself. Alix notices his clothes.

'Oh Eddy, you mustn't go out today. Your cold is no better. Stay inside.'

'But Papa is going out and Georgie still isn't up to it, so I think I must.'

'Nonsense. Why?'

'Because Papa will expect it, so I must at least try.'

His mother's reflection stares back at him.

'And when Papa expects, we must all, like Nelson, do our duty.'

She dips her fingers into a jar and rubs a cream into her hands. The scent of lavender fills the room, a burst of spring.

'Not long now,' she sighs, 'till my little Eddy is married.'

Her hand flies up and stops the hair brush.

'Promise me something.'

'Anything Mama.'

'Promise me that you will try, at least try, to give May the sort of marriage that I once dreamed of. That you'll endeavour to love her and not abandon her to herself.'

'I think I'm starting to care for May already.'

'Oh Eddy.'

When he walks out across the snow to where the shooters gather, he glances up at her window. She is waving down at him, gesturing that he should tighten his scarf. He raises his cap and waves it in circles round his head.

Considering the conditions, it is a fair morning's haul. But the fields and woods are desolate and the cold seems to slough the skin from his cheeks. The fingers of his gloves are wet where he wipes his dripping nose. May comes out to luncheon with the other women. He is pleased to see her, grateful that she has made the effort. Her smiles for him now are more relaxed, not the guarded ones she dispenses to most people.

'How many did you get?' she asks.

'I refuse to tell you. I refuse to be a bore even before we're married.'

'And I will make it my business that you're not a bore after it.'

'You're setting out to improve me then?'

'Merely to build on what's already there.'

He thinks again how wrong he was about Fat Mary's quiet, swotty girl. He sees now that they have both known loneliness and perhaps that is the essence of the hope for them, the hope that some kind of love will come in its own sweet time. Until then, when he fumbles or falters, he will look into that calm, contained face and into the eyes that once, for just a moment, showed him that they needed him. She may not be the dazzling one but she is, and he is sure of it now, the right one. And with this sureness comes an unfamiliar peace, powerful as any of the opiates he has tried. The smoking, the drinking, the fucking; all the pretty uniforms, the sparkling, undeserved medals, the collars and the cuffs.

Luncheon is arranged at one of the cottages. They sit on either side of his father. Eddy can tell that May and his Papa are a little nervous of each other. Bertie's ways are not her ways. But he likes clever women and he is beginning to get her measure. He is talking to her of Ireland. Such a beautiful country, he says, but so very troubled. We must double our efforts to find a happy resolution. There is much work to be done.

When Eddy begins to feel sick, he assumes it is the excitement in his belly about what lies before him. But then he becomes dizzy and his head starts to throb. He thinks he must go home. Dear May will walk back with you, Bertie decrees.

'Two sons in the sickbay now,' he shouts to the company. 'The Empire is doomed.'

May takes Eddy's arm as they walk through the woods towards the walls of the park, the glare of the snow hurting his eyes. Suddenly he disobeys his father and tells her about Ireland. She drops his arm and takes a step back. She slips and nearly falls on her arse, but her eyes are shining; the whiteness of the ground seeming to light her up.

'Do you think we could make a fist of it?' he asks.

'We'll do more than that. We will make a triumph of it.'

'I couldn't contemplate it without you.'

'I told you before. I will stand by your side. I will never leave you.'

He wants to say something momentous, something to be remembered in later years, but instead he sneezes violently and his nose drips like a faulty tap.

'If I weren't going down with some damn bug, I should like to kiss you now.'

'We'll have plenty of time for kissing,' May replies.

It is the first time any such words have come from the lips of shy May Teck. He feels a tiny current of shock, arousal even. Oh good, he thinks, I cannot be so very ill.

She leads him out of the woods towards home. When they reach the terrace, they can see into the Drawing Room. Alix and Fat Mary are at the piano singing songs; Mad Frank is dancing with one of the little cousins and bumping into the potted palms.

'Of course, it will be rather hard,' Eddy says, 'being in a different country from our parents.'

May gives him the guarded smile, then the unguarded one, then breaks out into that laugh of hers. It is the laugh of a navvy and he adores it. In the middle of the snowy terrace, they stand shaking together. He is not sure how much he shakes with laughter or how much with the damnable cold.

Georgie has taken refuge in the Saloon, throwing paper darts at the white cockatoo. He sends for a thermometer and rams it into Eddy's mouth.

'Bed,' says Georgie.

In his tiny billet, thank God, a fire has been lit. On the plain little iron bed, the sheets are fresh and crisp, the covers already turned down. The room is warm and dark as a womb. He decides that he will think of it as such and that, when he recovers, he will burst out of it reborn.

CHAPTER XXVIII

8 January 1892. Sandringham, Norfolk.

In the fever of his sleep, he finds himself lying on another bed in another time. Seven summers ago. A warm June evening. The windows are wide open. He can hear the shouts of his fellows heading for the river or out to the meadows. He can smell the new-mown grass in the quad, the heat in the old stone of the cloisters. He can smell the whole dream of this place, the dream that will soon end when the destiny of Albert Victor will come to reclaim him.

He thinks this is the most important moment of his life, lying there watching the clock while the blond boy with the spectacles sucks his prick. It is nearly the time when he has invited Jem to join them for a glass of sherry. He has planned it all so carefully. A scene to sear itself into Jem's soul, a recreation of the hurt Eddy felt on that day when he found them together and which he has nursed ever since. He knows it is a terrible gamble, but it is his last throw of the dice.

Punctual for once, the knock comes at the door. Eddy does not answer, does not call out. The busy blond does not seem to hear it. Another knock, the handle is tried, the door swings open. Jem is there. Big, sweaty, tennis jumper draped across his shoulders like a stole. His mouth is turned upwards, ready to smile and shout a greeting. First the face freezes over, then it crumples. The body flinches, takes a step backwards. Eddy's heart aches at his own cruelty, praying that this can soon be over.

And it is. Jem roars into the room, fishes the blond from between Eddy's legs, casts him out onto the landing where he trips and falls. His clothes fly after him, one piece after another. They cover him where he lies, cover his hardness, his wantonness. The door is shut against his indignity, locked, bolted.

Then Jem is on the rumpled bed. He takes Eddy in his arms, kisses his face, his neck, his chest and at last, for the first time, his lips. They both weep, then a little laughter, more weeping, more laughter. Jem swears that some way will be found to stop them being parted, some way to go on together. They say the things that have been held back for so long, the things felt since the day in the garden, beneath the Buddha, at the end of the avenue of pleached limes.

When the words are all said and the silence comes, when they give themselves to each other, Eddy begins to perform his usual role as the giver, the provider of comfort, the seeker of approval. But he is stopped.

'You need do nothing to please me,' says Jem. 'I want to please you.'

Jem wraps himself round Eddy, against him, into him. Eddy is aware of both the pleasure and the pain, but they are both feeble sensations compared with the one which floods through him. They lie in each other's arms, hearing the voices drift up from the cloisters. Familiar voices, the voices of those who assume that what has just happened, had happened long ago. Eddy knows, with utter certainty, that nothing and nobody can ever match what he feels at this moment, however long or short his life may be.

'We will find a way,' says Jem.

His party goes on without him. Absurd, really, but that is the way things are done. After all, he is Albert Victor, his father's son; a celebration must be held. The theatricals from the city have struggled through the snows and must perform. The talents of the banjo player and the ventriloquist cannot go unheard. Speeches have been prepared and shall be delivered. Everything will be perfect. That he himself is not present is tedious, but a minor point.

Earlier, he forces himself to go down and inspect his presents. How very kind people are. He feels guilty that the wedding is only weeks away and that they will be obliged to send another. He wonders if there is something from Jem, some little thing buried deep among the vast packages sent by the great and good. There usually is. He has a sudden urge to claw at the piles to find it, but perhaps there can be nothing this year. Not this year.

But his head aches even more than yesterday and he is dripping so much beneath his dressing gown there will soon be a puddle on the carpet. Even Bertie can see that he is not worth tuppence and orders him back upstairs. May blows a kiss as he trudges from the room. Fat Mary does too, then Mama, then the sisters. Papa and Georgie laugh and blow him theirs. Papa encourages the servants to do the same; a special impertinence is sanctioned. It is his birthday after all. He leaves the room as drenched in kisses as he is in sweat.

He heaves himself up the staircase, no longer the gazelle who skated on the lake. He is glad to return to his womb again and slide back between fresh sheets. Soon the carriages arrive beneath his window. How odd to lie here and listen to the distant sounds of people celebrating one's existence. For most of his life, he has not believed it to be any great cause for rejoicing. How strange that, just as he begins to believe that his space on earth is not completely wasted, he is not there to be part of it.

He lies in his tiny room and listens to the music from below. He hears a polka, a quadrille, a waltz. He wonders who is dancing with May and feels a sting of jealousy. Sleep tries to drag him under, but he must keep awake for his Mama. She has promised to slip away and bring up his special present. Why such a mystery this year? Usually, she likes to give it with a great fanfare, where everyone can see and make their 'oohs' and 'aahs'. What on earth can it be?

He drifts in and out of a doze. In his fever, many faces come and look down on him, guests from another party. Wind-burnt faces from the *Bacchante*; earnest faces from the turreted rooms of Trinity; rouged faces from Mr Inslip's soirees. Rose comes, carrying the puppy in her arms. Little Eddy, his godson, stands on a chair and rubs his nose against Eddy's as he always loves to do. Reverend Dalton booms down at him to stop being so sleepy and to get up at once. And then Helene, in her beauty and assurance. In recent weeks, he has tried to banish her, but she has refused to leave him forever. The locket with her picture inside it still rests round his neck. He has vowed to remove it on the morning of his wedding. He has already chosen the place where he will keep it hidden in memory of her good cheer and her gift of some kind of love.

It seems to him how much of his life has been inhabited by those who are loud. In this house, where they must all shout anyway, he has always needed to shout loudest for a hearing yet, most of the time, he has not shouted at all. If he had been surrounded by quiet, uncertain people, people who didn't notice that he was uncertain too, might he have found himself before? Oh well, *tant pis*, as his Mama says. He has found May now. She is far from uncertain, but she has that quietness, that silence which heals. May will bring him peace.

And Jem comes too, of course. He does not need a locket with a picture of Jem. He does not need a reminder of what he looks like or who he is. It is Jem who has created him. Jem is him. They can never be separated; they are always together.

Eddy tosses and turns on his plain little bed. His throat burns like hell now. The fresh sheets are already moist with his sweat and, though the fire still blazes, he feels the usual chill in the bones of the red-brick house. Once they are married, he and May will go somewhere warm and walk in the spring sun. And perhaps, by the time they return, his child might be in her belly. A child to love and accept, to mould and make in nobody else's image but the child's very own, whatever it happens to be.

The door opens. The rustle of silk crosses the carpet, the cool hand strokes his forehead. His Mama sits on the side of the bed; the diamonds in her hair dancing like fire-flies. She hands him a package wrapped with ribbons and bows. But his hands are too weak to open it, so she must do it for him. It is a battered old book, bound in faded green leather, gold leaf flaking off the broken spine. He recognises it at once; the book of fairy tales, given to her in her nursery by Mr Hans Christian Andersen himself. It is her most precious, most private possession.

'I want you to have this now,' she says, 'before you leave me forever. Wherever you are, you can open it and remember happy hours with your devoted old Mama.'

'I'll never leave you, Mama,' he croaks, his voice almost gone. 'Not truly.'

'Oh, but I think you will. I can feel it already.'

Alix strokes his wet cheek.

'Be careful, Mama. Don't catch this damn thing.'

'Fiddlesticks,' she says as she leans down to kiss his sticky cheek.

But she is right. He is going to leave her. If he could rescue her in some way he would, but her fate is sealed and he can do nothing about it. And he will never open the book she has given him. He will have no fairy tales now. He is a man and he will put away childish things.

He does not know how long it is before his eyes flicker open again. Below his window he hears muffled voices and the closing of carriage doors. The polkas and the waltzes have stopped now; the dance is over. Then he is aware of a new presence; someone else beside the bed. Bertie looks down on him. He takes a handkerchief and wipes it across Eddy's brow, as if he were a piece of china. Even through his stuffed-up nose, Eddy catches the whiff of cigar smoke, that scent he has known forever, both feared and adored.

'Happy Birthday from your loving Papa,' the voice says. Then the voice is gone and he is not sure if he is awake or if he dreams.

Footsteps, trained in silence, come and go. He half-hears the soft rush of more coal sliding from the scuttle. Again he dozes; again he wakes. The fire burns lower now, but the room is not quite dark. His eyes rest on the long mirror beyond the end of the bed. Suddenly he wants to see himself. Somehow, he heaves up onto his elbows. God, he thinks. I do look awful. Nobody will marry me looking like this. Maybe it is my punishment for so much pointless vanity. He is such a fright that he smiles at himself. The man in the mirror smiles back. For a moment, they contemplate each other and feel easy in their company.

Now he sees another face. It stands behind the shoulder of the man in the mirror. In the fading firelight, it is a little hazy, its edges blurred, but it smiles out at him too.

'You're all right now, Eddy,' the face says.

He lets himself fall back against the damp pillows and surrenders at last to sleep.

*

When Eddy woke the next morning, Saturday 9th January 1892, his flu had begun to turn into pneumonia. To the disbelief and horror of his family, he died five days later. In his delirium, moments before his death, he had murmured repeatedly, 'Who is that? Who is that?'

On hearing the news, Jem Stephen began refusing food and died less than three weeks later in his asylum, aged thirty-three.

AFTERWORD

Eddy was buried in a magnificent sarcophagus at St George's Chapel, Windsor. He does not rest in the main church, but in a separate chapel at the rear, beside Leopold, the uncle who had also died so young. It is probable that most tourists who shuffle past the flamboyant Art Nouveau effigy of the sleeping prince have no idea who he was. Eddy might have smiled at that.

At the funeral, Eddy's father wept throughout. For the rest of Bertie's life, Eddy's picture hung above his bed. The devastated Alix always kept the cap he had waved at her when he went out shooting for the last time.

The family soon decided that, after a decent interval, May of Teck would 'do' for Georgie, the new heir presumptive. They were married eighteen months later.

After Queen Victoria died in 1901, Bertie and Alix reigned as King Edward VII and Queen Alexandra. Against all expectations, including his own, Bertie made an excellent monarch.

In 1910, Georgie and May succeeded them as King George V and Queen Mary, later becoming the grandparents of Queen Elizabeth II. Until the day he died in 1936, Georgie always used Eddy's pen.

Helene d'Orleans, failing to land any other big fish, eventually settled for an Italian duke and, in old age, became a confidante of Mussolini. For many years, a simple beaded wreath bearing her name lay on Eddy's tomb.

The mental instability that cursed Jem Stephen's family continued its swathe in later generations. His much younger first cousin, the writer Virginia Woolf, would also suffer from what is now called bipolar disorder and would take her own life in 1941.

At Eton College, James Kenneth Stephen is still celebrated as the greatest-ever Keeper of The Wall. Every year, a toast is raised to his golden memory.

AUTHOR'S NOTE

If, in the new Millennium, the name of Prince Eddy is raised at all, it is usually in connection with two events: as a candidate for Jack the Ripper and his involvement, or otherwise, in the Cleveland Street Scandal. The former is ludicrous (as was the equally daft candidacy of Jem Stephen) and the second is still disputed among historians.

As a novelist, neither event much interested me. My aim in writing this book was to imaginatively chronicle the characters and emotions of two tragic, maligned but fascinating young men and, if possible, to rescue them from the two dimensions in which history usually paints them.

Obviously, this is a work of both fiction and fact, but for those parts in the former category, the characters, events, dates and places presented are, as closely as possible, based on the historical and biographical records. Since the Royal Archives at Windsor are rarely open to the historical novelist, I have naturally relied on other sources.

On Prince Eddy himself, the most recent and finest (though I differ from some conclusions) is *Prince Eddy* by Andrew Cook (History Press 2008). Others include *Prince Eddy and The Homosexual Underworld* by Theo Aronson (John Murray 1994) and *Clarence* by Michael Harrison (WH Allen 1972). On Jem Stephen, Deborah McDonald's *The Prince, His Tutor and The Ripper* (McFarland 2007) has been valuable despite its emphasis on 'Ripperology'. On Bertie and Alix, there can be no better sources than Jane Ridley's *Bertie, A Life of Edward VII* (Chatto & Windus 2012), Georgina Battiscombe's *Queen Alexandra* (Constable 1969) and Richard Hough's *Edward & Alexandra* (Hodder & Stoughton 1992). On May of Teck, the major work remains James Pope-Hennessy's *Queen Mary* (Allen & Unwin 1959).

ACKNOWLEDGEMENTS

To Professor Jane Ridley for the generous gift of her time, her knowledge and her deep insights into the characters and events of this book. To the late Professor Roger Lockyer for a historian's advice, enthusiastic support and, above all, his treasured friendship. To the novelist Sarah Bower for her invaluable comments on an early draft of the manuscript.

To the staff of The Wren Library, Trinity College, Cambridge, The National Archives at Kew, The Archives of The University of Southampton and The Garrison Library, Gibraltar.

To Rossella Spoerry for her thoughts on the psychology of the characters.

To my splendid agent Peter Buckman for his inexhaustible faith.

Last and by no means least, to my publisher, Louise Boland and her dedicated team at Fairlight Books: Urška Vidoni, Gabrielė Gaižutytė, Mo Fillmore, Lindsey Woollard and Emma Daley. My deepest thanks for their commitment, hard work and the great pleasure of working together.

ABOUT THE AUTHOR

Alan Robert Clark was born and educated in Scotland. He briefly attended King's College in London, before opting instead for a career as a copywriter and creative director with a number of leading London advertising agencies.

Alan has worked as a freelance journalist and, most recently, has ghost-written and co-authored a number of biographies. His previous novel *Rory's Boys* (written as Alan Clark) was widely praised.

FAIRLIGHT BOOKS

Also by Alan Robert Clark

Valhalla

The story of Prince Eddy's wife that never was...

Following the death of Prince Eddy, his intended wife Mary of Teck becomes, instead, the consort of his brother Georgie, who was later to be known as King George V.

Born into the lower ranks of royalty, and with neither beauty nor fortune, Mary of Teck never expected to find herself admitted to its highest echelon. Forced to be totally subservient to her husband, Mary lets her true self freeze over, sacrificing the person she might have become to do her duty.

The once warm and witty young girl pays a heavy price for her entry to 'Valhalla'.

Expected Publication Date – Early 2020

To keep up to date with *Valhalla* and other Fairlight Books' literary publications, visit *www.fairlightbooks.co.uk*